HOFFA'S WOMEN

The Slur They Made Their Banner

CHARLENE JONES

EDITED BY

JONATHAN LAMPLEY

A RED SPRINGS BOOK

Publisher's Note: This is a work of fiction. Names, characters, places, and incidents are the product of the author's imagination or are used fictionally. Any resemblance to actual persons, living or dead, events or locales is coincidental or used fictitiously.

HOFFA'S WOMEN
Copyright © 2006 by Charlene Jones

Red Springs Publishing
P O Box 916
Hermitage, TN 37076-0916

All rights reserved. No part of this book may be reproduced or transmitted in any form or means, electronic or mechanical, including photocopying, recording or any informational storage or retrieval system (except a reviewer who may quote brief passages in a review to print in magazine or newspaper) without permission in writing from the publisher.

First Printing 2006

ISBN # 1-888101-13-X

Library of Congress Catalog Card Number:
2006904164

Cover Design: "Designs with SAS"

Printed in the United States of America

This book is for my working parents, for Teamsters Local 480, for the International Brotherhood of Teamsters and for every wise and brave soul who has fought for fair benefits and workplace conditions. But, most of all, it is a tribute to Jimmy Hoffa who put America's working men and women on the middle class map. The man was truly an American icon and left us much to honor and to work by.

For a long time, I have wondered if this story should be told. My gut tells me, now is the time — May 2006.

CHARLENE JONES

❧❳❲❧ CHAPTER 1 ❧❳❲❧

The activity, the noise, trying to get back into the swing of the working world— all were baffling. Reeda couldn't imagine how time had moved so quickly from 1975 to 1985. Added to her dismay, her ten year reprieve from office work, machines and politics made for a hard adjustment. Her job skills creeping with rust made her nervous as a kite flying without a tail. At times she felt totally incompetent.

But— she was out of the kitchen she no longer wanted or could afford to be in. To say the least, the last two years had not been very good years. Actually, with the death of the good part of her marriage, they had been horrible years. She had shed enough tears to last forever. Somehow, God willing, this year had to be better.

But that was doubtful Six months after the holocaust of her near marital breakup subsided, she realized it should have been final. Nothing seemed right.

Reeda Davis, contented wife and homemaker, felt like a displaced person. Her satisfaction with housekeeping, loving her husband, and rearing their son was a casualty of domestic war. Days were eons, nights were boring and she constantly nagged the boy to, "Please, Jamey, be careful."

"Mom, I'm not a baby. Okay?" he always answered, in his teenage tired-of-being-overprotected changing voice."

In spite of her discontent and new frigidity, for the first time, when her husband was absent from home his location and activities kept her in a cesspool of fear and doubt. She really should have divorced Van because now she was kind of nuts where he was concerned. From trusting him completely, she had gone to not trusting him any further than she could see him. She actually didn't trust him then.

The aftermath also revealed how family problems cost dollars as well as tears. For several reasons, the smallest not being mounting bills and a cash flow problem, Reeda was forced to return to the working world.

To get her skills up to par, she initially went to work for a temporary help agency. In less than two weeks the agency got a job order for a full-time customer service position with Alpha Trucking Company. Her boss talked her into interviewing for the job.

God alone knew why Alpha hired her. Reeda was concerned about whether she could fit in working around a stable of burly truck drivers. With household finances degenerating every day, she decided to give it her best shot. The hourly wage was too good to refuse.

Her boss said, "Don't worry, I've been matching jobs and people more years than I care to admit. Trust me, Reeda. With your self confidence and gift of gab, you're a natural for the trace job and for the freight business. You said you needed to earn the most money possible. Everybody can't handle working in transportation. I think you can, if you really want top pay for office skills. Frankly, trucking companies work your ass off, but they do pay for it."

Now she was clocking in at Alpha, where orders were barked and questions were often screamed to be heard over clattering office machines or an eighteen wheeler warming up close to the building. Reeda was grateful her own case of nerves was unnoticed in a world where everyone seemed to be working in a state of sustained crisis.

Stanley Smith, the clerk drafted to train her, was constantly interrupted by questions and phone calls. After Monday and Tuesday working at Alpha, words like pro number, shipper, consignee, verbal delivery, proof of delivery, interline point, over, short and damaged were rolling around in her head like bearings out of their racer.

Eight hours a day, at a desk about ten feet from Reeda's desk, the over-the-road dispatcher talked incessantly on the Watts phone about teams, single men, two in the bed, horses, mules, rag-tops, flat-tops, and power. Clearly the trucking industry had a language of its own and learning the language was her first hurdle. Her second was conquering the yellow computer monster that had appeared since her working days.

After lunch on Friday, her boss Hank Carter walked up to her desk and inquired, "How are you getting on, Reeda?"

With a nervous smile, she lied, "Fine."

"Stan, is our lovely, raven-haired Reeda ready to take trace calls?"

She was appalled to hear Stanley assure, "Yes, sir. Reeda has great aptitude for customer service. She is going to do just fine." Near panic hammering in her ears impaired her hearing, but Reeda saw Stanley and Carter smiling at her proudly. As they stood shaking their heads in agreement, she felt like she might faint.

Carter said, "Good! I knew you were the girl we were looking for," and walked away.

"Stanley, you know I don't know what I'm doing!"

"You know more than you think. Don't worry; you'll do fine." He smiled at her and added, "Trust me," then turned his attention to the paperwork piled on his desk.

As she sat in a daze, hating him for ignoring her bewilderment, her phone rang. Her daze turned to a look of horror. As she beheld the black monster, it rang again.

Stanley's eyes questioned, she shrugged helplessly, another ring insisted. "Answer it," he urged. "You'll do fine— really you will!"

Her answer was a question, "Customer service?"

"Lady, where in hell is my freight?" a bass voice snarled.

"I... uh— I beg your pardon?"

"I want my cable. Got six men making twelve dollars an hour for sitting on their rears doing nothing. That order should have been here three days ago. Thought you people ran a truck line. My stuff should be here by now on a damn dog sled!"

"Uh... who is your shipper, sir?"

"Consolidated Cable out of Atlanta."

"And... how is your shipment consigned?"

"How is it what?"

"Who is the freight coming to?"

"Why didn't you say that in the first place? Bass Electric."

"One moment and I'll check." She pushed the hold button, then ran to Stanley's desk. "Stanley?"... louder, "Stanley?"... no response. "Stanley Smith, you answer me and I mean it!"

"Goodness! Now, what is it, Reeda?"

"A man on the phone wants to know when he'll get his freight."

"That's what they all want. Does he know the pro number?"

"Uh, I forgot to ask."

"Always ask for the pro number. Did you check the computer print out of the shipments billed on line last night?"

"The print out is late, Stanley. It isn't available yet."

"Did you get the other information?"

"Yes," she said, holding out her pad, feeling like a dog that had retrieved a ball.

"Huumm... see if he has the pro number, the shipping date, weight and number of pieces. Get all the information." Stanley's tone of an impatient school teacher with a slow student was maddening until he added, "Saves mistakes. Some customers receive freight every day. He might have received a two piece shipment yesterday and be looking for a four piece shipment now. That's another reason you need the pro number. Make him think he has another shipment coming today, when it was yesterday's delivery, he'll have your ears," he repeated, then absorbed himself in his own work.

"He... he seems real mad."

"Look, Reeda," Stanley's obvious irritation cut like a sickle, "if he can't take the time to give you enough information to help him, let him be mad. Just be courteous," he advised, dismissing her again.

Back on the phone, Reeda forged ahead, "Sir, do you have the pro number?"

"No. My shipper didn't know the pro number."

"Can you give me the shipping date, weight and pieces?"

"The what?" the man shouted.

"Sir, I'm sorry but I need to know the weight, the pieces and shipping date of your freight," she repeated, in a stronger tone. He didn't have to be rude, if she was dumb. He hadn't been born knowing all he knew about his job! Damn! Enough was enough!

"Yes, young lady, I have an invoice and shipping date here somewhere. Hold a minute." The sound of shuffling papers traveled the wire before the caller recited the information.

Then the computer started printing out the list of shipments Alpha had picked up the preceding day. Reeda checked her inbound list; Bass Electric was listed. "Hello, sir?"

"Yes, I'm right here."

"Now, I'm finally getting a trace list print out. Your three reels of cable were picked up in Atlanta yesterday. Just a moment, while I run the pro in the computer." Reeda entered the number. In seconds a copy of Bass Electric's shipment appeared on the monitor. Still, she didn't know how to use the information. "Stanley?... Stanley!"

A heavy sigh, then: "What is it now, Reeda?"

"We got the freight in Atlanta yesterday. He wants to know when it will be delivered."

"Has the trailer arrived?"

"Yes— it's unloading."

"Okay. Now check with the city dispatcher."

"The who?"

"You know Bob Crawford in the city dispatch office."

"Oh, yeah. Thanks, Stanley." Then into the telephone, "Sir, one moment while I run check with the city dispatcher."

Bob Crawford's desk, equipped with a radio system to the tractors of his city drivers, plus ten telephone lines, was deserted. She was near panic again when Howard Summers, Alpha Trucking's Operations Manager, walked in the door from the freight dock.

"Need some help?" he asked lazily, ogling her from head to toe.

Too involved to care, Reeda said, "I sure do, Mr. Summers. Can you tell me when this freight will be delivered?" she asked holding out a printout of the freight bill.

"Around here, folks call me Howard," he drawled. "And what Apache gave you them black eyes?"

"Okay, then Howard. My great-grandmother was half Cherokee— she had black eyes. My eyes are really navy blue. Can you please tell me what time this freight will be delivered to the customer?"

"Nope, hon, can't tell you what time. Just if it will deliver today," he answered, leisurely leafing through the delivery manifests. "You check your manifest copies?"

"My what?"

"City delivery manifest. You should have copies like these," he explained, as he extended a clipboard holding the manifest listing the day's deliveries. "Hon, the daily manifest looks sort of like a laundry list but it's our business Bible."

"I'm sorry, I forgot. Anyway this man wants to know what time he can expect delivery."

"Folks in hell want ice water, baby. I doubt even God knows how many red lights are gonna catch a city driver. If I was that smart, I'd be making more and losing less— Alpha Trucking would be, too."

"So, what do I tell him?"

"Listen, good-looking, let me say something, off the record, as a buddy. Don't take all these jokers calling too damn serious. Learn that right off. Hell, they'll bug you to death, if you let them, with all kinds of dumb questions. What time? What flavor? Any distinguishing marks?" Howard muttered, nevertheless, using his finger to carefully check down each page of the manifest. "You got any besides them navy blue eyes?"

"Any what?"

"Distinguishing marks?"

"None that are any of your business!" she snapped.

Howard chuckled, "Lord, I do like 'em fiery. Two days here and already sassing the supervision. I love it! Darling, you're gonna do just fine. Okay, here it is. Tell the bastard he'll get his junk today— if it don't rain. It's out for delivery."

"Can't you just estimate the time, Howard?"

"Damn the time, girl! Don't let these bastards snow you. Any time you give is setting yourself up to be accused of lying. Don't ever do that to yourself. Tell him it's out for delivery and if he still mouths about a time, tell him you ain't no fortune teller!"

Sensing she would get nothing further and somehow feeling better, Reeda smiled and said, "Okay, and thanks, Howard."

☙❧

Striding down the warehouse floor, his favorite place at work, Howard barked orders at two dockmen loading a Miami outbound trailer. The men moved immediately, but at their own pace to do his bidding. In spite of the fact he had never taken a course in employee management, Summers did well with the men. Sometimes he would walk out on the dock and give a yodeling rebel yell just from the pleasure of breathing before screaming at some dockhand, "Get off your ass and close that damn trailer out! You get any lazier, you going to need an automatic farter."

"What do you know about it, asshole?" a male voice came back.

"Bastard, it ain't been that long since I was loading trailers," was Howard's usual answer in the same harsh, joking tone. Well placed in an industry where common sense, combined with an acceptance of hard work and long hours, meant more and served farther than a college degree, Summers loved his work. He would work two shifts back to back if the need arose, and do it with relish. In quite a good baritone, he often sang along with country music radio that usually played on the dock P. A. system.

His love for his job was second only to his love for women. It was not unheard of for him to steal work time to see his latest favorite.

The way he looked at a woman— any woman— made it plain he never thought of them as friends. Indiscriminate as a bull, almost as direct, and uncomplicated as Adam, Howard too, would have taken a bite of Eve's apple. His appetite for all the things he loved was animalistic, without shame and never quenched for long. It was conceivable that he might have lately swung down from a tree. A rural product, he still walked as if crossing a field of furrows, but he possessed the physique of a Michelangelo creation, with wavy wheat colored hair and was a walking personification of animal magnetism. His green-apple colored eyes still carried shadows of the idealistic boy who had grown up in the school of hard knocks, but the graduate had lost much of his early sensitive self along the way.

Lately, there had been one particularly sloppy female involvement for Howard. She was a Panamanian immigrant, fifteen years his senior and her early beauty had faded to a shadow when they met. Still one rampaging night found him blind drunk and it started.

When he woke and realized what he had bedded with, he was deeply ashamed. Even though older women were usually great lovers and much easier to please, Howard's pride normally kept him after younger pickings. He hated her Spanish accent, but Moretza's appreciation of bed and of him was insatiable.

She was his first female with zero inhibitions— and loved to give head. He said, "Sure, honey, I say, if a girl's hungry, let her eat." Curiosity held him initially, then ready pocket money hooked him for a time. There was no trouble about other women, when he came or how often as long as, now and then, he did come.

On his way out, always wearing a new shirt or shoes or trousers, Howard usually rifled her purse. It was his first experience at owning a slave. He found it intoxicating. His relationship with Moretza lasted a year. That was a record for Howard.

Once promoted to operations manager with a healthy raise in salary, Howard began to break off with Moretza. He met with tears, her magnificent cursing in English and Spanish and even waking up with a knife at his throat.

His guilty patience lasted until she made the mistake of approaching him on the job. He got rid of her by promising to come that night, at which time he called her every obscenity he knew. He ended by telling her again he was through and would call the cops if she came about his job again. When she eventually did, Howard was as good as his word. He ignored her collect phone calls from jail. So far, he had not heard from Moretza again.

The women at Alpha condemned Summer's amorous escapades, expressing sympathy among themselves for his wife and kids. Still there was a begrudging awe of such a stud. General consensus was, "If you're not propositioned by Howard, at least once a week, better check yourself for body odor."

For a time, seeing Moretza diminished Howard in the eyes of his female coworkers. Consequently, two nude snapshots of his latest conquest began circulating the office. She was young, beautiful, buxom and knew how to pose to her best advantage. The ladies lounge began buzzing all over again: "Wonder what that Howard's got?"

This was Reeda's first encounter with the coffee break discussions of working women letting their hair down. At first it struck her as gross, perhaps even common. But with time she accepted it as get-down conversation of women among women— experienced for the most part at marriage, kids and life. Eventually, she too pondered openly on such things as, "Wonder what that Howard's got?"

In learning to tolerate and eventually contributing to such critiques, Reeda's revulsion at her husband's transgressions became, if not forgotten, less active. She began to understand sex in some quarters is accepted as sex, does not carry a pledge of allegiance, and is a simple failing of the flesh. She did not like the brittle shell of such a morality, but, God, anything was better than an open wound!

Like the woman named Cynthia told one of the younger girls, crying her eyes out over being dumped by the man she was engaged to, "Debbie, honey, there ain't no purple heart for getting wounded in a love war. Get over it, girl!"

Reeda's knowledge of transportation, like her awareness of human imperfection, grew almost by osmosis. There was little time for formal training in trucking's piston-paced world. Though, at times, her questions were ignored and were always answered in hurried tones amid the persistent ringing phones, Reeda's competence grew with the speed of a jungle vine.

She learned to interpret and use the information on the computer copy of a freight bill. When a customer started screaming for a shipment, almost any question could be answered if the bill was available. When the bill wasn't in the computer, she developed a sixth sense about when it had not left the shipper's dock, which happened all too often.

It was a total drag when the computer system was down, but like Howard said, "Hell, don't your washing machine ever break down?"

"Yes, but—"

"Still, hon, you don't wanna go back to a rub board, do you?" She learned great respect for Howard's grass roots logic. Unpolished or not, the man knew the freight business.

Her initial preference for the electric typewriter and dread of the computer monster changed. When she learned the computer, she realized it was as far ahead of the typewriter as the dishwasher was ahead of washing dishes by hand. Ten weeks a trace clerk, Reeda met her most critical test of competence, patience and endurance.

Nothing she said satisfied the insistent voice burning the other end of the wire. Stanley was out to lunch, she was on her own. Passed the point of tears and battling her temper, she heard herself managing to beg off by promising to check further and call the customer back within twenty minutes. On uncertain feet, she walked to the terminal manager's office. She hesitated in Hank Carter's open doorway, noting he was on the telephone. Ever the informal executive, Hank motioned her in and to a chair without interrupting his conversation.

"Now, Brewster, hold on a minute. If I have the picture, you are delivering with a road unit and the alley to the customer's receiving dock is too narrow to get in... Okay, how much weight is involved... No, they aren't supposed to send anyone after it... Take the shipment up to the dock yourself... Hell, man, you have a dolly, use it... Three cartons with a total weight of two hundred pounds hardly makes you a pack animal. Brewster, we sell store door delivery and that is precisely what we are going to give.

"No, it isn't your fault, or our customer's fault, you're in a rig too wide for the alley. Actually it's the city dispatcher's... Well, that's certainly your right. Get anybody you want in on it but, contrary to popular opinion, there are a few things the teamster's union doesn't run... Yeah, that's right... Well, maybe it's time we test that out but for right now, Brewster, you listen to me," Carter commanded.

"Take your dolly and deliver the freight. Now!... If you don't, I'll have your job, union or no union... Man, it's no threat, it's a promise and you know it! I didn't start in the freight business yesterday. If you want to work here, get on with your job!" Carter crashed the phone down and winked at Reeda before asking, "Now, what can I do for you, Miss Reeda?"

"Sir, Iron International is very upset."

"Honey, you look a bit upset yourself. What's the trouble?"

"They have a shutdown and need an eight hundred pound shipment on a trailer that just arrived. They say they must have it today."

"Is that a print out of the freight in your hand?"

"Yes, sir."

"Let me see." Reading the bill, he asked, "Did you tell them the truck is in town?"

"Yes, and that we just got the shipment off a connecting line in Akron yesterday. Was that wrong, sir?"

"Not wrong, darling, more like embarrassing."

"I thought it would help if the customer knew the freight was in."

"We don't sell overnight delivery from Akron or anywhere else. Second morning is as good as any line does, consistently. If a customer knows his shipment's in town, that's when he decides he needs it immediately, if not sooner."

"But we can't possibly make delivery today."

"That's right, no way. In some cases, where there is an extreme need, even though it's cost prohibitive to the company, we will pull the trailer to the dock, open the doors and pull the shipment off for pick up. See the number three next to the trailer number?"

"Yes, sir. I saw it."

"You may already know that LTL means less than a trailer load. We count starting with number one as LTL shipments are loaded in the nose of a trailer. Then so on to the back of the unit?"

"Yes, sir. Stanley taught me all about that."

"Okay then, Reeda, you know this shipment is right flat in the nose of the road trailer."

"Can we pull the freight off for their evening shift?"

"Do you know how long it takes to unload a trailer?"

"No, sir, I'm afraid not."

Carter smiled tolerantly, and said, "We always train our people after the fact. Lack of training time is why carriers are forever out to steal trained help from other lines."

"Well, sir, you don't have a worry about another line stealing me."

"Maybe not now, but there will be a day and it isn't going to be too long in coming."

"Thank you, sir."

"You're welcome. Now, with two good men unloading, a forty-five foot trailer averages between eight and ten hours stripping time depending on the type of freight. This unit didn't arrive until seven-thirty this morning, so it's actually tomorrow's business. We started working it about nine-thirty and if we hadn't pulled the men off to load outbound freight it would be somewhere around five-thirty this afternoon before this shipment would be on the dock, not counting the time it would take to deliver it across town."

"Mr. Carter, what shall I tell them?"

"What I've told you, in this case. Never explain this much if you can avoid it. Time is money and customers want delivery, not an education in trucking. Or excuses. But smile."

"Sir?"

"Honey, always keep a smile in your voice— that's why Alpha likes female trace clerks. And never tell a caller freight's in town we can't deliver. It really isn't."

To Reeda's surprise, the irate caller accepted what Carter told her to say and was satisfied with a promised nine a.m. delivery. It was possible to make a customer happy. It was sort of like minding a baby. Rocking might work, but you had to do whatever it took.

On this mystical day the glove of her job began to fit. At last it all fell into place. She started doing subconsciously what had required a constant effort. Being a part of the trucking industry began bringing her a new kind of satisfaction. In the weeks that followed, even Hank Carter commented, "Reeda, you have the rare constitution that can tolerate and even thrive on tracing and trucking."

In a booming economy, keeping inventory at an absolute minimum was paramount. The angry voice of a distressed consignee soothed by her diplomacy into the reasonable tone of a business person was the reward repeatedly forthcoming in her job. Her personal revelation that freight movement was the lifeblood of America lit in her a tremendous pride in helping that lifeblood to flow unhampered.

The endless activity on the dock, the interacting of men and cargo, the outbound doors yawning into the cave of a trailer, the inbound doors revealing the contents of a unit that might range from aspirin to zinc became as familiar as the pots and pans in her kitchen.

Inbound freight was handled in the a.m.— outbound in the p.m. Each had to make way for the other. A terminal manager's work nightmare was to find his dock covered with outbound freight when inbound freight was due to go on the city streets.

Never had she known such push, such pressure, such profanity. The freight business was many things— some good, some bad— but it was never, ever boring. In three months, she was comfortable in her job. In six months, she loved it.

After her first year, she had earned the reputation of being the best trace clerk in Alpha's thirty-five terminal system. Reeda preferred that reputation immensely to being the best housekeeper in her subdivision, even if she had ever had it— which she hadn't.

CHAPTER 2

One evening driving home from work, a sound like a snore came from the back seat of the car. Reeda hit the brakes throwing a heavy object to the floorboard and prompting a squeal of tires and protesting horn from the car behind.

"Damn! What's going on?" came a roar from the back floor.

"Howard Summers! What are you doing in my car?"

"Sleeping. What does it look like?"

"You almost caused me to have a stroke and a wreck!"

"Hey, lady, keep your bloomers on. Everything's gonna be all right," Howard drawled, as he go out of the car. The Buick that had almost hit them from the rear pulled up beside them. The elderly man driving screamed an obscenity prompting Howard to roar, "Stop tailgating and you won't have that problem you dumb son-of-a-bitch. And get that big wreck rolling before I beat your stupid brains in!"

The Buick jumped into motion with the white headed driver pumping a stiff middle finger back at Howard. Standing with his hands on his hips with a grin on his face, Howard watched the car disappear in traffic.

When he was satisfied the offensive driver was gone, Howard opened Reeda's door and said, "Glad I didn't have to beat up that old buzzard. Scoot over, hon."

"I beg your pardon?"

"Sweet baby, you don't have to beg for nothing I got," he said with a lecherous look. "But scoot on over, I got to get back to the terminal."

"Well, go around and get in and I'll drive you back."

"Hey, listen, it's your fault I'm stuck out across town. You're way too shook up right now for me to trust your driving. Honey, you know you almost killed my ass. Now, be a good girl and scoot over or I'll scoot you over."

Not doubting the man could and would, she agreed, "Okay! I'm scooting!"

Howard squashed the accelerator like stomping a roach and they were off.

Reeda screeched, "Lord, man, slow down!"

He said nothing and kept charging the car. At the next intersection, where he should have made a block to go back to the terminal, he shot across three lanes of traffic into the parking lot of the "Coffee Pot" restaurant.

"Howard, I really do need to be getting home."

"Davis, I really do need a decent cup of coffee, bad."

"There's plenty of coffee at the terminal."

"We ain't at the terminal. And, hon, you know how the coffee at the terminal is like axle grease this late in the day."

"You could make a fresh pot."

"I ain't no little coffee maker."

"Yeah, I know but it wouldn't kill you."

"Hon, I've been on the job ten hours already and don't know when I'm likely to get off. My wife has my car and it won't kill you to have a cup of coffee with me."

Seeing he did look like he was needing a good cup of coffee, she agreed, "All right, but it will have to be a quick cup."

As she met him in front of the car, he grinned, "If you had waited I would have opened your door for you." Reeda smiled. It was impossible to stay miffed at this green-eyed, overgrown boy, who was also one of Alpha's best supervisors.

"I said a quick cup," she reminded.

✥

By the time they were sitting over their second cup of very good coffee, Howard rambling on about work, kids, marriage, the high price of cars and the weather, Reeda sensed he was building up to something. Wanting to avoid any further complications, she finished her coffee and said, "I really must get on home. Van will be worried."

"Might do him good," Summers answered, making no move to leave.

Having no witty reply and unwilling to discuss her marriage, she merely shrugged.

"He's really given you a bad time," Summers said softly.

"I don't know what you're talking about."

"Come off it, honey. I know," he said pointedly.

"So you know! So what?"

"So, maybe it's time you had a little fun."

Though his statement had a certain appeal, she said, "I can't see how that would help."

"Davis, honey, you take just about every thing too serious. Don't you know some things don't need to help— they just need to feel good. Everybody plays. You keep on reneging, you'll be too old for anything but a rocking chair one of these years. Better have some fun while you still can, I always say."

"That's disgusting. You really do make me sick!"

"No, I don't," he said with a grin. "I know and you know what I make you, if you do have to fight it. But don't worry, hon. I got the time, I can wait."

"I don't understand making promiscuity a way of life," she hissed. "If you can't be faithful to your wife, why don't you divorce her?"

"Why don't you divorce your husband?"

"It... seemed wrong at the time."

"But it wouldn't have been?"

"Probably not. I don't know."

"Guess I know what you're talking about. I tried real hard to get a divorce, once upon a time," he said, with good humor.

"What happened?"

"Nearly starved to death, that's what. Living in a dump. Eating out of tin cans. Couldn't support two places. Don't make that kind of money. Besides, my wife ain't a bit like you, honey."

"Evidently not! She's got you working your rear off to feed her and pay her rent. That's a lot more than I've got."

"She don't have enough education to get a decent job to start with. And she was sitting squalling for me to come home. The kids too."

"So?"

"So, hell, Davis, I ain't that strong. I went home."

"And that was a big mistake?"

"Yep, I guess so— at least it was for me."

Watching his green eyes turn jade with sadness, she said, "Wonder what makes it so hard for people to get along and just be happy?"

"Shit, honey, I don't know. Wish I did. If you could bottle up peace of mind, you could sell it and name your price. But I do know what it's like to grow up without a daddy."

"Your father died?"

"Naw. My old man left us before I can hardly remember. Didn't see him again till after I was grown. You don't never forget not having a daddy. I won't ever let that feeling happen to my kids."

"Then, I guess you really do care."

"Hell, yes, I care. Told you that. What do you think I am?"

"But what kind of influence are you going to be on your kids? Your oldest son probably already knows what kind of life you lead."

"Yeah, if he's paying attention. I don't hide it. Anyway, Howard, Jr. was one squalling the loudest for me to come home. Lady, I ain't Jesus Christ. You ain't either. I just don't care who knows it. You really do need to grow up"

She told herself it was stupid to discuss aesthetic values with someone who had only temporal values. With an uncertain grin she said, "My mother used to say, we never get through with our education."

"What education?"

"Nothing, Howard. No kidding, I do have to get home. I have this son who is too much of a latch key kid at the best I can do."

— ✿ —

On her way home again, after dropping Summers at the terminal, she was truly concerned about being late. Van had started asking pointed questions lately, as if he fully expected to be repaid in kind for his unfaithfulness. She always answered his inquiries, not wanting a jealous husband on her hands.

When she finally did get home, Van wasn't there. Reeda felt relieved that no explanation on her part was necessary. Jamey was in his room watching TV and seemed fine other than hungry, as usual.

After dinner she talked with the boy awhile. Then they worked at the kitchen table on his homework.

Not long after Jamey was in bed, she realized how tired she was and went on to bed herself. Sometime later, unsteady footsteps awakened her.

"Damn," Van cursed at stumbling over a chair.

"Van, please turn on the light."

"You... you awake?"

"Not until now!"

He switched on the lamp, "Sorry I'm so late. We had a long meeting. Had to stay for the dinner and drinks afterwards," He rambled on, removing all doubt he was lying. When telling the truth, Van never explained. He came to the bed and as he bent down to kiss her she saw the smear of lipstick.

Rolling over away from him, her mouth against the pillow, she snapped, "Better see about your neck, Van. It looks like Vampira's had a hold of you."

"What?"

"There's lipstick on your neck."

"Lipstick? Can't be lipstick. Where would I get any lipstick?"

"See for yourself."

Checking his neck in the dresser mirror, he explained, "Must be from the cherries. Had cherry tart for dessert."

"I don't doubt the tart part."

"Huh?"

"Forget it! But sleep on the sofa, Van. I'm really tired and I can't stand sharing the same trough with you tonight."

He snarled, "Yeah, right! And bet you have a damn headache, too."

Reeda didn't answer. She lay with her eyes closed and thanked God for small favors when Van muttered, "Shit!" turned off the lamp and staggered out of their bedroom.

How strange, she thought, there really was a time she used to cry if he wasn't home at night to sleep with her.

❧✕❧

At breakfast, Van's attempts at conversation were met with polite, short answers. As he was leaving he said, "I'll try to get back early tomorrow night. Jacksonville never takes more than a day and a half. Maybe we can have dinner and catch a movie."

"Who cares," she said dully. Why she tolerated his peck on her check, was beyond her. He knew she knew he wasn't fooling anyone.

Van wanted to sidestep, but he had to ask, "You all right? You look kinda strange."

"I feel kinda strange, come to think of it."

"Is it that time of the month again?"

"Always is when I'm upset, according to you. I was wondering what you might say if I told you a man asked me out."

"You take him up?"

"I can't imagine why not. But, no, I didn't."

"Good, girl," he said, pleasantly.

"Sounds just like you are praising a bitch dog. Don't you even care who he was?"

"You didn't pick up on his come on, so it doesn't matter."

"God, you've gotten weird, Van."

"I've gotten weird? Hell, you always have been off the wall. Don't be thinking since you're making your big trucking company pay check, I'll be your fool. Maybe I shouldn't say it, but if you ever run around on me, like I have you, I could never forgive you."

Seeing the flicker of dismay in her eyes, he added, "That may not be fair, but I couldn't. I'd just have to divorce you and take Jamey with me. You just wouldn't be a fit mother."

"Right! I deserved that. When you lay down to be walked on, there's always some ass glad to do it. Then it goes on and on."

"Reeda, I can't help the way I feel."

"Three years ago I would have said the same thing."

"You feel different now?"

"I am different now. And I know we don't really know what we will do till the time comes. It's bad business to count your actions before you react. But I strongly agree that a divorce is what should happen when a twosome becomes a triangle. Because afterwards, Van—" she paused for effect, taking bitter satisfaction in the pain she was about to deliver, "it's never the same."

It was pure delight to watch him wrestle with hiding his pain before he asked, "You mean you don't love me like you used to?" Reeda ignored the warning sounding somewhere deep inside her.

Maybe she was going too far, but what did it matter? He had hurt her too much to miss her shot. "Van, if we divorced tomorrow, in a way, I would probably still love you. You were my first love, we have a son, we've been together a long time and there had been some good times. But love you like I used to? No, not now— not ever again!"

She brushed past him and was in the car and five miles down the interstate before her mental processes returned to normal. How curious she felt no anger or pain, but only a weary disappointment and a tired acceptance of the inevitable.

A rotten apple is a rotten apple is a rotten apple and no amount of polishing will make it anything but a rotten apple. How stupid of her to have taken so many years to realize such a kindergarten fact! Still she couldn't shake the idea that it was her rotten apple and somehow of her own making. Therefore she had to take some of the blame.

Once she was at work and at her desk, answering the phone, talking to the customers, running the computer, Reeda worked like a sewing machine and forgot her personal problems while the phone rang with the regularity of a heartbeat.

For eight hours of questions and answers, offers of steak dinners, punctuated with blasphemy and threats to never give Alpha Truck another pound of freight, she was free from pain.

But that night, Van was a no-show again for the promised dinner date and movie. She and Jamey went on to dinner and a movie without him.

Later, after her son was asleep, the tangle of her life came to haunt her. Knowing she couldn't sleep, she tried to watch television. The hovering blackbirds of her thoughts wouldn't let her get into the talk show. It was past three a.m. when finally, with no answers and no hope, she turned her wet pillow to the dry side and slept.

❧❈❧

At coffee break, after a bit of idle conversation, Cyn zeroed in, "Aren't you ever going to say anything about it? Reeda, a rock could see you're having a hell of a time at home."

"Is it really that obvious?"

"Maybe only to those who know you. Want to share?"

"Not especially."

"Okay, whatever you say."

"I don't mean to block you out, it isn't anything that can be helped."

"Okay. Reeda, uh, when I left work, one day last week, I saw Howard sleeping in your car. That was the day you got hung up on long distance with that idiot in California. Was Howard still in your car when you came out?"

Reeda faltered only a moment before saying, "Yes, but I didn't know it until I was half way home. He started snoring and just about scared me to death."

"And?"

"And what?"

"God, Reeda! You can be so dense. How do you like the man?"

"Not much. When you look past the beautiful physique, he's just another womanizer. And don't be giving me that raised eyebrow look. You know him as well as I do." She waited, but Cynthia said nothing. "Damn, Cyn! You don't think I'd lie to you?"

"Sometimes, the way you look at him, makes me think you'd lie to me and you, too."

"What way?"

"The way a woman looks at a man she finds attractive. He looks at you the same way."

"But he isn't attractive."

"Maybe I should say attracted to— you tell me. Don't be phony enough to say nothing."

"I've never been phony in my life. Howard Summers isn't very much of anything, I suspect. Oh, he's all male, I'll give him that."

"Like... stud? Or do you like the word hunk better?"

"There's something wild and virile about Howard. Like a stallion sniffing wind."

"I hear that! Yes, ma'am!"

"But that doesn't mean I want to go to bed with him. I have a little more respect for myself than that."

"To be a wife and a mother, you're the most naive female I know."

"It's not a matter of being naive, it has more to do with hygiene. I know people don't have to be married to have sex. But I don't understand being intimate with a man you know is subject to be intimate with any woman who wants him. Aside from morals, for cleanliness sake there are some things you just don't do."

Cyn laughed as if she had heard the joke of the year. Then she gasped, "Please hush. You're killing me," and continued to laugh.

"What's so funny? Come on now, share the fun."

Finally, Cyn stopped laughing and asked, "Where did you find this cut and dried little world of yours?"

"I don't think it's cut and dried. And it isn't my little world. We're all in it together." Reeda realized, she sounded on the defensive.

"You've never had anyone but your husband, have you?"

"Cyn, that's personal!"

"Have you?"

"No. Of course not."

"You're not the first woman to tell me that— you really are the first one I've believed."

"Did it ever occur to that racing mind of yours, I might be in love with my husband?"

"Yeah. I gave you the benefit of the doubt, but I rejected that idea the first week after we met. You don't send out the right vibrations."

"What vibrations?"

"All sorts of things. Mainly, unless it's illegal, a woman talks about the man she loves. You seldom mention Van's name."

"Just because I have no patience with these rampant dime-a-dozen affairs doesn't mean I'm some kind of freak."

"Reeda, I said naive. Lord, One of these days you'll go wild over someone and you'll understand. It's like losing your cherry, no one can explain it. It has to happen to you before you get the picture."

"You're over my head. Let's get on back to work."

All afternoon, every wholesaler in town seemed to have a hot shipment in route. Reeda was thinking maybe it was going to be a full moon night when she answered her most disturbing call of all.

"What are you doing?"

"Tracing. What else?" she said, not catching the voice.

"How have you been?"

"Fine," she said, still in the dark.

"Are you happy?"

"Who is this?"

"Am I embarrassing you?"

"No, I just don't know who you are."

"Bryan Kelly, of course. Cynthia?"

"I'm sorry, Mr. Kelly, you have the wrong party. The operator must have misunderstood. Cynthia's out. Can I have her call you back?"

"I— no."

"You might try back around two, she should be back by then."

"Thank you," he said, leaving Reeda feeling strangely guilty.

On Friday after lunch, in the ladies room brushing on more blush, Cyn said, "Reeda, please don't mention the mix-up on the phone the other day. Patsy is the flakiest switchboard operator in captivity."

"No problem. Patsy just pushed a wrong button. It's no big deal."

"If I have to draw you a picture, this friend happens to be married."

"You're not serious?"

"I wish."

Reeda frowned. "Why does someone beautiful as you want to see a married man?"

"Thanks. Things happen. Besides, he hardly knows he's married."

"But you do."

"Don't get excited, I'm not going to date him, I just like to tease. Make him think I can't wait, then when he asks, utter a sweet no."

"Why?"

"Hell, Reeda, I don't know."

Reeda's puzzled grin took the sting from her, "Don't you realize how cheap that is?"

"Yes, but when you are, in the words of my divorce lawyer, built like a brick shit house, you get to despise men, in a way, because they never notice anything about you except your behind. Your needs and your feelings don't count. Guess it makes you spiteful and a little bitter. Know what I mean?"

"Nope. I never had such a problem, not being blessed with a behind like yours."

"You're lucky."

Reeda grinned. "Well, your secret's safe with me. Listen, we better get on the clock if we want to keep working for good old Alpha."

"It's time to repeat my motto, it pays good, it pays good. You go ahead. I'm going to brush my teeth, right quick here."

Surviving hard times made Cynthia and Reeda natural allies. Reeda knew that Cyn was a wife and mother before she was seventeen.

They didn't have the typical shotgun wedding, but Cynthia's parents found some notes and decided that because of what had transpired between Cynthia and John, their marriage ceremony was mandatory. According to what Cynthia told Reeda, not all that much happened. At least not enough to railroad two curious teenagers into premature matrimony. But they were excited over their tentative investigations of each other's bodies, as much in love as teenagers usually are, and not opposed to marriage.

The first year was fine. John finished high school and Cynthia finished her junior year. An exceptional athlete, John won a sports scholarship to a first-rate college. He probably would have been set for life, despite his inclination toward laziness if he could have spent the college years unhampered and gone on into professional football. John Madden never truly loved anything but sex and sports, in that order. College satisfied his love for sports.

His appetite for sex suffered with Cynthia a hundred miles away living with her parents and finishing her senior year of high school. There were plenty of willing coeds around. Out of desperation, he finally had a go in the back seat of a new red convertible belonging to a beautiful brat who had been after him for weeks.

That next Saturday, John was so full of guilt that he missed an easy touchdown pass and vowed to himself never to cheat on Cynthia again. Every time he felt himself on the brink of another transgression, he cut classes and football practice to go home to Cynthia. Cynthia, too shy to get fitted for a diaphragm and John, hating condoms, brought on the inevitable. It was a hard pregnancy. Cynthia vomited every morning; and some days vomited intermittently all day long. Still, she managed to graduate from high school with honors and the flowing graduation gown hid her condition beautifully.

That summer, John took a counseling job with a boy's camp two hundred miles up state. The money was so much better than anything he could get closer to home refusing was out of the question. Lonely and pregnant, Cynthia passed the hot summer eating. By fall, when the baby came, she had gained fifty pounds, delivered breach and almost died. She was in the agony of labor four days and recovered hating sex, men and babies.

It was six months before she was physically or mentally ready for sex. Then an overly zealous John broke the condom. In Cyn's words, she "Got knocked up the second time without even breathing hard." Her husband had never been the target of such loathing, that grew more intense in Cynthia's eyes as her stomach swelled.

Before voting age, John had two sons he couldn't support and a wife who despised him. He made no martyr announcement, but after Christmas break his junior year, John simply did not return to school. As though for self-punishment, he found a terrible job in the furnace room hell of a glass plant and worked all the overtime he could get.

Initially, John and Cynthia were overjoyed with their new cracker box house and cheap modern furniture. Along with their two sons, Cynthia thought they were living the American dream. As time passed it became the American nightmare. John became what she called a "slob in living color". When he was home, John sat in front of the TV with a can of beer, watching sports and singing along with the beer commercials. He never shaved, showered or changed clothes until she raised hell or he had to go back to work.

Cynthia acquired a diaphragm and lost some of her apprehension about getting pregnant. Still her husband very rarely approached her for sex. She dismissed the possibility of his cheating on her, since he was always at work or hanging out in front of the big TV at home. Her efforts with special dinners and even a new black negligee were met with half-hearted acceptance. With the rage of a woman scorned, she began to berate John even more about his appearance and his beer.

John began drinking after work at a sports bar. He would come home drunk, fall into bed and answer his wife's frustrated anger with impudent snores.

When it occurred to Cynthia that she was losing her husband, right before her eyes, she put aside her own disillusionment. For once, since her first pregnancy, she tried to be tender and loving and understanding. It was one more case of too little too late. John's response was evasive and half-hearted at best. Cynthia came away from each session of trying to "communicate with him" feeling more confused and alienated than ever.

Ever the athlete, John was too much of a good sport to tell her that when their sexual relationship was destroyed, then his future in sports, he had for any good reason ceased to live. Since their marriage precluded his chances in either direction, he merely regarded her, without any animosity, as his executioner. Still, he couldn't stand to make love to his executioner.

Similar to the dread and hopefulness a parent applies the razor-strap, Cynthia filed for divorce. Her cunning lawyer, determined to "tie John up hand and foot" was foiled by a wise judge permanently saddened by the multitude of couples arriving in his court in mortal combat. The judge persuaded Cynthia to give her husband another chance on the strength of his promise to do better.

And John truly improved. He stayed home and stopped drinking until his wife grew tired and bored again from too much house work, too much baby work and too little money and affection. Deeply hurt from feeling he no longer cared for or about her, Cynthia opened up with the big guns of her tongue. John promptly returned to the sports bar, drinking and staying out till the wee hours.

Another year ground by before he began to miss work. He never felt feel well and complained, "I have this awful tiredness all the time, Cyn." After seeing the doctor again, who could find nothing wrong again, John would spend a day or two in bed.

Then he would drag back to the plant, preferring the discomfort of working and being on his feet to the chaos of home and his wife yelling, "Drunkard, you can't work because you're hungover! If you would lay off the beer you wouldn't feel so bad."

"Cyn, I drink to numb the pain."

The constant yammering of two kids still in diapers was almost as horrible. His "bad tiredness" progressed to pain, smoldering initially in the pit of his stomach, then later graduating into fingers of fire licking up his back and down his legs. There were trips to new doctors, treatment for everything from heartburn to hypochondria and an impending nervous breakdown. His drinking was replaced with tranquilizers and anti-acid pills.

They could not revive John the day he fainted at the plant. The ambulance made good time to the hospital and they managed to revive him there.

After ten days and a round of tests, other than losing thirty pounds, the hospital doctors still found nothing wrong. Still the man who was getting weaker by the day. His doctors decided that exploratory surgery was the only option left to John.

Cynthia would always remember it was cold and it was raining on the day of John's surgery. After only two hours in the operating room, the surgeon emerged and advised her that John's operation revealed advanced cancer of the pancreas and liver. In less than three weeks, when John died, he was the brightest neon yellow she had ever seen. Cynthia thought John looked more possessed than dead. Maybe that was because she hadn't really slept in forever.

In the aftermath, Cynthia suffered a near breakdown and was totally exhausted. Along with her two small sons, she moved in with her parents. Mawmaw and Pawpaw were delighted to have their grandsons in the house and enjoyed taking them out on day trips and showing them off.

Weary Cynthia got the first real rest and peace of mind she had know since her first son was born. After a year, feeling somewhat mended, she found a day job in the office of a shirt factory. The office was dingy, her clerical desk was heavy, dull and low pay, but she felt it was a start. At last she could do something besides change diapers and weep for the dying.

In four years, she jockeyed from minimum wage to the ten dollars an hour she made working for Alpha Truck Lines. Liberated from always losing, feeling scorned and unappreciated, she proved herself intelligent, capable and impervious to hard work. These were the rare qualities needed to successfully work for a common carrier.

With the unending help of her parents, whom she had learned to appreciate and dearly love, Cynthia lifted herself up from living off them and government food stamps.

Currently, she was in a comfortable apartment, had dependable day-care for her boys and a wonderful cleaning lady twice a month. For the first time in her adult life, Cynthia was happy, proud of her achievements and loved working for Alpha Truck Lines.

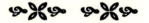

CHAPTER 3

As Reeda stood reading the manifest on the work table just inside the trailer, Howard walked up close beside her. She could feel his body heat as he purred, "Hon, maybe I can help. Whatcha looking for?"

"Uh, well, Howard. Whiz Electric is wild for a reel of wire that's supposed to be on this inbound Chicago trailer."

He checked the manifest. "The shipment's unloaded. It's on the floor in front of twenty-two door. Be delivered tomorrow."

"Can Whiz send a man over to pick it up?"

"Sure, I'll tell the dock men not to load it out."

"Thanks, I appreciate it."

"No problem. Listen, hon, I sold an old car I had and got a pocket full of money. I'd like to take you out and spend it on you."

"You couldn't pick a worse prospect for a night on the town. I'm not feeling very well."

"You just look to me like a woman feeling real blue."

"Guess that's part of it," Reeda admitted.

"You'd feel better if you got out and had some fun."

"We've been though this. Can't you take a nice no for an answer?"

"Yeah, I can, if I have to. But I know when a woman's saying no and wants to say yes."

"Wrong, Howard."

"Don't much think so, honey. I got a sixth sense about women."

"And your wife? Do you have a sixth sense about her?"

"Hell, hon, done told you about my wife. Janey knows how I am."

"Then how does she bear it?"

"Reckon, that's her choice. Sure don't beg her to live with me."

"Men! You all make me sick, you think you're so smart."

"With them eyes blazing, baby, your Cherokee side is showing something beautiful."

"So! Just look at you, standing reared back with your chauvinistic side showing like you know all the secrets of the universe."

"Hon, don't take no guru to see the heart of your marriage stopped beating awhile ago."

"I can't help it, if it has, Howard."

"Naw, angel, you can't change your dead marriage any more than I can mine. You can accept it. You'll feel better if you take things like they are, your old man too, probably."

"Do you hate the mother of your children that much?" "

"Naw. Don't hate her none. Don't hate or hurt nobody, if they just let me alone."

"Surely, you don't pretend to care for her?"

"Don't pretend about nothing. I do care for the woman. Every damn paycheck I work for, that she gets the most of, proves that."

"But how does she stand your fooling around with other women?"

"Hell, I don't know. That's her problem. I told you about that and she knows I'm not in love with her. She strangled that part years ago."

"I know she wasn't unfaithful. You're too chauvinistic to forgive an unfaithful wife."

"Wouldn't make me no difference, if I loved her and she was loving me back good."

"Howard, you're nuts."

"Davis, you're hung-up on unfaithful. There's a hundred ways to ruin your love life besides somebody being unfaithful."

"Like what?"

"Like, Janey got pregnant and blamed me."

"Guess you weren't there."

"We were sort of out of protection that night. She's the one crawled on me. After the baby, she got fat and lazy and sloppy. She knows I hate that. And back when things were rough, she raised hell cause I couldn't set her on a satin pillow. Cussed me for any disappointment that came her way. Drove me out of love with her years ago. She knows it, cause I told her. I'd say we're about even."

"Then leave her."

"Like I said the other night, can't afford it. But I do care for her and I love my kids."

"But not enough to be faithful."

"No, ma'am. My job and women are all I got left. Ain't giving up either one, if I can help it. But I care for Janey. Like family— like a mother or a sister."

"Your feelings sound perverted to me, Howard."

"Could be, but they're my feelings. And, like you say, she's the mother of my kids. Plus... she's done things for me nobody else would. Like when I burned my hands."

"Burned your hands?"

"Couldn't do one thing for myself. Janey fed me, bathed me. Did everything and I mean everything for me."

"When was that?"

"Several years back, way before you ever knew me. For three weeks I was helpless as a baby and the whore I was running with at the time didn't have time for me. But Janey seemed almost happy I was hurt so she could do all those things for me. Made up my mind to be the kind of husband I should be. Was for a couple of months after I got well. But— hell I couldn't keep it up."

"Why not?"

"Know it's crazy, but I couldn't stay excited about her. I gotta have that kind of excitement. All I could think about was I just had to be wild over someone one more time. To be out of your head, stinking wild about someone, ain't nothing else like it."

"Good Lord, you say things other people don't let themselves even think except at night with the lights out and everybody else asleep."

He grinned. "I know. Guess that's what makes me a bastard."

"Guess so," she agreed. Reeda realized his honesty was contagious as she asked, "Am I... uh... built like a brick outhouse?"

Still grinning, he said, "That ain't the right word."

"Whatever," she said impatiently. "You know what I mean."

"Yep, I know. Who told you that? Old Hank? I've seen the way he's inspecting you."

"No, nobody told me that," Reeda said irritably.

"Hey, you can talk to me without being embarrassed."

"I'm trying. I admire the way you talk about your feelings. Without being embarrassed. Anyway, am I?"

"Nope, you're built like more for flying. Like a dark, jet plane, long and slim and curved, Not too much, not too little, in just the right places." His eyes praised her body as he said, "Darling, it's a God awful shame, all them goodies you got just plain going to waste."

"Well," Reeda said, her face crimson, "Guess, I asked for that. I have to get back to my desk and call my customer."

"Girl, listen, I know the time ain't just right yet, but when you do wise up and realize what's going on, let me know."

"When deserts need sand," she snapped.

But in the weeks that followed, Reeda became the slave of depression. All the joy had gone out of her life. This is how it's going to be, she kept telling herself. Just accept it. Once you do, things will seem better, only fools refuse to accept the truth. But oh, God, how horrible it is! Hey, don't go off the deep end. You have problems enough without exaggerating. I'm not; horrible doesn't nearly express it. Every plan, every dream, my every conception of love and marriage mocks me. If I ever start orally expressing how terrible I feel about my marriage and Van, they'd wind up sending for a net.

That bright young man I married, who was going to be a leader of youth, protector of the innocent, the perfect husband and father; where did he go? Oh, he turned out to be a lush, a liar and a letch.

And that wife? Where is she? Why, she's a breadwinner, my child. And the mother, the one who was going to guide her children and be close to them and understand their problems and remember what it's like to be a kid and want to do so many things and seemingly, get to do so few? Well, she only has one son, couldn't fit another child into the budget. Like everything else, another child costs too much.

And is she listening to the plans and dreams of the one child she does have? Why no, my dear, her ears are deaf, her mind drowned with her own disillusionment. Her heart is too saturated with pain to relate to her son like she should and wants to. And instead of the perfect son with high hopes and high marks and high ideals, that son is becoming a sullen teenager substituting being hip for dreams and TV for ideals.

And what about those days not long ago when she was going to be a model of forgiveness and understanding, when she would overlook anything for the sake of her home and marriage, when she couldn't face being a divorcee with a son to rear alone and a living to earn? Why did that life seem so unacceptable then and the better part of valor now? Who thought up this marriage-saving bit anyway? The state, of course. Keeps the welfare roster down.

It simply wasn't civilized to save rancid things. Nobody wanted to eat chicken that had died a natural death. Marriage was no different. They've brainwashed us, she thought. By the time you realize you couldn't face burying a corpse, it seems too late to bury it.

Reeda's depression plummeted deeper as the weeks went by. Howard's hungry eyes at work and Van's lying eyes at home did not help matters or her state of mind.

She continued to refuse to share Van's bed. His "business" absences became longer and more frequent. But she didn't question him. What did it matter? The pressure of the freight business filled her day. At night, she used the anesthesia of TV and sometimes sleeping pills. She was in the gestation period of a plan for what to do with the rest of her life. She knew there was no rushing it. It would take— however long it took.

Eventually, she started feeling some better. Finally, a morning came when she woke clear headed, strong hearted and determined to accept what she knew now must come. Acknowledging she couldn't walk on water, accepting defeat, realizing she had to separate herself from the present to make a future.

That night she again approached her husband as gracefully as she knew how with, "Van, I don't want to fight with you but our fiasco of a marriage has gone on long enough. It's high time we filed for a divorce."

"I wondered how long that would ferment before it came of age."

"You've anticipated my asking?"

"Of course. I knew you'd never really forgive me. You always held yourself above me."

"Not before the woman."

"Reeda, before the woman was ever thought of. You tried to hide it but I knew. I've always known. You have always held yourself higher than the rest of the herd. Admit it."

"The herd, yes. But I never considered you part of it."

"Yes you did. You've always had a withdrawal, a certain reserve. You never could let me quite all the way in. I felt it all along, I just never could express it before. You always wanted to know why I did the way I did. Couldn't tell you then, because I didn't know. I know now. The only time in our marriage I had one hundred percent of your attention was when you thought you were going to lose me. And it wasn't losing me that concerned you so. It was the thought of losing your ability to hold me."

"I don't know what you are talking about."

"And the only time I get that, 'I don't know what you are talking about routine' is when I have you pegged."

"Van, I'm not going to argue with you about that or anything else. It's too late for two adults who have made as big a mess as we have to rehash. Let's just end it as soon as possible, for all our sakes."

"Uh, uh, baby, nothing doing."

"Surely, after running around on me for years, you don't intend to fight a divorce."

"You bet I am."

"But why? It doesn't make sense."

"Just for the hell of it, Reeda."

"What's to gain? You don't care about me, you haven't for years."

"That's where you're wrong."

"Don't make me laugh. If you had one grain of respect for me, you wouldn't hop on and off of mattresses like some bed bug."

"It's you who don't care for me— for who I am. Always has been."

"That isn't true, Van Davis, and you know it isn't."

"Sorry to tell you, Reeda Davis, but it is true. Anyway, it doesn't matter, I like it this way. You'd be surprised the situations having a wife and son can get you out of."

"One situation it can get you into is a divorce."

"Oh what grounds?" he asked, innocently.

"Adultery!"

"After we've been living under the same roof? Don't be dumb!"

"But I haven't lived with you. At least, not in the physical sense, since the last time I knew there was another woman in our marriage."

"We are under the same roof, darling."

"Not for long! I'll have you out of here in forty-eight hours."

"Not if I don't choose to you won't— and I don't choose to go. And since our reconciliation I've kept my nose clean."

"That's a lie."

"Prove it! Little lipstick on my neck with no witness doesn't prove a thing, Reeda. Any courtroom bum in town will tell you that."

"I hate you, Van. Can you possibly, even remotely, conceive of how much I really do hate you?"

"Probably. You always have. That's why you always tried to change me. Better learn to live with it. As far as I'm concerned, we are going to have a long unhappy marriage."

"You bastard! I should have known better than to try and talk any common sense to you. I'm going to bed!"

Knowing Van never lied when he could be checked on, Reeda still consulted a lawyer. She didn't look forward to a divorce. She sincerely doubted she would be any happier as a divorced woman, but a bad marriage, like a bad appendix, was a progressive thing. It had to be eliminated before it killed.

Cecil Evans was one of the most prominent attorneys in the city. It disgusted her that her hand shook as the suave gray-haired man lit her cigarette. "Now," he said, settling himself on the plush chair behind his desk, "I believe you said you were having domestic difficulty?"

"Yes, Mr. Evans. I... I need a divorce."

"What seems to be the trouble?"

"Other women."

"Hummm... tell me about it."

"Well, the main trouble was three years ago. We managed to patch things up, but it hasn't worked out."

"Same kind of trouble? Other women?"

"Yes. I suppose anyone is liable to try and live through one infidelity. I can't imagine trying again."

"Many women do," he said, "and successfully, or so it seems."

"Yes, that's why I forgave my husband three years ago and agreed to try again. But— Mr. Evans, it was a bitter pill to try and swallow."

"I would imagine."

"I have had to realize I'm not like many women. As we speak, I'm trying to come to terms with what is, instead of what I'd have it be. Bottom line, Mr. Evans, I have a horrendous marriage. I can't live with a womanizing husband and I want a divorce in the worst way."

"Have you asked your husband for a divorce?"

"Yes, he refused. He said I can't get a divorce because I lived with him after our separation and that I have no proof of anything since."

"If you don't have any proof, legally, he may be right."

"But I know he is being unfaithful."

"Knowing isn't proof. Some hungry lawyer might try for a divorce action based on your husband's past infidelity and your present suspicions. It would be a messy business if your husband fights it. I don't need clients that badly. In fact, as I said on the phone, I no longer handle divorces. I would turn the case over to Mr. Bird— under my supervision, of course. Mr. Bird is a junior partner here and quite capable. You can't imagine the muck slinging in domestic court. The first cases most lawyers refuse, once established, are divorce cases. Divorce is at an all time high. Our domestic judges have become very strict. Once a marriage goes through a reconciliation, what caused the split is passe' in the court's eyes. You have no witness to your husband's transgressions since then?"

"No, but when a man stays out all hours and comes in with lipstick on his neck, he hasn't been out with the boys."

"No, I grant you that, and I even sympathize. But this office goes into court to win. You haven't anything to win on."

"Well, Mr. Evans, what am I supposed to do?"

"You have lived in a bad situation all this time, Mrs. Davis. You surely don't want to lose the last round."

"No, I don't. How can I keep from losing?"

"Get the goods before going to court. Hire a detective. I can recommend one, but reliable detectives are expensive. A friend would do as well."

"I don't know that I have that kind of friend."

"Anyone reputable who will act as your witness will do. But let me warn you, a fish that has thrown the hook once is a hard dude to catch again. If possible, your best bet is to make up with your husband. Put him off guard. Let him think you suspect nothing. Suspect everything, check out everything till you get what you need."

"You mean sleep with him?"

"Of course."

"But I can't! Not after he has slept with God knows what! You should have seen what he went wild over before."

"Beauty is always in the eye of the beholder, Mrs. Davis. When it comes to sex— who knows? But if you deny him the marriage bed, you're beat before you start."

"Oh, good God!"

"If my firm represents you, I want you to win."

"I see why you have the reputation of being a super attorney. What you are suggesting is ludicrous."

"My dear, so is losing and so is a divorced couple sharing the same house. But it does happen. I want to see that it doesn't happen to a client of mine. Also, I never advise a client to file for divorce if I detect the slightest iota of a chance for a reconciliation."

"There isn't. Not the slightest."

"Maybe not, but verbal missiles are one thing. Legal language, down in black and white, is another and becomes an almost impossible barrier to hurdle in the continuance of a marriage."

"It doesn't matter in my case," Reeda said evenly.

"When it involves their sexuality, men are complex creatures. They go through periods of sexual self-doubt. It reacts like a fever and they will stoop to almost any depth of degradation for reassurance. Sometimes, if their wives can bear with them, one day they drag themselves up from the mire and again become responsible husbands and fathers."

"I don't care."

"I don't blame you. I just wanted to explain why I don't like anything in writing, if I detect the chance a wife might put such a period behind her. I don't know whether it's a plus or a minus trait, but I doubt you are such a woman. It was probably a mistake for you to continue the marriage after your husband's first indiscretion."

"I don't know. At the time, I thought the most horrible thing in the world was to be single and rear a son alone. I thought my pride wasn't nearly as important as my son having a father. How wrong I was!

"Live and learn, that's the name of the game, so consider my suggestion. If your husband is having an affair, I think you are smart enough to get what you need. You would come out so much better. Seducing your husband can't hurt anything either," Cecil Evans said and hid his amusement at the shock in her eyes.

Rising from her chair, Reeda said, "I have never made love for any reason except the pure pleasure of it. I'm too old to change now."

The lawyer smiled sadly as he said, "In over sixty years of living, there is one thing I have learned for sure. One is never too old to change, and you aren't old. By the way, keep your own nose clean."

"What do you mean?"

"Don't fall victim to the woman scorned backlash."

"I don't understand what you are saying, Mr. Evans."

"Don't jump into bed with the first man that asks you to and don't get caught if you do."

"Why on earth would I do something as foolish as that?"

"Only the gods understand that one. I have seen women of your same conviction and high moral caliber make the most awful fools of themselves in your situation."

She swallowed before saying, "You don't have to worry about me."

"Let us hope not, my dear. Let us most certainly hope not," Evans said. This time he did not bother to hide his amusement. Reeda Davis had much to learn but he did not doubt her ability for a moment.

※

All things considered, it had been a good eight weeks for her since consulting with Lawyer Evans. Divorce or no divorce, she would never be able to make love to Van Davis again. She was over Van. There had been too many nights of not knowing where he was or who he was with, but knowing exactly what he was doing. A woman could only stand so much.

Besides, she liked having her own pay and doing what she wanted with it. With a decent paying job, it was much easier to support herself and Jamey. It was easier to do as she saw fit, rather that answer to a husband who had never been what the word "husband" implied. Without Van muddying up things and making her life miserable, she could support herself and Jamey standing on her head, if she had to.

And she couldn't see that life was any worse for Jamey. As bad as she hated to admit it, her son had become a latchkey kid like so many children these days. Without a father, he would always be a latchkey kid. That was the part she hated most and, she supposed, what had kept her hanging on.

But, thank God, Van had finally agreed to a cooling off period. Initially he had refused saying, "Nothing doing. What's going on? Got you a truck driver on the string?"

But finally he had agreed. Actually, he had started changing his mind after she had said, "What have you got to lose? You will have a chance to do or see whoever you want to and no questions asked."

"You mean just like I was single?"

"Yes, of course, just like you were single. You will be single!"

But when she pulled in the driveway, Van was in the yard with Jamey flying a model airplane. "Hey, Mom," the boy called, "Look at the neat plane Dad bought me." Van's sudden interest and generosity was as astonishing as Jamey's joy at having his father pay him the slightest attention after all these years.

"Yes, it's very nice," Reeda called, hiding her surprise, advancing just outside the circumference of the airplane's circle.

"Dad's going to take us to dinner and a movie when we get through flying the plane, Mom. Okay?" It was impossible to refuse the boy's blue-eyed exhilaration, again she digested the hard fact of enmeshing reality. There was much more than right or wrong or the law to seduce one into continuing a bad marriage.

Without looking at Van, she said, "I'll freshen up. Let me know when y'all are ready."

When Jamey and Van came into the house, Reeda was leafing through a magazine.

She saw her son's delight again as he said, "Ready to go, Mom"?

"Yes, darling, but wash up first and brush your teeth. A clean shirt wouldn't hurt."

"Okay, I'll be right back."

Her eyes hardened as she asked, "To what do we owe this rare occasion of being graced with your presence and attention?"

"What do you mean?"

"Just because Jamey's soaking it up, don't think I'm that naive. This is the first time you have shared an evening with your son in years."

"Well, he's getting older and as you say, he is soaking it up. Let's not spoil it for him."

"One question, how did you manage to drag yourself away from your other activities?"

"Reeda, let this just be Jamey's evening. Don't bitch it up. Please?"

"You're right. There's really no point in it, anyway."

Jamey bounced into the room and said, "Do I look okay, Mom?"

"You look mighty handsome to me."

Van said, "Yeah, you even parted your hair straight, for a change."

All evening it was pitifully clear how fervently Jamey had hoped for the companionship of his father. Van was not only present but receptive, attentive and loving. Reeda saw the eager forgiveness of the young render a long wait unimportant. All evening the boy's eyes danced, and his laughter was as joyful as a toddler's on a carousel.

When it was over, and at the moment of good night he said, "Mom, tonight was wonderful. We were all together like we used to be."

"Yes," she said, kissing the boy good night.

Outside his door, Reeda paused a moment to gather herself. The joy of her son from just a simple family evening had renewed her sense of confusion and loss. The pain of her sadness was almost inconsolable. God, she wished she was big enough to beat some sense into Van. She knew him too well to be deluded. Van was just copping an attitude— this wouldn't last. Fist to mouth, she steadied herself against the wall.

Van had refused her a divorce. Maybe he did care. They had both had some cooling off time for Jamey's sake. The lawyer did say it was possible for a man to stoop lower than a snake's belly and still straighten up.

In all truthfulness, divorce offered about as much allure as a bottomless pit. Thirty-three was rather old to start a new life. At twelve, Jamey was too old to ever accept a step-father. Like he had said, tonight was like it used to be. Lord, sometimes out of the mouths of babes for sure.

Gathering her strength to face the man in the living room, she managed to enter smiling and asked, "Want a cup of coffee, Van?"

"Yeah, think I do." Van stood in the kitchen doorway making small talk while she prepared the coffee.

When the coffee was ready she asked, "Still drink it black?"

"I haven't been away that long."

"One never knows. Just checking."

"Yes," he answered.

"Okay, here you are." Turning to hand Van his cup she caught his appreciative eye on her figure.

With an acknowledging grin, he said, "That dress wouldn't be anything without your hips, Reeda."

"Thank you. That's the first nice thing you have said to me in ages."

"Your moods don't give me much chance. Do you mind?"

"Let's go in the living room," she evaded.

"Okay," he said, following the handsome woman who, whether she liked it or not, was still his wife.

They placed their cups on the coffee table and took seats at opposite ends of the sofa. "Reeda, you didn't answer my question."

She lit a cigarette before saying, "A woman who says she minds compliments is a liar."

"You were never one to lie. I'll say that for you."

"Is that a sin?"

"When a woman's strong, maybe straightforward is a better way to put it, she can make it harder for a man who may be weaker or at the least finds it hard to always be straight up."

"I've never thought of you as a weak man, Van."

"I know, that makes it worse. Being weak is terrible, pretending to be strong is as bad as it gets. Other people see through me."

"By other people, you meant other women," she said softly, surprised that she could say it so calmly.

"Other women accept me for what I am."

"I've always accepted you for what you are."

"No, you accept me for what you are— strong."

"Maybe, here is where I should ask, what are you?"

"I'm just a guy. I have no special qualities, no outstanding characteristics and no distinguishing marks. I'm not going to set any records or conquer any worlds. Trouble is— you always made me think I could."

"Was that bad?"

"Yes, when it gets to be too big a load to support."

"But a woman in love feels that way about her man."

"Believe it or not, some women love what a man is, not what she wants him to be."

"But I always loved you."

"You always goaded me about a better job."

"I only wanted you to get ahead."

"Getting ahead isn't all that important to me."

"Why haven't you told me this before now?"

"Like I already admitted, I'm weak. So weak, I accepted your values. And it has taken me a long time to figure all this out. All of it didn't come together for me till the past weeks. Guess I went a little crazy when you asked for the divorce."

"I thought that was what you wanted."

"It was different when I was doing the asking." Van moved closer. His blue eyes were begging as he said, "I can't lose you, honey. It's taken way too long for me to admit it, even to myself. But I can't live without you and Jamey."

Somehow she didn't believe him. Maybe she was the burned child. What if he really was sincere? She was past the crucifying hurt of knowing he had been with other women.

"Darling, whether you appreciate it or not, you still mean the world to me. You always have." Her lawyer's statement that men often pulled themselves out of detours came to mind as Van insisted, "Please, Reeda, you're the only woman I love— the only woman I have ever loved."

"Even at this late date, I suppose it would be better, especially for Jamey, if we could revitalize our marriage. If you honestly mean to try, I can't see as we have much to lose."

"You don't sound as if you give a damn one way or the other."

"The fact I'm discussing it with you proves I give a damn. I just don't have much faith."

"God, you do lay it on the line."

"Man, it's time to lay it on the line. Like you said, that's the way I am. You want me to accept you as you are. Accept me as I am. Let's give each other the freedom to be ourselves. Okay?"

"Anything you say," he said taking her hand. "Would it be all right if I kissed you? It's been forever."

"Van, I don't think—"

His lips touched her lips and suddenly felt as warm and wonderful as they had in those long ago first years. When she opened her eyes he was smiling. It was as if the in-between years of pain had never been. This was the same boy-man she had fallen in love with. The same winged brows, white teeth and curling black hair. It was all alive again. Love was on his lips and in his eyes. Tenderness and caring was in his hands. She felt new, giddy as a girl, and followed his lead like a downhill stream. Old hurts welcomed the healing hands of love.

But the fool has to gloat, the insensitivity of the self-indulgence, the insecurity of the weak had to crow and thus destroy what was being freely offered. "Reeda, the old charm still works doesn't it?"

There was enough light in the bedroom to see his triumphant grin. Her breath was arrested as if an anvil had been dropped on her chest.

"Now, honey, all you have to do is ask. Come on... it's right here waiting for you." Revulsion hit Reeda with the force of a slammed door. For a moment she felt she might faint.

He went on, "Don't be bashful, darling. Ask. I love a woman who don't mind asking." The lights from a passing car hit the room and she saw his eyes, horrible with victory.

"No!" she snarled and threw him off, scrambling from the bed as though it were suddenly infested with vermin.

"Reeda, what the hell?"

"You scum!" she rasped and switched on the lamp. "You're the lowest form of son-of-a-bitch that has ever contaminated my life." Then aware of her nudity, she yanked a duster from the closet and ignored the hanger that clattered to the floor. "After all you've done, after all you've put me through, you have the brass to ask me to ask you! Van, you're insane! Anybody would have to be totally nuts!"

"Come on, Reeda, it was only bed talk."

"No, it's who you are! Who you've always been. Pumped out of sight by small victories. Why it has taken me so many years to see that, God only knows, you smeared my nose in it enough. Now, Van, you get the hell out of here and if you ever attempt to lay another hand on me, I'll kill you and I mean it. You hear me, bastard?"

"But I thought—"

"I thought, too, but I thought wrong! Your mother should have smothered you in the cradle. A he-whore is all you are! All you have ever been or will ever be, mentally and physically." Then, remembering the boy, Reeda lowered her voice and her control ruled out any possible way to credit her words to anger of the moment as she hissed, "I despise you! Worst of all, you make me despise myself. I feel as if I've let maggots crawl on me."

"You're really serious," he said, softly, wondrously.

"You can bet your precious scrotum on it!" His face sagged with pain. For a long moment she thought he was going to cry.

Instead, he forced a sneering grin and said, "Sorry about that, Reeda. Sometimes you have to learn to live with maggots... or whatever." Still his eyes were filled with pain. It was her first time to realize she had hurt someone and felt good about it.

He gathered his clothes, then standing with them bundled under his arm he growled, "Can't blame a husband for trying to get a little from his own wife, once in a while."

"To be a handsome man, I don't know how you got so ugly inside."

"Hell, we both have always been good looking. Those black eyes of yours could set a saint afire. Specially when you're mad. If looks made good screwing and a good marriage, we'd be close as a closet."

She hissed, "Get out! Get out of this house! And don't come back. It's over. My lawyer will call your lawyer."

"Screw you and your lawyer," he snarled. Then with great dignity Van swaggered from the room.

For some time, Reeda had known he had no integrity. For the first time she doubted his sanity. She stood a moment feeling passed paralyzed. Hearing his car screech out of the driveway, she moved to lock all the doors behind him.

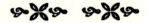

CHAPTER 4

"Customer service. Reeda Davis speaking. May I help you?"

"Miss, this is Mrs. John Fanning. I stayed home all day yesterday waiting to get my new chair. I haven't seen it yet! Would you please be so kind as to tell me what is going on with you people?"

"Ma'am, I'm sorry you didn't get your chair. I remember your call. Your chair really was out for delivery yesterday when I checked. Hold on a moment and I'll see what happened." Reeda pushed the hold button and rang the city dispatch desk.

"City dispatch, Bob Crawford speaking."

"Bob, yesterday, I promised delivery on a chair. We had it on the street consigned to a Mrs. John Fanning on White Plains Avenue. She didn't get delivery. What happened?"

"Reeda, who had the delivery?"

"Smithson had it on 214 pickup."

"His pickup broke down. Got three shipments delivered then the clutch went out. We had to tow his truck in. The maintenance shop got the truck fixed last night. The freight will be delivered today."

"Do you have any idea what time?"

"Should be by one, two at the latest. We didn't load any new freight on 214 so we can get yesterday's shipments delivered first."

"Thanks, Bob." Reeda punched the other line and said, "Mrs. Fanning, I am so sorry. The truck your chair is on broke down yesterday.. It will be delivered today for sure."

"Well, I certainly can't be tied up here another day all day. Tell your driver to leave the chair in the garage."

"I'm sorry, Mrs. Fanning, but the driver isn't allowed to leave freight without someone home to sign for it."

"I'm to spend another day waiting for a truck that may not come?"

"Ma'am, I'm terribly sorry for the inconvenience. Your shipment should deliver by two o'clock. If it doesn't, you call me back."

"My hair appointment's at ten, my bridge game starts at one."

"Isn't there a neighbor or someone who could sign the freight bill?"

"If I say leave it, why not leave it?"

"We aren't cleared of the shipment till we have a signature. If something happened after the driver left, Alpha would be liable."

"That is ridiculous. Nothing would happen. This is a respectable neighborhood. I've been reading about that strike your union is involved in up North. If y'all spent less time cutting tires and more time cutting red tape, I dare say everybody would be better off."

"Ma'am, I'm not in any union, I'm inclined to agree with you." Knowing it was time to end the call as gracefully as possible, Reeda said, "I'm truly sorry we have inconvenienced you, still a signature is necessary before we can deliver any shipment."

"Oh, all right. I'll wait for my chair. All my time is spent waiting anyway!" The emphatic hang-up prompted Reeda to rub her ear, then her phone jangled again.

She answered, "Customer service," and started writing down information that was almost shouted over the wire. When the male voice hushed, she said, "Hold on, sir, while I check for you." She found nothing on the man's freight. She went back in on the line and said, "I'm sorry, sir, but I have no record of your shipment."

"I just hung up from long distance with my shipper. You people did pick my freight up this morning and I need it like yesterday."

"Sir, if your freight was picked up in Chicago just this morning, that's why I have no record. It can't possibly be here until tomorrow and it isn't due here until the day after."

"You don't have overnight?"

"Chicago is second morning, excluding weekends and holidays."

"Lady, I'm in a real bind for that shipment."

"I'll be glad to put it on the hot sheet and try my best to have it here for you tomorrow."

"I'd appreciate that and I'll send a driver to pick the freight up off your dock. But level with me, do we even have a chance to get the shipment in my hands by tomorrow?"

"Yes, there's a chance. Bottom line, it depends on if Chicago has a full trailer to run to Manchester tonight before midnight."

"Put it on the hot sheet and hold it on the dock for pick up if we do get lucky. Will someone be there say, six in the morning?"

"Yes, sir. Someone's here twenty-four hours a day."

"I'll check back then and thanks, you have been mighty helpful. By the way, do you like the candy my factory makes?"

"Yes, sir, I love it."

"What's your favorite?"

"The chocolate covered pecans."

"Get me those containers in here and I'll have my driver bring you a five pound box. That's chocolate covered pecans?"

"Yes, sir, but you don't have to do that."

"No, problem. I scratch backs that scratch mine. And thank you."

"You're welcome." She hung up and suddenly thought of her impending divorce. She didn't believe Van would fight it.

"Better run that brain of yours down, baby, before it gets away permanent," a voice said. "It's an ocean away".

She looked up to see Summers standing at her desk, and joked, "Doubt I'd know what to do with it, if I caught it."

Seeing her smile failed to brighten her dark eyes, he said, "Rough night?"

"Rough life," she admitted, and could have cut her tongue out.

"Hey, pretty lady, I can fix that." Leaning closer, with his broad hands on her desk, he added, "Make your nights smooth as honey and twice as sweet."

"Thanks, but no thanks. Just feeling sorry for myself. It will pass."

"So will the years, darling."

"We can't stop time."

"Nope, beautiful, but we can enjoy it." As her phone rang again, she waived him away.

Late in the day, when she entered the city dispatch office to check on another delivery with Bob Crawford, Howard was sitting at the dispatch desk. Scanning the dock through the glass partition, she asked, "Where is Bob?"

"Gone," Howard said.

"When is he due back?"

"Won't be back."

"Did he get sick?"

"Nope."

"Did he quit?"
"Nope."
"Fired?"
"Yeah, Reeda, something like that."
"Don't sound so concerned," she snapped.
"Hell, why should I be concerned?"
"He was your friend, wasn't he?"
"I guess. Never done nothing to me, I never done nothing to him. Lots of folks are my friends. That don't mean I mind their business, fight their battles or tote their cross."
"You're a real sport."
"Girl, this ain't no football game."
"You're right. What happened?" she asked reasonably.
"Nothing. Nobody can do the job they want done with the equipment we got to do it. When the home office gets on Carter's ass, he's got to get on somebody else's. Just like in the army. Crawford knows that."
"Hank had no right. Bob's a fine dispatcher."
"That's right! And Bob's been knocking around in trucking long enough to know, all he had to do was take old Hank's chewing with a grain of salt and go on."
"Must have left his salt shaker at home today."
"Guess so, or I wouldn't be sitting in his chair."
"Really, Howard, how can you be so callous?"
"Hey, Carter didn't fire no cherry. Like me and anybody that's been in the army or in freight supervision awhile, Bob's took a lot more for a lot less pay."
"As the number two man around here, if you had put in a good word for Bob, he might still have a job."
"He might. Then again, he coulda kept his mouth shut. Could be, if I had opened mine, neither one of us would have a job. Look, honey, I'm the number two man here because I know when to keep my mouth shut. The number two man before me didn't. Like Bob the dumb bastard ain't here no more."
"Why do you talk like that?"
"Like what?"
"You use good English when you want to."
The grin fell off his face, as he growled, "I talk and live like I want to and don't apologize for neither to nobody."

"That's obvious."

"And while we're at it, I'm like the three monkeys. Don't see, hear, or speak no evil where the boss is concerned long as he ain't on my case. Don't nobody care when the boss is on my case."

"Man, do you ever have an attitude!"

"You better believe it! Wasn't born with it but I'll damn sure die with it."

He held her eyes till she said, "Have it your own way."

"I try, hon. Been flat on my ass and flat on my own too many times for the boy scout shit, anymore. As a piece of friendly advise, Reeda, the sooner you wise up to the real world, the better off you'll be in trucking. Don't wake up one day with no job from sticking up for some ass, before you see don't nobody worry about you, but you."

Whether she agreed or not, it was impossible for her not to feel some admiration for this maverick of a man. He did have his own world figured out.

"I'll keep it in mind. Listen, have you have seen this shipment," she said, keenly aware of the tanned muscular arm he extended for the freight bill she held out.

"The dock has been so goofed up today I ain't seen nothing," he said, reading the bill. "Dallas picked this freight up yesterday. You know it probably ain't here yet. What's the trailer status?"

"The trailer arrived at four this morning. No update since then."

"In that case, I can tell you the trailer's parked on the yard. I was typing the trailer log in the computer when Bob went home. We quit stripping new arrivals at five this morning. Won't start back stripping till after six tonight."

"Sounds like my customer is out of luck."

"We gotta concentrate on getting our city deliveries made before cluttering the dock up with new freight."

"No way for an evening dock pick up?"

"Nope. Talk him into an early a.m. dock pick up."

"Okay, but he won't like it. Would you put out the fire, if he gives me a hard time?"

"Sure. If he gets tacky pass him to me. Ain't due till tomorrow, anyway," he said, handing the bill back to her.

For years, she would wonder when she had made up her mind to say, knowing the growl of the computer would cover her words, "You once told me if I wised up to let you know. I feel real wise."

Howard came off his chair as if it had been electrified. Suddenly, he was standing close enough she was moved by his breath on her cheek. "Knew you'd come around to my way of thinking, hon. The first day you walked in this joint, I knew we were alike."

"Don't tell the world," she cautioned, her courage faltering. Still she said, "Be in the parking lot after I clock out. Make it look like you're checking trailers on the yard."

"Anything you say, honey," he breathed as the phone rang. He picked it up and barked, "City dispatch," his eyes locked on Reeda's. "Yeah, I'll tell her. Reeda, Cynthia says your kid is on line five."

"Tell her I'll be right there."

Jamey was fine. He just wanted permission to go over to a friend's house. Still, the next hour was racked with misgivings about Howard.

You'll be sorry, she thought. Being sorry is no novelty, she snapped back at herself. But this is against everything you believe in. Right, like everything that has happened to me in the last five years. The lawyer said not to crawl into bed with the first man that asked. Pretend this is the second man and to hell with the lawyer.

Cecil Evans would probably jump at the chance, if some desirable woman asked him to crawl into bed with her. He was short on ideas anyway, if you ask me. And if there's no justice, maybe there is a little revenge. Howard Summers is doing as bad as Van. Well, in the words of the handsome Mr. Summers, he ain't doing it to me.

The phone rang in on her thoughts, but smooth as cake icing, she answered, "Customer service. Reeda Davis speaking."

"Reeda, honey, I'm Charley Toliver, owner of Toliver Bolt and Nut. I got a copy of one of your freight bills for fifty pound carton. I have no record of said carton ever being in my stock. Would you be sweet enough to tell me who signed for that carton?"

"Could you give me the pro number and date of the bill?"

"The what number, please ma'am?"

"Look in the upper right hand corner of the bill. Would you give me that number, sir?"

"It's 00731485, and it's dated March the third of this year."

"Mr. Toliver, hold the line and I'll check our delivery copy for the signature." She crossed the room to the files, found the copy and returned to the phone. "Sir, your carton was delivered March tenth, signed for by Paul Roberts. Does he work for you?"

"Mr. Roberts did work for me, little lady. Such as this is why he doesn't work for me now. But that's my problem. You answered my question, I thank you very much."

"You're very welcome, sir."

"Reeda, do you look half as good as you sound?"

"Thanks, I try," she said and hung up. Since her phone didn't immediately ring again, she started typing trace messages into the computer.

Sending messages was too routine to block out personal problems. A nagging dialogue played in her mind: I agree you've had a bad time, but don't make it worse. Call city dispatch and cancel with Summers— it's a bum idea. Hey, don't start again, I got work to do. Where's your pride? Pride? Ha! And don't get bitter, just because you married a pig, you don't have to turn pig yourself. I used to buy that. Now you don't? I don't know. Something's gotta give. I can't go on like this and I mean it. I really can't!

When they clocked out for the day, Cynthia said, "If you don't have anything else to do tonight, come help me hang my new drapes."

"Thanks," Reeda said, "but I can't. Uh, got a hair appointment."

"But you already had your hair done this week."

"So, I feel like pampering myself. Listen, I need to make a pit stop before I leave. You coming in?"

"Gotta get on home. See you in the morning."

When Reeda left the building Summers wasn't in sight. By the time she was starting her car to leave, he was suddenly leaning on the window. He caught her eyes with his for a moment before saying, "You seem in a hurry, hon. Hope you didn't change your mind."

"I didn't want to goad you into anything."

"Hell, had to let the others clear out. You busy tonight?"

"No," she said, softly, but determined.

"Well, you wanna see me?"

"Why put off till tomorrow what two can do tonight."

"Girl, that's just what I always say. Wanna have dinner?"

"No, Howard, I'll have dinner with my son."

"We could honky tonk a little— do some dancing."

"Not tonight."

"What, then, hon? You suggest something."

"How about a motel?"

His eyes widened. "God, girl, when you decide, you decide."

"I don't want to be seen. Isn't that what it's all about anyway?"

"Hey, lady, you don't have to sell me."

"All right, where?"

"Highway 169, Reeda, about three miles past the city limits there's a place called Express Way Manor. It's clean, private and room 22 is on the back side. We won't have any visitors or any trouble."

"I take it you have been there quite often."

"Does it matter?"

"No. Around nine?"

"Sounds good, hon. Know what?"

"What?"

"I'd sure like to kiss you right now."

"Not now," she cautioned, then drove away.

✣

It was twenty to ten when Reeda pulled in at the motel. The man doesn't skimp, she thought, parking beside his car in front of door 22. After switching off her car she began to tremble. It was one of those marker moments when things would never be the same again. Maybe she ought to forget this nutty idea and take herself home.

She considered leaving for several seconds, then lifted her chin as she thought, don't sit here like Avon calling trying to get up the courage to knock on a door. And damn, don't take it so seriously, nobody else knows or cares.

As she was about to knock on number 22 it opened.

Summers, in a well cut business suit was amazing. His smile was wonderful as he said, "Thought I heard a car. Girl, I was getting afraid you'd changed your mind."

"Not yet," she said, trying to match his smile.

"Well, good looking, come on in."

Even as she walked in, Reeda couldn't believe she was walking in a motel room to do what she was walking in to do.

She jumped as he closed the door. "It's okay," he said, seeing she was nervous. "Hon, the blue chair. Sits better than the green one."

Reeda sat on the blue chair, placed at right angles to the green one. The occasional table between the chairs hosted a fifth of vodka, two glasses and bucket of ice. A carton of Seven Up was under the table.

The room wasn't what she expected. It was tastefully wallpapered and furnished in a decent grade of Danish modern. Still, Reeda saw the most prominent piece of furniture as the king size bed.

He took the other chair. Mixing the drinks, he asked, "Have any trouble getting here?"

"No. My illustrious estranged husband is out of town and I have a reliable sitter with my son."

The lamp was low, easy listening music floated from the radio. She saw there was no other word for his green eyed good looks except beautiful. And, she thought, smiling back at him, he does go all out.

"Here, hon, this will settle you down," he said, extending a glass.

"Why not?" She tasted the drink.

"Mixed to suit you?"

"Yes, thank you."

"Tried not to make yours too strong."

"It's fine, Howard."

"Does it need more vodka?"

"No, it's fine," she said, then took another sip as proof and tried a smile that make her lips tremble.

"Good."

"Is this part of the routine?" she asked, raising her glass again.

"Don't know about a routine, to me a good drink after work's part of enjoying living."

"You believe in that?"

"Drinking?"

"Enjoying yourself."

"Above about everything," he said, with an intimate smile. "Know anything better?"

"What about God?"

Something close to anger burned in his eyes before he said softly, "God who? Does he work for Alpha?"

"He's supposed to work everywhere."

"Gives Him lots of terminals to cover."

"You doubt He covers all of them?"

"Hope he ain't covering this room. At least right now. Don't you?"

She was surprised by her laugh before saying, "Yes, I suppose so."

"Drink up, it'll get you past feeling funky about being here," he said, then took a swallow from his glass.

"Is it that obvious?"

"Sticking out just like a sore toe."

"Sorry about that."

"Me too, baby, so drink up and that funky feeling will go away."

"Are you always this open with your thoughts?"

"Nope. Just with myself and once in a while with someone worth being open with," Howard said, his eyes going very soft.

"Thank you."

"You're welcome." He squinted his eyes against his cigarette smoke and said, "If I make up my mind I want to do something, I don't believe it makes me better to feel extra guilty about it. Do you?"

"No. But most people can't or won't be that honest. That's what I admire about you, Howard. You don't lie to or for yourself."

"I don't think you do, either."

"I'm not so sure, anymore."

"Do you need to tell me about your husband?"

"Do you need to hear about him?"

"Naw. It ain't no seldom story. I'm living one about like it."

"I sure didn't realize that."

"Details vary. Outcome's about the same. Heard a song on the radio about it before you got here called *They Lost All The Love*. That's what all the divorces and TV soaps are about. Hon, if you need to talk, I got all night. I'm a real good listener."

"Well, it's just that I thought I could forgive him. Actually I couldn't. Not really. He might have straightened up, if I could have forgiven him." Howard's eyes filled with such naked sympathy, she had to look away. She didn't know how to take that kind of support and this was the last scene she wanted to cry in..

"I doubt that, honey. Once he gets a taste, it's rare a dog that quits sucking eggs. What you can't forgive him for ain't the other woman. It's making you doubt yourself, as a woman. That's what it always is."

"How— "

"Not rushing you, but it'd be better if we got on with the loving. In your own way, for your own reasons, you need a good loving much as me, angel cakes. That's the real truth of it."

Though his words wouldn't have been the envy of any poet, his eyes were so knowing, his voice so gentle, there was no way she could be offended. She confessed, "I... don't know if I can, I mean— "

He stood, drained his glass, placed it on the table, took her glass and placed it beside his. Taking her by the hand, he pulled her gently to her feet. "Ain't nobody gonna give you a test, but won't ever be a better time to see. Besides, practice makes perfect."

Since it was all her idea, she whispered, "Okay."

Still she turned away from his kiss. He waited. There was no pressure, she knew she could withdraw— could stop at any moment, could leave at any second. His breath was warm and sweet on her cheek and she felt the patience and tenderness of him, strangely coupled with the strength and zest for life that was the essence of him. This was no husband exercising conjugal rights.

"Lord, girl, you're a beautiful woman. Don't ever let anybody tell you different. I dreamed of this since the first day you twisted across the office. But, if you'd rather not, it's okay. Just cause we're here don't mean we have to do a thing but talk and enjoy a few drinks."

Whether his words were true or not they were wonderful to hear. She turned her head to see the pleasure that was in his eyes. His kiss was as gentle as a baby touching a petal. Then, as though a silent question had been answered, he took his lips from hers and tucked her head under his chin. Holding her like he might comfort a child, stroking her hair, his voice was hoarse and his whisper was full of wonder, "Know the best part about times like this?"

"What?" Her lips brushed his neck as soft as she spoke.

"The loneliness is all gone. That's such a sweet feeling."

"Oh, yes. For the first time in so long I hardly remember, I'm not feeling lonely," Reeda purred. This time she was ready for his kiss.

Then he said, "You all right, now?"

"Yes." Fiercely she put her arms around him. Feeling the hard, wonderful muscles of his back, she said, "I'm just fine."

Then she was clinging to him after affection like a lonely child. Summers gave her the kiss he knew she wanted. When he raised his lips he said, "I just knew we'd be great together. God, girl, you're gorgeous." He kissed her again.

This truly was sex without love, but to be wanted, to feel lovely, to see her dark beauty reflected again in a man's eyes had it's own value. She kissed him back, kiss for kiss, honest enough to acknowledge how wrong it might be without letting it ruin how good it felt. When his tongue ventured into her mouth it was as welcome as a new playmate. When it withdrew, her tongue, not wanting to be left alone, had to follow, had to touch, had to taste inside his mouth.

When his hands were softly at the buttons to her blouse, then her bra to lightly touch— then kiss her breast. She gasped from the surprised thrill that zinged through her. God, it had been forever— if ever— she'd felt this good— this way.

She felt her nervousness subsiding in perfect harmony with her rising desire. It was going to be okay, giving to him, making love to him would be no sacrifice— no problem. He was so sweet and easy— so gentle— the perfect lover. Thank God! She wasn't going to freak like some nut. Feeling the man's kiss, his touch, made her realize how vanilla her sex life had grown.

Even her fantasizing was not on a par with how excited she was when her hands slipped under his shirt and began to explore... to caress. As she felt his quickening heartbeat it felt very right to whisper, "Oh, man, you are so warm."

"And you're something wonderful! Yeah, knew that first day I watched you twist across the office, you and me had to be, baby-doll."

CHAPTER 5

Cynthia stood at the wide mirror over the sink perfecting her makeup as Reeda walked in the ladies room.

Reeda greeted, "Hey, Cyn, how goes it?"

Cynthia frowned at her in the mirror a moment before saying, "Lord, you either got a lousy set or canceled your hair appointment last night."

"Well, a big old thanks to you for putting a damper on what started out to be a fine morning."

"Now, I don't mean your hair doesn't look nice. Always does— just doesn't really look like a fresh set."

"Actually, it isn't. Changed my mind. I was too tired to keep my appointment."

"Hope you're rested up. It's gonna be another one of those days," Cynthia cautioned. "I've been here about ten minutes and the phones are ringing off the wall. Howard said tell you to get on the clock as soon as I saw you. He's going nuts with the phones."

"Thanks, but I have a couple of things to do in here first."

"And look out for Carter today. Patsy called me at home last night. The old bastard's got the hornys again. He has been after Patsy all week long. Said she might get fired, but she has waltzed Hank as long as she can. He flat out asked her if he could come over. Patsy told him she didn't think her boyfriend would like it."

"Ugh! Why don't Hank book himself with a nice hundred dollar prostitute and get it upside down, inside out, frontward or backward or whatever would let him get his dirty mind out of his crotch for an hour or two?"

"Beats me. Just watch out his mind or worse ain't in your crotch, baby girl. Listen, see you later. I got here early so I could use the calculator before I have to clock in. Gotta balance my stupid checkbook. I can't stand to ask the bank man to help me again."

◆◆◆

It was lunch time before Reeda and Cynthia had a chance to talk again. As they were brown bagging in the breakroom as they did most days, Cynthia said, "That Griffin's such a smug little office manager, just like a fifth grade hall monitor."

"Lord, I feel like the Road Runner. I've been running up and down the dock all morning checking out one trace call right after the other."

"I know. I have to listen to them bitch cause I have them on hold."

"Seems like everybody's freight is hot today."

"Why? Is service running that late?"

"No, but all our nine a.m. deliveries are late because every city truck we have was late getting out on the street. Howard said they started calling at five this morning. I guess the natives are just restless today. Anyway, Cyn, what's going on in the office?"

"We weren't on the clock any time till Griffin came after Molly again. She looked about ready to faint when Griffin walked her into Carter's office. They have kept her in there ever since. I really doubt Molly can stand up to much more, Reeda."

"They have been giving Molly a hard time for the last two weeks."

"I haven't worked the cashier desk, but it doesn't look to be that complicated and Molly doesn't seem incompetent."

"She isn't, Cyn, and it ain't. You know I worked relief cashier. Molly's been cashier over three years. Did a fine job till just lately."

"Could be problems at home. We both know she's married to a prime asshole. But if she was going to mess up, it should have been a long time ago. Bet Carter's building a case to get Molly out of here. Making room for a new girl, if I'm any judge, Reeda.."

"That's a little hard to believe. He doesn't impress me as the type of man to conjure up a case just to get rid of someone."

"My God, Reeda, grow up!"

"If Carter isn't happy with Molly's work, why not fire her?"

"Too obvious. Hank don't want to get his office organized."

"Organized?"

"Getting the teamsters union in here, Reeda."

"But the dock and shop and road are already union."

"That don't help our paychecks or our job security. Matt Fletcher, back in billing, is talking union big time."

"You mean in the office?"

"Right. If Carter fired Molly outright it could cause suspicion as well as union sympathy."

"Think he's having an affair with someone he wants to hire?"

"You got it."

"Cyn, if he has a girlfriend, bringing her in his terminal to work would be so dumb!"

"Right. But who plays it smart when they're incensed?"

"You're always looking for hanky-panky."

"Yep, and it's usually there. Time will sure tell."

The breakroom door was shoved open and a weeping Molly rushed in. She sat down at the table and continued to weep. Reeda and Cynthia exchanged a helpless look.

Reeda asked, "Carter and Griffin giving you a hard time again?"

"Yes, over errors!" Molly said, her brown eyes swimming in tears. "They keep hounding me about making errors".

"Have they shown them to you?" Cynthia asked.

"No, that's it. They won't show them to me. I've asked and asked to see what kind of errors I'm making. So far, I haven't seen a one."

"Reckon why won't they show them to you?" Reeda asked.

"They've already gone to the home office. It's the home office that's complaining. So they say."

"That's weird," Reeda said.

"How can I correct errors when I don't have any idea what I'm doing wrong?"

Cynthia said, "It ain't errors! Molly, you've worked in trucking long enough to know a scam. It's the old freeze out."

"I'm so upset, I don't feel like I know anything."

"It's simple, that old fart has come on to every female working here with no success. He's got his eye on some bitch to put on your desk who'll work and play."

"Well, if that's what he wants he can have it. I don't have to take his abuse or his lies and I mean it. I feel as low as whale doo doo and that lays on the bottom of the ocean."

"Shake it off, girl. You can't let that old son-of-a-bitch get to you."

"Cyn, he already has! I have a husband who can feed me. I'll quit before I'll be treated like this. Art will probably make me quit anyway, when he hears the latest."

Reeda said, "But you need a job. You' would have a hard time replacing the money you make here. Molly, honey, please don't quit."

"I don't see as I have much choice."

Cynthia growled, "Sure you do! And you and Art need a second paycheck or you wouldn't be here working with four kids in the first place. Hang in and fight! Make Carter fire you if he wants shed of you. Make the bastard come on out with it."

"Don't think he won't! He threw everything at me while ago but the front door."

Reeda said, "I hope it won't come to that. But make him fire you if you do leave. At least you can draw your unemployment."

"Reeda's right. Besides, if Carter sees he can't intimidate you, the whole thing might blow over. And stop crying! You cry too easy."

"That's what Art says, Cyn."

"Art is right for once— dry up and brace up. Reeda, you and me better get back to work or Carter will be on our butts."

"I know," Reeda agreed, then added, "Molly, you have to stand up to Carter. Don't let him blow your mind and don't quit!"

Once outside the breakroom, Cynthia whispered, "A coke says she'll hit the door bawling before the week's out."

"I hope not. All she has to do is ride it out."

"Wrong, Reeda. When trucking management wants rid of you, they don't stop till you're gone ready or not. That's what Hoffa was all about stopping and why they hated him so."

"Speaking of Hoffa, it looks to me like we really do need a union."

"Hush, child! Don't use such dirty language."

As Reeda approached her desk the phone rang. She forgot all else as she swallowed hard and answered pleasantly, "Customer service."

"Honey, yesterday I shipped a crib to my daughter in Miami. Her first baby's due next month," a middle aged female voice said, "When will that little crib be getting down there?"

"Ma'am, Alpha's schedule to Miami is third day after pickup."

"Good. Now, your trucks run all night. Right?"

"Yes, ma'am, that's right."

"We see them on the road at all hours when we drive to Florida to see our daughter. I was wondering if that crib might get in Miami, say three o'clock in the morning. They wouldn't wake my daughter and her husband up at that time of night, would they?"

"No, ma'am. We make appointments for residential deliveries."

"Fine. I was worrying about that. It would scare those kids to death, if someone came knocking on their door in the wee hours. Well, you have been very kind and I thank you."

"You're very welcome," she said gathering her paper work, then turned to the computer to send out her tracing messages. After typing in the first message and waiting for the system to accept it, she was conscious of someone standing by the machine and looked up into Howard Summer's eyes.

He stooped down and said intimately, "Hi, doll."

"Don't talk like that in here," Reeda said in a low voice, "someone might hear you."

"With all these printers running, they couldn't hear hell roar."

"Well, don't look like that. Nobody here is blind." The possession in his eyes made her feel acutely uncomfortable, not to mention the blush burning her face.

"Like what?"

"Like you could eat me."

"Anytime, sweets. Just say when," he said with a maddening grin.

"Man, get away from me and let me do my work."

"See me tonight?"

"I don't know."

"Girl, I could stand here all day looking in them black eyes of yours. But I am standing here till you say, yes."

"All right, Howard! Now go see about your dock or something."

"Relax, hon. No one's gonna know us nearly a hundred miles from home. If anybody saw us, they wouldn't say anything. They never do. I want us to dance to some good country music and eat a decent dinner for a change."

"I know and that's nice of you, but Van's just hoping to catch me with a man in a place like this."

"Van ain't here. I doubt he even knows about this place."

"That's easy for you to say. You don't have anything to lose."

"Not much, Reeda, just my job. Quit worrying and sip your wine. If it's as effective as my bourbon and coke, you'll feel better shortly."

She sipped her wine, then asked, "How does our being together affect your job?"

"Babe, the first commandment for Alpha supervisors is, don't plug the help."

"Don't talk trash, Howard."

"Hey, that's not my line. That's straight from the President. Like old Alex Vance, himself, used to say, 'If you got problems, we want to help. Financial, marital, anything at all, just ask. You're all good men. Experienced in freight, not afraid of hard work and long hours. These qualities are vital to the trucking industry and they aren't easy to find. We want to keep you and we prefer happily married people. If you just must dally, make it outside the office. Pick on somebody else's employees. Plug Alpha's help and get caught, you're through here, people. And that's a promise.'"

"When did you hear Alex say that?"

"Lots of times when he was in Manchester back before he retired. His number two son, Nathaniel Vance, mostly runs things now."

"What happened to his number one son?"

"Joe Vance is a fool and a drunk. Now and then after hours, the supervisors meet with Nathaniel and some of the other brass. We talk constantly on the watts line. Unless there's major trouble, they pretty well let me and Hank run things."

"You have a good job, Howard."

"Yeah, but sometimes I get to wishing I'd stayed at city driving and in the union."

"City driving is no easy job."

"Anywhere in the kinky kingdom of trucking you work your ass off. Even the office. But carrying a union card and working hourly, you put in your eight, maybe some good overtime, then you punch out and forget it. Management's a twenty four hour job."

"How do you like working for the crown son?"

"Nathaniel's okay, pretty much a copy of his old man. Just more polish from his college education and being raised in the money."

"Wonder what being raised in the money feels like?"

"Ain't got the slightest, baby. Anyway, I'm not as free as you think. If it means anything, my job is on the line when I'm with you. You are the only woman from the office I have ever risked it for."

"Didn't think you'd let anything interfere with pleasure."

"Hon, there's hardly anything that comes before my job. And don't you forget it. Don't believe the bull you hear about the supervisory burden. Telling someone else what to do beats hell out of doing it any day of the week."

"That sounds reasonable," she drawled.

"Imagine loading the nose of a forty-five footer in mid July. Your sweat's rolling like rain off a roof. There's barely enough air to breath, anyway, then the hayseed bastard helping you load decides to unload a monster fart and you're about gassed to death."

"Oh, God!"

"Oh, God, is right. You come as close to suffocating as you ever will and live to tell it."

"But it pays good, Howard." Reeda smiled sweetly.

"And worth every penny. I hope I never have to work at stacking freight in a trailer again. A dockhand deserves every dime he makes."

"Over-the-road drivers seem to have a good gig. They rarely unload trailers."

"Most road drivers think they're some kind of eighteen wheeling cowboy. Guess it depends on point of view, like most anything."

"Like different strokes for different folks?"

"Yeah, Reeda, but there ain't no creme puff jobs in trucking. Your tracing job would drive me crazy. Out city driving, you're jockeying for position in up-town traffic and that ain't no picnic. To make big money over the road, you got to live in a sleeper cab. Now, that ain't my style sure enough," he grinned.

"What is your style?"

"Rob from the rich and give to the poor. Like Robin Hood."

She said, "I know that's right," and they shared a laugh.

"Naw, hon, I been in freight all my life; don't know anything else. Took twelve years of being a dock mule and first line foreman for me to make operations manager. And like the midget said, it ain't much but it's all I got and I want to keep it. You're the only woman I ever laid my job on the line for, and that's a fact."

She turned her eyes from his penetrating gaze and said softly, "Maybe we should stop seeing each other. You know I don't want any ties. Seeing me might not be worth the risk you're taking."

"Hon, I'm a big boy. I'll make up my own mind whether the risk is worth it or not."

"Apparently, you're not the only supervisor who has seen a woman he will lay his job on the line for. Not to mention trying to fire another girl so he can give his girl a job."

"What are you talking about?"

"Haven't you seen Molly's red eyes the last few weeks?"

"Yep. Figured she had more husband trouble. Carter loves you girls talking to him about husband trouble. Makes him think he might be able to slip one in."

"She isn't in Carter's office about here husband. Carter's down her throat every other day about making errors."

"Well, hell, tell her she better quit making errors."

"That's the point, Molly isn't making errors."

"How so?"

"Because he never shows her any errors. That would be the first thing he would do if she was. He just keeps chewing Molly out about complaints from the home office. Cynthia says there's hanky-panky going on. She thinks Carter's involved with someone he wants to put in Molly's place. If he can goad her into quitting, he's got it made."

"Ha! I thought Carter was too old for that kind of deal."

"Apparently not."

"Old Hank ain't dead, after all," Howard laughed.

"You're not one bit concerned about Molly!"

"Yes, I am, hon, but you ain't seen Hank's old lady. I'm talking major ugly. That's the only human being I ever saw who really does look like a cow. And I mean it. Every time I see that old broad, I keep watching for her to start chewing her cud."

"Good, Lord, Howard!"

"I been worried to death the old girl is going to come up smothered," he said, seriously.

"Smothered?"

"Well, don't you just know Hank has got to put a pillow over her face to get any."

"Okay, have your fun. But surely you can see how lecherous it is for a man to use a job to sleep with a woman."

"Reckon you and Cyn might be letting your minds run wild?"

"I think not, for Carter to be putting the screws to Molly like he is."

"Even if you're right, what else has the old boy got? Every girl in that office draws damn good money. Outside trucking, nobody in town pays women what you girls get."

"Why is it a disgrace for women to make good money? You aren't always oohing and aahing over what you men make."

"Hey, I got no problem with that. I'm just talking about Hank—trying to figure what he's up to. Don't mean nothing against you, or the girls or women in general. Okay?"

"Okay."

"Now, if what y'all suspect is true, he ain't pulling no first. For years, management has been known to use those big salaries y'all make to buy a little sweetening."

"Ugh!"

"Yeah, well, whatever. You know what I'm saying!"

"Unfortunately, yes."

"Then, it ain't unthinkable a terminal manager might fire a girl, who don't give him no sweetening, to hire a girl who does."

Reeda snapped, "What about Alpha's first commandment: about not plugging the help."

"Honey baby, in and out of trucking, commandments get broke. Just like trace clerks and dock hands, terminal managers get fired every day."

"And nobody does one thing about it, Howard. An old buzzard like Carter should be put in his place and you know it."

"Maybe so but who is gonna do it?"

"I'd like to. I wish so hard sometimes I was a man for two minutes and could whip the tar out of some of the filth in the world."

"Hate to tell you, Reeda, you could be big enough to cuss, stomp, whip ass, whatever... still wouldn't have a job after you got through."

"The dock does! The road does! Sometimes they have fights and get in trouble. They don't always get fired!"

"But they do get fired at times. Depends on the circumstances. Besides, hon, they got something you and me ain't got."

"What?"

Howard finished his drink before he answered, "A union card. Come on let's dance one before our food gets here."

ง•✕•ง

Molly Luna had always been a good girl, but she had never been strong emotionally. She had always been quick to cry, easy to persuade, anxious to please and ready to forgive. She might have weathered Carter's conspiracy to fire her if life had been tranquil at home and her husband had been supportive.

When Molly clocked out at Alpha her work day was only half over. At home she put in almost another eight hours cooking supper, seeing to four kids, the laundry, the housework and all the countless household duties that went along with having a family. Art stationed himself in his Lazy Boy chair and busied himself with the morning paper, the evening paper and criticizing Molly on everything from cooking to housekeeping to motherhood and barking, "Can't you please make the kids be quiet, Molly, so I can rest."

Besides holding two jobs to Art's one, every morning driving in to work together, he picked her apart. On this sunny morning, he found how Molly was dressed displeasing. There had been no recent change in her figure. The dress she wore was not new, but suddenly, according to Art, it was too short, too tight and showed everything she had.

Art often dwelled on the fact that she had been intimate with him before marriage. He even questioned her virginity, which had been indisputable, with such jibes as, "Since you did it with me, you probably did it with others." Actually, she never consented to do it with Art. In a lover's lane one night, he forced himself on her.

After that, Molly didn't see much use in trying to refuse him. In no time, foxy Art had Molly believing the sexual side of their relationship had been as much her idea as his own, hinging his argument on the fact she hadn't screamed. He had no problem ignoring the fact that no one had been within range to have heard her scream. Molly's pleading no's the whole time he was tearing off her panties and then raping her didn't count.

Men couldn't help it if women were always saying no, when they meant yes. He got it, didn't he? And it wasn't anytime at all till she was enjoying it as much as he was— maybe more. And that didn't seem quite appropriate for a good Christian wife.

In four months after the first time, Art had Molly pregnant and convinced it was her fault. Still, since he was a preacher's son and terrified of his father's wrath, not to mention God's, Art decided, in the interest of doing the righteous thing, they should elope.

In the classic syndrome of the passive-aggressive soul, Molly convinced herself everything had worked out for the best. The only two people who were truly disappointed were her parents. They had been saving the money for their only child to go to college on since she was a baby. Like Molly told her mother, "Mama, you can finally have your house done over and still have the money for you and Daddy to take that trip to Hawaii you have always dreamed about."

Thus far, the marriage had produced four kids, a big house, a new car every year, still fifteen thousand dollars worth of furniture and a registered Bouvier Des Flandres, all bought on time payments and credit cards.

Art had resentfully accepted his role of father and husband until recently. His growing lust for the full-blown blond in his office was turning a resentful ass into a demon of a family man. The affair, outside of Art's fantasies, had only progressed to the lunch date and the dozen roses he sent to the object of his lust. Art was sure their after hours motel rendezvous was eminent.

His displeasure with his wife mounted daily and her complaints about the pressures of her employer met deaf ears and no sympathy. A husband, reared by a tyrant of a father who was also a Hell Fire Bible Belt preacher, building resentment strong enough to overwhelm the guilt of pursuing another woman and trying to launch an affair, feels no sympathy for his wife.

The previous Friday, there had been another session in Carter's office concerning Molly's alleged errors. Thinking about what Reeda and Cynthia advised, she managed to contain her tears, but she could hold them no longer when Art picked her up that evening. Art dismissed her tears as a bid for sympathy he did not have. She was interrupting his running fantasy about the blond back at the office.

Molly was on edge all weekend. It was one of the few weekends she refused sex with her husband. Sex was one of the few things she enjoyed with Art even though he kept saying she was too passionate to be a Christian wife, whatever that meant. She knew, like father like son. Sometimes Art said things just to hear himself preach.

On Monday morning, the idea of going back to work with probably more of the same to face was excruciating. Molly was near tears all the way in. When Art braked the car in front of Alpha, she was still trying to talk things out. "Art, do you think I should resign? You never said all weekend."

Art had not seen the object of his lust since Friday. The fact that Molly sat rehashing her problems instead of leaving the car irked him immensely. Not wanting to go through one of her bawling sprees, he tried to be patient. "Molly, I think you should do what Reeda and Cynthia said, stick it out. Sounds like they know what they're talking about, and we need the money. If you aren't doing anything wrong don't let your boss intimidate you. If you are just straighten up."

"I... I'll try— "

"Come on, Molly, I'm going to be late," Art barked, checking his watch. "You've done nothing but talk about this all weekend."

"This is so painful to me. I just wish you'd show more concern."

"Goddammit, Molly, if you didn't always go to work painted up like a whore, maybe Carter wouldn't always be chewing on you. It's probably frustrated sex on his part."

Molly's speechless mouth fell opened, then her eyes filled with helpless tears. Finally, she cried, "Art Luna, what on earth do you mean? I've been wearing this makeup over a year. You never said a thing before."

"Well, I didn't want to start a fight. And I thought you'd finally wise up. Look in the mirror if you don't believe me. No, stupid, not now! I'm sorry, Molly. I mean when you get inside. I've got to go! God, will you please hush bawling before you get in high gear and get the hell out of the car so I can get to work?" Humble as a chastised child, she scrambled out of the car that was financed through her credit union.

☙✖❧

Reeda breezed into the ladies room anxious to check on her makeup. Her new shade of blush was good, but she wasn't sure if she had on too much or too little. Also, she had eaten a sausage and biscuit on the way and wanted to brush her teeth again before work time. "Why, Molly, why are you washing your makeup off?"

"I'm afraid maybe I put too much on this morning," Molly explained, with a weak smile, then bent to the sink to rinse the soap off her face.

"Oh," Reeda answered, then checked her watch. Seeing it was fifteen minutes till clock in time, Reeda sat down.

Drying her face on the towel roll, Molly said, "If I ask you a question will you give me an honest answer, whether you think it might hurt my feelings or not?"

"Well, sure, if you want me to."

"Do... do I look like a... do I wear too much makeup?"

"No, of course not. Where did you get that idea?"

"Art mentioned it this morning."

"Well, some mornings you can't listen to husbands."

"Art says something like that every once in a while."

"Don't guess men have PMS, but they do have their cranky days."

"These days, nothing I do seems to please Art."

"What do husbands know about cosmetics anyway?"

"Guess he knows what he likes. And... well, he said I paint up like a whore."

"You do no such thing! Why did he say a thing like that?"

"I don't know— unless he thinks I do."

"Well, he's wrong! He's even more wrong to say such a thing to you. You're a beautiful woman and you always look nice. Maybe he's upset about something else."

Inspecting her face in the mirror, Molly said, "Maybe I should just wear lipstick."

"No, you shouldn't, Molly Luna! You put your face on like always and forget Art. He's bound to have a bad burr under his saddle from something else. There's not a thing wrong with the way you wear make-up. You are a very well groomed woman."

"You really think it's okay, Reeda?"

"Of course but hurry and get your face back on. You don't want to be late punching the clock. That'll just give Carter fuel for the fire."

"Lord," Molly said, rubbing pancake on her face, "I hope he doesn't start on me again today. I triple checked the work I turned in Friday."

"If he does, play it cool. Be strong. Don't let him upset you again."

"That's easier said than done."

"Everything is but you can do it."

"I'll try, Reeda, I really will try."

They had been on the job hardly an hour when Molly was taken to another session in Carter's office. In twenty minutes, she dashed out and frantically began dialing her telephone. Her voice was too loud and it was plain she was crying, as she said, "Art Luna please... Art?... Art, you have to come get me!... No, now! I can't stay in this place another minute!... Yes.... Okay, I'll wait in the coffee shop across the street. Please hurry!"

Molly was taking her purse from her desk drawer when Reeda got to her and said, "Settle down, honey. Don't be foolish. This way you won't even get your unemployment benefits. There's no point—"

"Reeda, I can't stand it anymore!"

"Let's go in the ladies room so you can calm down and think."

"No! I have got to get out of here," Molly slung her purse strap across her shoulder, moved around Reeda and ran out the door bawling as Cynthia had predicted. Cynthia met Reeda's eyes and shrugged, knowing the anger her friend was feeling.

She motioned Reeda over to the switchboard, then whispered, "Don't mouth off— there's nothing we can do, now. She brought it on herself. Molly chose to walk out."

"I can't believe that bastard Carter!" Reeda snapped.

"Believe it! Be mad or be glad, but trust me— it's over! Molly Luna's long gone!"

"It didn't have to be this way, if she had listened to us."

"No, Reeda, it didn't, but shake it off. You can help a friend and lead a friend, but she's got to have a little backbone of her own."

༄༅ CHAPTER 6 ༄༅

Sara Majors, Molly's replacement, reported to work the following Monday. She was not as young or as sexy as her women co-workers had expected. As Cynthia said, Sara was no Marilyn Monroe. The woman wore thick glasses, medium heels, was a bit long in the tooth, wide in the beam and never would see forty again. She had been working at Alpha Trucking just over two weeks, when Cynthia to signaled Reeda for a meeting.

When they were safe behind the door of the women's lounge, she whispered, "Reeda, I finally got the straight story. For sure, Sara is sleeping with Carter."

"Oh, God, we might have known."

"They started before she came to work here. A good friend of mine works at Can Do Trucking, where Sara used to work. He told me the whole story. She was the office manager at Can Do, then suddenly got laid off. That sure is why Carter railroaded Molly out of here just like we suspected. The bastard!"

"Actually, Cyn, Molly railroaded herself. I told her not to quit, you told her not to quit. It is so horrible that Carter won't even have to pay her unemployment. Molly might still be working, if she could have only listened to us."

"Maybe. But I really doubt it."

"I don't! It was a planned deal. Everybody knew that when they started calling Molly on the carpet for errors she never got to see. Even Matt Fletcher says so. Matt is as laid-back as rate clerks come."

"She could have still been working if she hadn't gone to pieces. I didn't realize how fragile she is. I was going to talk to Carter for her."

"Hell, yeah. That's sure you all right, Reeda. Sticking your neck out, thinking you can fix anything. When you was a kid you read too many Wonder Woman comic books, lady."

"Honestly, I didn't intend to brave it alone. I was going to ask you to see Carter with me."

"Double hell!"

"Well, we could have made a difference. Hank would never have fired both of us."

"Don't bet on it. Listen, it ain't our fault Molly's soft and high-strung and won't listen to her friends. She still believes in true love and true husbands and all that crap. They knew she would be the easiest female here to pressure into quitting. That's why they picked on her in the first place. And like Molly said, she does have a husband to feed her."

"But if Carter and his henchmen had left her alone, Molly would still be working. She's going to need a good job before it's over. I'd hate to think I was depending on Art to feed me."

"Me, too. But I don't reckon she sees it that way. Guess she had a right to her choice. But you can't beat them. When they want rid of you, they get rid of you. I've seen too many come and go. Some put up a healthy fight but they're gone. Anyway, Carter wanted his lady-love close at hand and when a man's that hot over a woman, better stay out of his way. It's like trying to stop an eighteen wheeler with a fly swatter."

Reeda protested, "I think he must be nuts to give her a job in his own terminal. They are going to stick out like a sore toe, Cyn."

"From what I hear, he didn't have much of a choice. After Sara got laid off at Can Do Trucking, her husband found out about Carter and threw her out."

"Isn't there any end to fooling around?"

"Not as long as people are people and are born male and female."

"Well, don't sound so pleased about it."

"Why be bugged? We didn't invent the human condition.."

"We ain't doing much to improve it either."

"Reeda, how long you been seeing Howard?" Seeing Reeda's eyes pop, Cynthia went for the kill, "Hey, tell me what's happening. We're supposed to be friends! How long, Reeda?"

"I... well, awhile now, Cyn."

"Knew you were ripe and yet..."

"Yet, what?"

"Nothing. You're just the last person in the world—"

"You would suspect of seeing a married man. Know how you feel. I was the last person I would have suspected of seeing a married man. But I'm real slow about some things."

"Don't be too hard on yourself. It isn't the worst sin in the world."

"Just one I never wanted to be guilty of. I don't even know how it got started, Cyn. It isn't me."

"Honey, I don't want to bust your bubble, but you pull your bloomers up and down just like the rest of us."

"I know. But the innocence kids lose at nine or ten, the idea that it's a do as I say world, not a do as I do, never happened to me. I kept on doing what I said and saying what I did— till Howard."

"So?"

"So, I was dumb enough to think everybody else was wrong. It was me all the time. When you're the one out of step, when everyone you know is stepping different, you have to be the wrong one. Right?"

"Well, Alpha's girl trace clerk is finally beginning to grow up. What you're getting at is me seeing Bryan. Why did you let me think you believed my lie?"

"You wanted me to. Would it have changed a thing if I hadn't?"

"Guess not," Cynthia said slowly. Then her face brightened, "But I'm glad you know. Now we can be better friends with no secrets."

"Friendship needs respect. Right now, I don't respect either one of us very much."

"Oh, crap! Reeda, stop trying to live by some storybook! Life ain't no fairy tale!"

"It could be."

"Naw, it can't. A fairy tale ends with, they lived happily ever after. But a fairy tale doesn't go into the ever after. After— we were both treated like dirt. John treated me bad, but Van has treated you like shit. Now you're getting your licks in and I'm proud of you. At least be woman enough to admit how sweet it is."

"I don't know, Cyn, I have my regrets."

"If you'll stop feeling properly guilty and just be honest, I'll bet next week's paycheck, regret is the last thing you feel when you're with Howard. That new glow on your face says you're having the best you ever had. Since I been knowing you, anyway."

Suddenly Reeda saw the rotten side she had always denied in Cynthia. Softly, she admitted, "I don't feel regret when I'm with Howard, but later I do. And— I feel so ashamed."

"Why? No one ever had more cause. Everybody has to reach out to somebody, at some point, or go nuts!"

"That is the point! I don't want to be like everybody. Now I am."

"Well, you might be better off and a better person. That's your real hang-up, trying to be different and better."

"Cyn, I'm sorry, but I hate being like people like Carter and Sara Majors."

"Who said you were? If Carter and Sara wanted to have an affair that was their business and their risk. The crummy part was screwing poor Molly out of her job."

"And we're better since we only screw wives out of their husbands," Reeda said sarcastically.

"That's bull! A dumb guilt trip, pure and simple."

"Hell, Cyn, we're guilty!"

"Bryan and Howard were running around on their wives before we ever heard of them and still will be if we never see them again. If it wasn't you with Howard, it would be Howard with someone else. And Bryan would be, too, in a New York minute."

"But it isn't someone else with Howard. It's me."

"I say, feel good about it, and stop pricking yourself with guilt needles! If you really don't enjoy what you're doing, stop doing it!"

"That's the first real intelligent thing either one of us has said."

"Girl, you're past help. Let's get back to work before we get fired and our kids wind up hungry. We ain't even got an Art to help us."

❧✖❧

Soft music drifted from the bedside radio while they talked through touch, trial and response. Taking competence for affection and passion for love, practice was making perfect. The crescendo of feeling took them high and rendered them as languid as smoke with the peace that comes from doing anything well.

Howard lifted her battered ego like a hit record lifts a down and out singer's career. It was, Reeda acknowledged, fairly late to be learning the difference between love and sex and just great sex. While it was not the same, there was a certain feeling of freedom that was not unpleasant. Her conversation with Cynthia had not dampened her pleasure from being with Howard.

On leaving this room, they would go their separate ways. She would not be responsible for him, nor he for her. What they did outside this place, this night, was of no consequence to either. It was like cooking, eating your fill, then leaving the mess to someone else.

Reeda smiled and said, "You make wonderful love, Mr. Summers."

He was lighting two cigarettes. After passing one to her, he said, "I've given up all my other extra women."

"Really?"

"You don't sound impressed."

"Well... maybe, it's because I thought one extra woman at the time should be enough for any married man."

"Never has been before." It was strange the way his solemn honesty stripped his words of conceit.

"Then don't be any different that you've always been. I accepted you as you are. I don't want you to change in any way for me."

"Know you don't. Maybe that's why I don't mind."

"That's weird."

"Yeah, guess so. For me, anyway. And I'll leave Janey, any time you say." Her rush of guilt prompted her to move away from him.

Her hand trembled as she drew on her cigarette. It was devastating to think of one's self as the dreaded other woman— the home wrecker. She shrank from those labels as she would have a maggot.

"Don't leave your wife for my sake."

"I thought that was what you wanted."

"It isn't and I never said it was."

"But that's what women always want."

"Not this one. My intentions toward you are strictly dishonorable."

"Damn, you're serious," he said bewildered.

"I'll sign an affidavit."

"Girl, I may break your neck if you dump me."

"Listen, Howard, let's get out of here."

"I can see you're terrified."

"I don't have time to be terrified. It's late and I need to get home, but I need a quick shower first." She rolled out of bed.

He growled, "Damn," to the closing bathroom door.

At home, having milk and cookies, she knew it was a ridiculous time of the night to be eating, but an evening with Howard always produced hunger— then wonderful sleep. It's all that exercise, honey, her conscious mocked. Have to admit, you know your stuff. Got him ready to desert his wife and kiddies any time you whistle.

Suddenly the phone rang and made her jump. At this hour it had to be an emergency. As she hesitated the alarming ring erupted again.

Some irate husband has probably blown Van's stupid brains out, Reeda thought as she said, "Hello."

"Reeda, uh, this is Patsy. Patsy from the office?"

"Yes, of course, Patsy. What's wrong?"

"It's my roommate. She's... she's sick."

"Have you called a doctor?"

"Well, uh... no, that's just it, we don't know any doctors down here. Sissy's from up home in the country. We moved into town together to get work, but we still use our old doctor up home."

"Can't she wait till morning?"

"Well, we really don't know what to do."

"I see," Reeda said, hearing the trauma in Patsy's voice.

"We haven't worked together long, but you're the only one I know to call. I wonder if you might come over, I think Sissy needs a doctor bad, but she doesn't. Could you please come? Our place isn't too far from you."

Reeda checked the clock over the kitchen sink. Two a.m. was too late to call Dr. Wassermann unless it was a true emergency. Better check into it first, she decided and said, "Give me your address. I'll be there as soon as I can."

Half an hour later she was ringing Patsy's doorbell. Patsy opened the door, her face stiff with fear and said, "Oh, Reeda, I'm so glad to see you. I really do appreciate you coming."

"What's really wrong, Patsy?"

"Uh, come on in, Reeda." Patsy said, and closed the door behind Reeda. Leading the way, Patsy went on, "Sissy is having a lot of pain. She's in the back bedroom."

A scared-eyed girl, who couldn't be over nineteen, lay in bed, her face shinning with sweat. Her blond hair was plastered to her head with sweat. Reeda guessed she was about five or six months pregnant.

Patsy said, "Sissy, this is Reeda from the office. The woman I was telling you about."

Trying to smile, the girl uttered, "Hi," then bit her lip from pain.

Reeda knew even before asking, "What seems to be your trouble, Sissy?"

The girls exchanged a questioning glance. Patsy said, "I hope you won't be offended, Reeda, but well, Sissy's having a miscarriage. And, we just don't know what to do."

"You haven't called a doctor?"

"Well, yeah, kinda... Like I said on the phone, we don't know any real doctors down here in Manchester." Patsy's eyes were as sad as a broken hearted dove's.

"I'll call my own doctor, Patsy. Where is your phone?"

"No!" Sissy moaned.

"We can't call a doctor," Patsy said weakly, then added with more power, "not now".

"This ain't indigestion. Patsy, Sissy needs professional medical attention. Like now!"

"I know but... it's an illegal abortion. Sissy could get in trouble if we call a doctor."

"And she could die if we don't!"

"Reeda, Sissy will die if we do."

"Then call the animal that did it," Reeda hissed.

"We have. He... he won't come. Says he doesn't see anyone except the first time. Says it's too risky. I promised, Sissy, I'd help, but I don't know what to do."

"Patsy, what do you think I can do?"

"I thought since you are so good at the office. You know every job there and you do have a son of your own, I thought you would know."

"Oh, God!" Reeda said.

"He... he said this one would have arms and legs."

"He who, Patsy?"

"The man who did her abortion. He said, it might move but it wouldn't live but a minute— and to lay it in a wastebasket till it died."

"Patsy, do you know what you're saying? That's murder for sure!"

"But we thought it would all be over when we left his place. He didn't tell us all this other, till after. There's nothing else we can do," Patsy moaned, as she started crying.

"Oh, yes there is. I'm calling an ambulance!"

"Patsy," Sissy begged weakly, "please, please, don't let her do that!" Then the girl's eyes rolled back in agony.

"You can't do that," Patsy argued. "Sissy thought the boy was going to marry her but he skipped town. That's why she waited so long about the abortion. He kept putting her off, getting her back in the bed and then he ran off and left her like this all by herself."

"But what kind of monster could do a thing like this? What kind of pig did y'all go to?"

Patsy's young eyes looked like blue ice as she spat, "Maybe the kind of pig that tried to help her when nobody else would!"

"There's no time to argue now. I'm calling an ambulance."

"Mrs. Davis?" Sissy moaned.

"Yes, Sissy," Reeda said gently.

"Please, ma'am, please don't call a doctor."

"Sissy, you are very sick. You should have already had a doctor."

"Yes, ma'am, I know," the girl said, then paused for a pain to roll past. "I went to the real abortion clinic, like somebody, where they do it right with real doctors. That was right after missing my second period. There was bad trouble from a hateful bunch, mostly men, picketing. They don't want women free to have abortions. With all the cops and reporters around, I got scared my picture would be in the paper or on TV and left.

"That could intimidate anybody," Reeda sympathized.

"Well, I have to do this on my own— without any doctor."

"But you don't have to be embarrassed. Doctors know about things like this, a doctor will help you."

"You don't understand," Sissy said, then her tears and more pain began to roll. The girl waited until the pain had passed, then brushed her tears aside and went on, "You see, Mrs. Davis, I'm all my mama and daddy have. They think I'm about the finest thing that ever happened. Knowing I've got myself in this shape would kill them both. They can't ever know about me being like this." Sissy looked at her swollen stomach.

"Sissy, if you die, think how bad that will hurt them."

"I thought about that a lot. I won't have to face them if I die. You don't know how it is back up in the country; everybody knows everybody. Folks are all from the old school. Getting a baby and not getting married is still awful. And... since I got in such a fix, I don't know but what they are right. Anyway— my folks never understand anything. And I doubt they could ever forgive me."

"Give them a choice. Sissy, if they love you they will forgive you. Besides, God is the only One you really need forgiveness from."

"You think God will forgive me?"

"If you have asked Him, He already has."

"I haven't. I've been too ashamed before God, too, Mrs. Davis."

"But God can be your comfort. He can take the place of your parents, now that you're grown and away from home."

"He can?"

"Sure. Remember when you were little and pricked your finger maybe trying to pick roses or blackberries. Then your mother would dry your tears, hold you close and make it all okay?" The girl nodded. "Let God work the same way— then you're never alone or ashamed. After we get grown, He understands more than moms and dads."

"Does He do that for you, Mrs. Davis."

Reeda's throat constricted on the lie she wanted to tell and couldn't. "Uh... no. I'm sorry to say He doesn't. But I would give five years of my life if He did."

"I doubt you could talk about God like you do, if He didn't."

"Thanks. Now I've got to make that phone call." Seeing the objection in Sissy's eyes, Reeda added, "If you lie here and die, your parents are sure to know. Maybe, this way, they never will. In any case, I have no choice."

—✌✖✌—

It was six a.m. when the intern told Reeda and Patsy, "Sissy is going to be fine.."

"Thank God," Reeda said.

"Yes. After we took the dead fetus she came around well. It could have been a different story, if you hadn't brought her in when you did. A damn butcher abortionist again. Why didn't she go to a clinic?"

"It's a long story and you probably wouldn't believe it," Reeda answered sadly.

"Can we see her?" Patsy asked.

"Not yet. She's in recovery, heavily sedated and should sleep most of the day. Rest is what she needs most for now, but Sissy is young and strong. She will be well again soon."

"Thank you ever so much," Reeda said.

"You're welcome. I'm sorry we had to report this to the police. They'll be here any moment. They may have some questions."

The stricken Patsy looked to Reeda.

Sounding more secure than she felt, Reeda said, "We understand and thanks again. We'll be in the waiting room."

※

Reeda resented the sneer on the detective's face from the moment they met. Her irritation and resentment grew with each of his questions. She felt they were on trial from the start. It was her first time to realize what one did to one's own body was not always a private or a personal matter.

She answered the detective's questions patiently until he rudely asked, "Did you have anything to do with this?"

"Are you crazy? No! Did you?" Reeda hissed, scalding him with her eyes.

"Hey, lady, you don't need to be getting huffy with me. I'm just trying to do my job."

"And you don't have to be getting huffy with me, I'm just trying to be a friend. If I had one dumb thing to do with this, I wouldn't be stupid enough to be sitting here now. Why don't you get huffy with those bastards, sitting in at the abortion clinics holding up the work and killing the doctors and nurses, who caused poor Sissy to get into such a mess and almost die?"

"Mrs. Davis, those people care about the lives of babies."

"You really think that is what they do?" Reeda sneered.

"Of course they do! That's why they take their time to try and shut down abortion clinics. Anyway, what other motive could they have?"

"Controlling women."

"Ma'am," he said, with a indulgent smile, "I really doubt that."

"If they care about babies, why don't they concern themselves with the millions of babies already in the world starving? Why don't they go after the vermin, in just Manchester alone, who don't pay their child support?"

"Actually, ma'am, I'm not here to discuss that."

"And why don't you check out those SOBs obstructing the abortion clinics and see if they paid their child support?"

The detective said, in a noticeably nicer tone, "Really, ma'am, I'm just doing my job. If I get sent out to check on those guys, like I got sent in here to check on y'all, I certainly will be doing that, too. You can rest assured."

"Thank God for small favors. Detective, I think we've answered enough of your questions. It's got so late it's early and we are beat. You know where to reach us."

"At home?" the detective said.

"No. I'm just going home to dress and get my son off to school. Then I'll be at work. You can reach me at Alpha Trucking from eight till four thirty, weekdays. You have my home and work phone numbers. Come on, Patsy, we're out of here!"

On the way home, Patsy said, "I really thought Sissy had better sense. That Danny is such a creep. Low-rent's written all over him."

"Sissy's awfully young. For that matter, so are you."

"We're both old enough to know right from wrong."

"Knowing the difference and being able to live it, darling, are always two different things."

"I tried so hard to tell her, she kept saying they were going to get married. Even after she was pregnant, Danny kept right on promising and promising. Sissy kept right on believing him."

"We all can be such fools for approval sometimes."

"One night about six weeks ago, he brought Sissy home and then he just vanished. That trash didn't even call her up or come around to say goodbye— and he knew she was carrying his baby."

"Sometimes, folks can be so cruel."

"Sissy's better off without him. She would have been miserable, sure enough, married to white trash like Danny."

"Know you got that right."

"I couldn't desert her then, and I can't desert her now till she gets able to work. Then I'm moving. Reeda, I can't live with a fool."

"Maybe she just made a mistake. We can all be fools at times."

"I know but I can't keep going through with this kind of thing. Sissy is stupid or something, where men are concerned. Her daddy ran her out of his hayloft with an eighteen year old boy, when she was only fourteen. I thought it was all just kid stuff, but I can see now how wrong I was."

"Wrong?"

"Till lately, I didn't know she went all the way with that boy. She was lucky and didn't get pregnant that time. You can't tempt fate every time you turn around. Sissy is crazy for male attention. She goes all the way with any man half way nice to her. Might make sense if she was over sexed."

"She isn't?"

"No. She doesn't even climax. Never has experienced an orgasm with a man. Sissy's just easy. She never listens when you try to tell her something for her own good. Some women are like that."

It was a moment before Reeda was able to comment, "I thought you younger people believed in free love."

"Some do, it happens. Like divorce happens with you married people. That doesn't mean all of us think it's the right way to live."

"No?"

"No. I came off a farm, but my parents aren't ignorant. They both graduated from high school. They're simple, but they're good people. Got married right after graduation. I'd bet my life both were virgins and have never thought about anybody else since. Daddy still lights up when Mama walks in the room. Don't have to be around five minutes to know she still thinks he hung the moon. Reeda, that's what I want someday."

"I guess that's what we all want."

"They brought me down here to go to business school before I started working at Alpha. It knocked a hole in their savings but they won't hear of me paying them back. I'll never forget, Daddy saying, 'Patsy, I'm not going to lecture you. We tried to raise you right. It's up to you now. You're calling your own shots, just don't ever forget who you are. And remember, if you plant corn, you get corn. If you plant wheat, you get wheat and if you do wrong, you get trouble.'"

"Your Daddy's a real smart man."

"Reeda, I'm just now seeing how smart he really is."

CHAPTER 7

She avoided his kiss.
"What's wrong, hon?"
"Nothing."
"You ain't much good at lying."
"No, but I'm improving everyday."
"We don't have much time. You said you want to get home early," he reminded softly."
"You're right, I do," she said and kissed him. He touched her breast and began, like always, gently working her nipple. She slipped her tongue in his mouth and tried to give herself to the moment, but her nipple stayed soft, her pulse would not quicken.
Howard moaned, "Hell, Reeda, you'd think we was married. You feel just like a wife."
"I know, I'm sorry. Please don't you start acting like a husband."
"Want me to turn that bathroom light out?"
"No, the light's fine. I like a little light."
"Babe, something don't suit. You're as cold as a sun perch in a frozen pond."
"Tell me something I don't already know."
He moved back from her and searched her sad eyes. His eyes were neon green with pain and anger. Still his voice was gentle as he said, "Pretty kitten, if you can't play without feeling guilty, it's no good for either of us."
"Yeah, that's what Cyn said."
"She oughta know."
"I'm just having a little trouble sometimes with planned sex."

"Sweet darling, how can you have sex or anything else without planning it?"

"You're right, Howard, and it's not your fault."

"What's different about tonight than any other time?"

"Nothing. That's the problem. A couple of quick drinks, the quick kisses, then the shuffle under the sheets. It's too regimented. Makes me feel like I'm rehearsing for the real thing or something."

"Girl, that didn't give you any trouble till lately."

"Don't remind me."

"Wanna take a weekend and go away someplace?"

"No, not really."

"You just need another drink. Here, give me your glass."

"Why not?"

The drink he brought her with a tender, "Baby, try this," was terribly potent. She took several swallows. Why disappoint him? Being here was as much her doing as his. Probably more. Anyway this was their swan song.

He lay back on the other piled pillows and said, "How's the drink?"

"Beautiful," she replied, smiling.

"Talking about routine, what could be more routine than going home every night to the same boring supper, the same boring, bitching woman, the same boring TV programs and worrying about the same damned boring bills?"

"I don't know."

"I do, Hon. Nothing. Not a damn thing."

"I don't have any answers, sweet man. I'm justa drinking my drink like a good girl."

"You'll feel better in a few minutes. You know what makes one of the saddest things in the world?"

"Yep, a lover who won't talk to me. What's the saddest thing in the world for you?"

"Going to bed with a woman, who's so familiar she's a stranger because you can't remember what you saw in her in the first place."

"That's pretty sad, Howie."

"Even worse is seeing she feels the same way about you, even if she lies to herself and to you too much to admit it."

"She's too afraid to admit it. She's afraid she might disappear cause everything she ever dreamed has already disappeared."

"Whatever. Anyway, you go through the same motions then try to get to sleep in spite of the same old disappointment and heartache. In that scene, you think you're rehearsing for your own funeral, because that's all that's left in your life you don't already know about. You ever felt that way?"

"God, yes."

"Then how in the hell can you think us being here together is any worse that two people keeping each other penned up like that?"

"Maybe, you're right. Maybe it isn't."

"Hell, once old Dr. Bourbon takes hold and starts making you feel better, we'll both go home with a smile on our face. What's got next to you, anyway?"

"Actually, the other night, I got involved in something I'll never forget if I live to see a McDonald's on the moon."

"What, hon?" he said tenderly. She wished for the ten thousandth time he wouldn't call her hon, but he was being too sweet to complain.

"Howie, I can't say who, but this young girl had been in the hands of a butcher abortionist. She was as close as air to dying. Now, she won't ever be the same because of an aborted pregnancy that meant absolutely nothing to the ass who knocked her up."

"Reeda, those things have been happening since creation."

"How can you be so insensitive?"

"Guess smelling farts loading hot trailers in August does it."

She laughed. The whiskey was doing it's work. It wasn't a pretty laugh but at least she laughed. "But you got out of loading trailers."

"You better believe it, doll baby. Had all I could take of trailers and pulling a damn dock buggy like a dumb jackass."

"But it paid good, it paid good."

"It done that. Per hour I never made more. On overtime, I made a hell of a lot more. But it's worth every penny I'm losing to be out of it. I did enough sweating and stacking freight, all cooped up in a trailer, to know I'd rather starve than spend thirty years doing it. Even at union wages and with a union pension coming at retirement."

"So, you got in management."

"After I worked on the dock over four years. Then I took the first dock foreman's job I could get— if it was straight midnights. Hell, Hoffa himself woulda got out of the union if he had to load forty-five footers in the summer time."

"I'll say one thing, Summers. You do know who you are and why."
"Well, you might explain a thing to me I never have understood."
"I doubt it." She took a swallow from her glass. "But what?"
"I'll tell you straight up, if I was a woman, I wouldn't let no son-of-a-bitch poke at me. But hell, if he ain't her husband, she knows he ain't with her to have no baby. Probably with her to get away from his babies at home. Know what I mean, hon?"
"Yes, Howie, hon, I do."
"So why does a woman turn herself up to a man, like here it is, darling, come and get it, then bitch about getting pregnant?"
"Mister, I don't have the slightest. Maybe it's the dumb nature of the female beast," she said, and was suddenly ready for their evening to end. "Like I said, I don't have any answers. Besides, I'm sure you don't really want answers from me, cause that's the last thing I want from you." She moved into his arms and kissed him.
Then he said, "Yeah, hot stuff, this is more like it. Things were sure looking real pitiful awhile ago."
"You're feeling good to me now," she said, then seriously kissed him again and slipped her hand from his chest down to stroke his stomach. He took her hand and moved it on down farther.
"Lord, man, you're already ready."
"I was ready when you walked in here with me." Knowing no matter what the foreplay, the most she could hope for tonight was to please, she moved on top of him.
"Hey, you're coming on real strong now. Good whiskey always comes to the rescue."
"Hush, Howard, and just love me."
Later, when Reeda locked the bathroom door, after throwing the latest in disposable douches in the wastebasket, she turned the shower to a torrent to muffle her sobs.
When they left, with fresh makeup on and no worse for wear than a shopping trip would have made her, she said, "Don't take this personal, you have been grand, but I don't want to do this anymore."
"Ah, hon, I know this ain't been a real good evening for you. You haven't got over Carter running Molly off."
"It's more than that."
"Think you just getting a bad case of the PMS. Angel, I know you're gonna be feeling better tomorrow and feeling different about us. We got too much good going for us to forget it."

She allowed him to walk her to her car, kiss her good night and see her off without further comment about her feelings. Why should she be redundant? What was the point?

When she eased in her front door, her effort to be quiet was wasted as Mrs. McGammon met her with, "Mrs. Davis, there's been an accident. I called for you everywhere, but you weren't to be found."

"Jamey? Has something happened to Jamey?"

"Oh, no, ma'am, Jamey is fine. It's Mr. Davis, the police called. There's a sergeant's name and number by the phone. He said for you to call as soon as possible."

"Did he say what has happened?"

"He said there's been a bad wreck. Mr. Davis is critical."

Reeda went to the phone and dialed the number written down in Mrs. McGammon's large oval script.

That next morning at four a.m. in Good News Hospital, Van Davis died without regaining consciousness. He preceded his companion, Madeline Jean Harbold, by only twenty minutes. The good doctor said with their blood alcohol level, both were oblivious of the impact with the bridge abutment that split Van's new convertible in half.

There were occasions, Reeda supposed, when it was just as well to be drunk.

"Mrs. Davis, I know how hard this is for you. Is there someone I can call? Mrs. Davis?"

"I'm sorry, doctor, what did you say?"

"Is there someone we can call? Do you have family in the city? Or perhaps a friend?"

"That won't be necessary."

"Would you like to stay here in the hospital tonight? I could give you a sedative if you won't be driving."

"I... I want to go home. I'll make the arrangements in the morning."

At Van's funeral, the general consensus was how well Mrs. Davis held up. Never shed a tear, still in shock. It would hit her later, another woman and all. A son to raise all by herself. Just terrible. Everybody knew what a drinker and chaser Van was. Rather poetic justice. But it would be hard for the boy as well as the mother.

And it was hard for the boy. He knew more about his parents quarrels than either suspected. Because of his mother's tattletale swollen eyes, he often hated his father. It was very hard on the boy.

For Reeda, it was like the end of a long illness that defied all treatment and then, at last, miraculously cured itself.

She was immensely relieved that Howard honored her request and displayed the good sense not to appear during Van's wake and funeral. He was most understanding and supportive with his phone calls, but Summers was not a man to accept denial for long.

The day she returned to work, he cornered her in the breakroom, "Reeda, baby, I just gotta see you. You don't know how I been missing you."

"No. It's over, Howard."

"Reeda, you didn't love that bastard and I need you. You put me off too long now."

"I'm not putting you off, I'm through."

"Girl, nobody puts me down. I put them down when I'm finished."

"Consider yourself put down, finished or whatever but I'm through." Reeda walked around him and out of the breakroom.

Later, when she was checking with a dockhand about when a shipment on the trailer he was unloading could be picked up, Howard walked up and said, "Can I help you, Reeda."

"Yes. When can this freight be picked up?" she repeated, indicating the pro number listed on the manifest.

"Hon, it's manifested smack in the nose, the trailer is less than half way unloaded. The men are going on coffee break in ten minutes. They'll be put to loading outbound when they come back. That shipment won't come off till after the midnight shift comes on."

"Howard, this customer badly needs his freight. It's critical, a shut down situation. Can't you make some kind of exception?"

"I don't know, hon, come on. Let's see what the load looks like. Maybe we could put a tow-motor in here."

She followed him into the trailer, he stood a moment inspecting the cargo. "Well, it ain't too bad, lots of big stuff, a bunch of TVs. A tow-motor could have them off in an hour or so. Then we could probably see how to dig your little shipment off the unit."

"That would be great. This is for the glass plant and you know they give us a lot of trailer loads outbound. They want to send over and pick their shipment up by seven tonight, if there's any way. Can you do it, Howard? We need to be good to them."

"Well, hon, that all depends on can you be good to me?"

"I've always been good to you."

"Yeah, you have. But would you be good to me tonight?"

"No."

"Damn, hon, why not?" Reeda glanced over her shoulder to check on the dockhand. He can't hear us now. He's pushing his buggy over to the city delivery door."

"Howard, I've told you, as gracefully as I know how, I'm through."

"What did I do?"

"Not a thing, it's me. I can't... anymore."

"Why?"

"I don't know, I just can't."

"Girl, I could slap hell out of you."

"I don't care if you do, but you won't."

"Don't be too damn sure, Reeda."

"Like you told me once, you have a job to protect." It was clear she no longer wanted him and she wouldn't scare.

His voice changed, "Why be cold to me? It ain't my fault you had to bury that clown."

"I know that."

"What we did don't have a thing to do with him being dead. Your old man wasn't worth a damn alive, he sure ain't worth ruining us dead. But that's it, ain't it?"

Reeda shook her head and said, "No! Don't be absurd."

"Then what? I been trying to see you four weeks and you keep putting me off. I can't live like this. Promised myself when you came back to work we'd get things worked out."

"Jamey needs me. He is still upset over his daddy and probably will be for some time."

"That bastard didn't give two hoots about Jamey. Sooner the boy realizes that the better off you and him both will be. You're going to see me tonight and lay this thing out. It can be the motel, your place, a park bench or anywhere you say, but I've got to talk to you."

"I'm not seeing you again, ever!"

"Yes, you are. I'm coming to your house tonight and if you're not there, I'm coming every night till you are. Now, girl, there was a time when you wanted me for something. I don't guess I understood what it was but I filled the bill, whatever it was. Hon, you're going to talk to me. You know you owe me that much!"

She was about to say she didn't owe him anything. But the desperation in his eyes testified he could be pushed to where he might create a scene. Job or no job, hers or his. "Okay, if nothing else will do, my house at nine-thirty. Jamey will be in bed by then."

"I'll be there, hon." He does have a great grin, she thought.

"Now, Howard Summers, you get my shipment off this truck and I mean it. It's already late coming in and one of our best shippers has an emergency. I'm telling them the freight will be available for pick up off the dock at seven sharp and it damn well better be."

"Doll, you got it. Lordy, , you're something else, when you get really bad pissed."

"Give me a break!"

"Your eyes are shining like two black stars."

❧✖☙

Jamey was asleep and Reeda was watching a video till he knocked at nine-thirty. When she opened the door, Howard gave her his best smile and a warm, "Hello."

"Hi. Come on in."

He took the chair she indicated and offered, "I noticed your grass needs cutting. I could do that for you."

"You probably need to cut your own grass."

"It ain't going nowhere."

"Jamey will cut the grass this weekend. He lost some school time and has been staying over to catch up. Would you like some coffee?"

"Nope. You wouldn't happen to have a cold beer?"

"No, I cleared all the alcohol out of the house."

"Guess, you're turning over a new leaf, strictly clean living."

"Trying to revive the old leaf is nearer the truth. The way I was with you was a new leaf for me."

"Hell, I didn't see nothing but good about that."

"It's just not the way I want to live."

"Meaning, I struck out."

"It has nothing to do with you. It's me, my values and my self-esteem. Van's not here to blame it on now. I need to like me again."

"Loving me don't make you indecent."

"It isn't just you. Every day I lived with Van after I knew what he was, was a disgrace. I used every excuse in the book. Divorce is a sin... Jamey... all kinds of things. But I let fear keep me from divorcing Van, and now I'm ashamed of myself. I need to respect me again. I can't do that sleeping with another woman's husband."

"Would it make any difference if I were free?" he asked, sometimes that worked when a woman started copping an attitude.

"Breaking up a marriage is about all I haven't stooped to."

"I haven't had much of a marriage in years," he said, humbly, knowing that usually eased their guilt pangs.

"But you are married, you have kids that call you daddy and know you'll be home... sometime. That means something to a child no matter how bad things are between their parents. I could never accept responsibility for changing that for your children."

Giving her his saddest look, he said, "You can't just cut me off. I've never known a woman to touch me like you do. I... I might kill myself!" that one usually broke down the rock of Gibraltar.

A burst of laughter erupted from Reeda, then she said, "Don't be dumb. You aren't the type to kill yourself and we both know it."

"I don't know, I'm bad blue. Never have been this blue."

"Man, you love living too much to kill yourself over a woman or anything else."

Unable to comprehend that a simple truth can't be manipulated and that she was telling him a simple truth, Summers said, "You know, there's a pretty little lady named Fay wanting me to meet her later tonight. Good looking little thing. She's got a husband, he looks right feisty. Don't know what she could want with me."

"God! You don't mean Fay Russell from work?"

"Well, as a matter of fact—"

"Forget it. It's none of my business and I don't want to know."

"She called me right before I left work, wanting to make an appointment. Told her I couldn't possibly see her before eleven and didn't know if I could then or not. Don't really care about going. Haven't seen anyone but you since we started, I'd like to keep it that way. All you have to do is say the word, hon, and I won't go."

"But that's what you should do, Howard."

"You're serious!"

"Yes, completely," she said, so honestly all doubt left his mind.

"Hell, Reeda—"

"You better be on your way. Shouldn't be late; especially for the first date."

Smiling wistfully, he acknowledged defeat, "I don't understand why you're doing this. Now you have no one to answer to, but I see you're hell bent on doing it. The Devil himself couldn't change your mind right now."

He rose and moved to the door. With a last piercing look, he searched her deep dark eyes again for doubt. Her need to be rid of him was all he saw.

As if she knew, she whispered, "I'm sorry, Howard." It broke his heart to realize that all she wanted was enough time to pass so that she could consider him a memory. He had been here before.

"Me too. Ain't used to being the rejectee instead of the rejecter. But... when someone wants out, all you can do is let go. Bye, hon."

"Don't say it like we will never see each other again. We still work together and we can be friends. I do consider you a friend, and I'll always love your beautiful green eyes."

"Hon, you got my eyes mighty blue tonight, cause we won't ever see each other again like I want us to."

"No," she said, in spite of the plea that spoke from his eyes.

It was midnight when he pulled along side Fay's car at the airport. She came out of her Chrysler and was into Howard's Camaro by the time he cut the motor.

"Hi, there," he said.

"Howard, where were you?"

"Uh, well, I got called back to the terminal. Sorry I'm a little late. A major problem came up and I had to run back and handle it," he lied.

"I should've known. You stay as busy with your job as Bob does his. It's mean how they make management people work all the time."

"Well, we gotta do what we gotta do. Girl, you're looking good. I sure was surprised to hear from you," he said, eyeing her appreciatively. "Course I was mighty pleased."

"Can we go somewhere else and talk? All these planes flying in and out are making me nervous. I'm nervous enough worrying someone might see us."

"Sure thing, but don't worry. An airport parking lot is the best place in the world not to be seen," he said, backing out of his parking space. "Everybody around an airport is always in a hurry."

"I did notice that."

"Hey, Fay, you want to stop somewhere for a drink or something?"

"I'd love a coke, but that would be taking another chance on somebody seeing us. Is there a private place where we could talk?"

"My cousin owns a motel, but I wouldn't want to rush you."

"Uh, that sounds fine, if no one will know we are there?"

"No one that matters. Fay, trust your old Uncle Howard. You're as safe as you would be in your mama's arms."

"Is it far?"

"No, and don't worry, old Howard knows how to handle these things. We can still have a little drink. I got a bottle under the seat and we'll get coke and ice at the motel. Do we have to worry any about your husband?"

"No, Bob's in St. Louis. He won't be back until tomorrow evening.

"Good. We can take our own sweet time." He cut his eyes to appraise Fay as she stared straight ahead. Never could figure women or quail. No way to tell which way or when either one would fly. Just like this gal, from the first day she walked into Alpha she couldn't say two words unless one of them was Bob. He never had seen her look cross-eyed at nobody. Then, boom! She comes on. He hadn't meant to get involved with anyone else from work. Too damn risky, but it was a true case of hard times when Fay called.

He knew already all bets were off with Reeda unless she got real lonely. That could be a long damn time, knowing how gutsy Reeda was, and he'd cut all his other women off but Janey. Like always, the best thing he could do was get over one woman being with another woman. All any man could rock-bottom-count-on was not counting on a woman— any woman.

Hell, they didn't know what they wanted their own self most of the time. So how could a man know? And, Lordy, he hadn't had a decent piece in over three weeks. For sure he needed Fay. Even if she did work at Alpha Fay was the only good looking woman in sight. Janey wasn't hardly even a sport fuck anymore.

Fay read the Expressway Motel sign as Howard turned in and parked at door twenty-two. She hadn't thought crossing over into the world of motel lovers could happen this quick or this easy for any married woman who loved her husband.

"Hold on a second, little honey," Howard said, fishing under the seat for his bottle. Then he was out of the Camaro and around opening her door, smiling his best smile. "Come on in, darling, where we can talk and not be seen."

"Don't you have to sign the register or something?"

"All taken care of, baby. My own blood cousin owns this place, we got a mutual thing going. He and his help knows my car. Don't worry your pretty red head about a thing."

He put his hand on her waist possessively as he guided her through the door of the motel room. The sick feeling in her stomach started churning worse, her courage was registering zero. Suddenly, they were behind the locked door and she was being thoroughly kissed.

"Why, Fay, baby, you're shaking."

"It's okay, don't pay any attention. Howard, just let me undress and we will get this over with," she said sitting on the edge of the bed.

"Whoa! You're way ahead of me, seems like. I think in more ways than one," he said, catching her hand that was removing her shoe.

"Well, sex is really all men like you want, isn't it?" she said, suddenly feeling almost calm. At least her shaking had stopped and she could control her voice.

"Sure, darling, but not cold turkey. I may be some kind of animal," he said, grinning. "My old lady says I am. If I am, I'm a good animal. So, relax, sweet thing. There's no hurry. I don't have to be at work till seven, you don't have to be there till eight. Your old man ain't coming in till tomorrow evening. We got time to do each other some justice. Let's have us a drink or two first."

"Howard, you don't have to give me the routine. I'm ready to co-operate and I certainly don't expect you to argue."

"I'll be damned," he said, taking a chair. "Ain't this night is just crammed full of surprises." He lit a comforting cigarette, enjoyed a deep inhale, then said, "Oophs, sorry, Fay. Cigarette?"

"No, thank you. I don't smoke and you shouldn't either."

"You're right," Howard agreed and took another deep drag. "As for the routine, as you call it, I need the routine even if you don't. Now, I'm being honest with you, so how about you being honest with me."

"Honest about what?"

"We all got our reasons. Fay, hon, I want you for the pleasure. Now why do you want me? Revenge? Heard that one lately."

"Oh, no, Howard."

"Then why? You have already let me see my wonderful looks ain't overwhelmed you," he said with a dry laugh.

"It doesn't matter. Really, Howard!"

"Does to me. I need to know what kind of pond I'm swimming in. Specially with a married woman."

"Can't we just get on with it?"

"Nope, not till you tell me why. But hold on a minute. I'm going get some Seven-up and ice. I want a drink, you want a coke?"

"Seven-up will be fine." Fay realized she had misjudged him. He wasn't as crass as she thought. While he was gone she better use the bathroom. This evening was making her kidneys over active. It never occurred to her a stud like Howard would even question her offer. She hated having to explain. Apparently, there was no other way.

When Fay walked out of the bathroom, Howard was sitting by the lamp table mixing two drinks. He looked ready to sit all night. If she didn't go through with her plan now, she never would. She held his eyes a moment before saying, "To save my marriage!"

"What?"

"I want to... well, to be with you to save my marriage. You and your wife must have some kind of agreement. She has to know that women are your... hobby. For want of a better word."

"Well, I do like beautiful women."

"And... you have children of you own and you and Bob are near the same size and coloring, except for your green eyes. Bob's eyes are hazel but I guess something would be different with any man."

"Here, Fay, this one's your drink. I didn't think you'd want yours as strong as mine. Most women don't."

"I don't want a drink."

"Well, I do. If you're saying what I think you're saying, I need a drink real bad. Do as you like." He set her glass on the end table, took a long drink from his glass, then smiled and said, "That's what I call good. I'll be right back."

After he went into the bathroom, Fay decided maybe she did need a drink. She took a sip from her glass. The man did know how to make a good drink.

When Howard came out of the bath room, Fay was sitting on the side of the bed, holding her half empty glass and looking gorgeous He asked, "You're drink okay?"

"Actually it's really good."

"Thanks. I like a good drink and I try to make one."

"Howard, why are you dragging this out?"

"I still don't know what's going on. Girl, straight up, what do you want from me? I know it ain't love."

Looking directly in his green eyes, Fay shrugged, then whispered, "Sperm."

"What?"

"Sperm. Bob is sterile and driving me crazy to adopt a baby."

"So?"

"So, I can't stand the idea. Don't ask me why, I don't know. I'd just as soon let well enough alone. I always wanted a child of my own, but I don't want someone else's mistake. That might not be the proper way to feel, but it's the way I feel. I spent too many years denying my own sexual appetite to want the responsibility of someone too loose to keep her own legs crossed."

"Can't blame you there. Raising kids ain't no picnic, if you ask me."

"I was raised in the middle of eight kids so it's no picnic to me either. Bob is an only child and he was a very lonely child."

"Guess that would make a difference."

"I might feel differently, if there was something wrong with me."

"I can see how anybody would."

"But there's not and Bob says we adopt or we divorce. I love him too much to lose him but I can't adopt, and he is set on having a child. That's the whole truth of why I'm here and why I called you."

"Lord, I've heard some wild reasons. You can't believe the excuses a woman comes up with when she wants some strange. You sure take the cake, gotta hand it to you."

"But that's how it is, we've seen two doctors. They agree there isn't a chance in a million for Bob to father a child. You still interested?"

"Well, darling," he drawled, "I've broken up a few marriages and I've interrupted a few. Guess it's about time I quit thinking of only me and saved one. Come on over here," he invited with a smile. "Let this old marriage counselor get started counseling."

"Let's just get in bed. Foreplay isn't necessary. Really."

"May not be for you, but it sure as hell is for me. A wine taster don't gulp and a chef don't shovel his food. Experts don't get in no rush. They know to savor the flavor. Won't take no more from Bob if we enjoy saving his marriage."

"Howard, Bob is my husband!"

"Bob might be Christ Almighty to you, but he ain't nothing to me."

"I can't enjoy another man."

"Hon, don't be dumb and for God's sake don't think I am."

"No, I never could do any good with any man till I met Bob."

"Betca can and double your money back if you can't."

"Howard!"

"Hell, girl, Bob's the one wanting the baby. You're just trying to be a good wife, if any wife ever did try."

"I really am, Howard. I'm sincere about that."

"I know that's right. And me? I'm just trying to be a friend and save your marriage. At your request. And I ain't asking you to say you love me, I don't even want you to love me. But if you don't want to come over here and make love and act like a woman to me... fine. I can understand that and we'll still be working together friends. If you can't, let's get the hell outta here, honey, if you don't mind," he said, his voice gentle. "I can always get a sacrifice piece at home."

"But, Howard— "

"Fay girl, this is your party. Contrary to popular opinion, I ain't no bull standing at stud. I sure don't want no woman looking at me like she's getting up courage to take an enema with no soap."

"Really, I'm sorry. I don't mean to hurt— "

"Baby, when there ain't no sweetening happening or about to, a bedroom's the most depressing place I know of. So I'm about to get outta here and take you back to the airport. The night's running out, and it's damned late not to be pleasing you or me."

Knowing he meant every word, despite his boyish grin, she hesitated only a moment before saying, "You... you want me to take my clothes off?"

"Naw, darling, I'll do that when it's time. Right now, just come on over here and sit on my lap and talk to me a minute. Course, if you prefer, I'll come sit on the bed with you."

"You come over here, Howard. We'll be more comfortable."

"Okay," he said and moved to the bed with his drink. "By the way, do you folks want a boy baby or a girl baby."

"I just want a healthy baby, Bob prefers a boy."

"Well, maybe we can get started at trying to make him one. You got mighty soft looking lips, give me a little warm up peck, right here on my cheek," he said, tapping himself on the cheek, "that's the first step." Fay kissed him on the cheek, then he turned the other cheek, tapped it and said, "Hon, this other side wants a kiss." She kissed his other cheek. "Now right here in the middle, if you don't mind," he said, tapping his lips.

Fay kissed him warmly on the mouth, then smiled in spite of everything. Howard said, "Girl, you do have soft lips, and I like your perfume, you smell real nice."

"So do you." She finished her drink and sat the glass on the floor.

Howard got up for his drink on the lamp table and drained the glass. Then he knelt in front of Fay still sitting on the bed and said, "A baby ought to be conceived with good feelings. It's good luck for the baby, so let's take things just slow and easy, okay?"

"Okay."

"Why don't you try kissing me one more time. Lady, you do have the softest lips." This time he felt her began to kiss him with confidence and knew she was okay. "Sugar, you're gonna make a beautiful mother."

"I hope so."

"I know so, take my word for it," he said with a grin and kissed her forehead. He moved to sit on the bed beside her and kissed her, just touching her lips till he felt her respond. Then he put his arms around her, lay back on the bed with her and thoroughly kissed her.

"Howard, I..."

"What, pretty baby?"

"I didn't know a man could be so gentle. Where did you learn to be so tender?"

He drawled, "Well, Sunday school, I guess."

"I didn't know they teach making love in any Sunday school."

"Not how to make love exactly. But they teach about love in Sunday school and all about treating folks like you want to be treated. I try to treat a woman like she wants to be treated so maybe she'll treat me like I want to be treated."

"Do you mean some women want to be treated rough?"

"Sorta. Sometimes."

"You mean like whips and stuff?"

"Naw, I ain't into mean stuff. Life's mean enough without making it a part of loving."

"What then?"

"Well," he said, kissing her neck, "some women like to be shown who's boss. I really like a willing and tender lady like you." He unbuttoned the top button on her blouse so he could kiss where her breasts began, then said, "They say the best chance of making a boy baby is when the woman really enjoys the loving. Since Bob wants a son, we gotta make sure you have a real good time."

"You know something," she said, unbuttoning his shirt, "you really are right." She started stroking his chest. "We should do this with real feeling, Howard. It won't make me one bit more unfaithful. Besides, it is just because of Bob that I'm even here."

"That's what I been telling you, angel cakes." Smiling he slipped his hand inside her blouse. "Now just play along with me. Help me show you a good time and we'll be sure to make your Bob a real fine boy baby. Darling, I'll even try my best not to give it my green eyes. And you can even call me Bob if you need to."

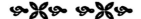

CHAPTER 8

After all the years of heartache and humiliation, Reeda thought it might be psychotic to want to flee the split-level house she had loved so much when she and Van bought it. But she did. In fact she had reached a time when she found it impossible to continue life in the same house. Van's choosing, her choosing, or fate's choosing, with him out of the house she should feel more comfortable. She didn't.

Consulting with a very highly recommended real estate agent enlightened her about the housing market. The agent assured her that the house would rent profitably and he would manage it for a fifteen percent fee. The real estate market was down and a sizable amount would be lost to taxes if she should sell. For the present, renting out the place seemed to be her best option.

Jamey going into junior high in the fall meant a school change and a busing situation that was incentive enough to move. Reeda started checking on apartment houses without a busing bottleneck.

She found that accommodations for Jamey and her rented for a little less than the amount the house would rent for. She found a complex that she liked with a pool, tennis courts, cable hookup, several teenagers Jamey's age, and a view she couldn't resist. After signing a six months lease, she took a two month leave of absence from work for the move, some R & R and to spend some badly needed time with her son.

He seemed elated about their new home. They spent her first two weeks of leave with getting settled and taking a daily swim. A park was in walking distance and he made friends with several other kids. Things seemed to be going well till the day Reeda came up from the pool to find him sitting at the kitchen table obviously depressed.

"Hi, Mom," he replied, lifelessly.

"I thought you would still be at Billy's apartment."

"I was tired. I'd better take my tennis stuff on up to my room," Jamey said, picking up the gear he had stashed under the table.

Suddenly, she longed for the days when it was an everyday struggle to keep him from littering the house with his toys. "Are you hungry?"

"No," he answered from the stairs, "ate a bunch of junk at Billy's."

"I'm having a coke," she called, "you want one?"

"Sure, Mom, I can always use a coke."

She couldn't get used to the long legs he sprawled under the breakfast nook table. The hands that picked up the coke bottle were the size of a man's and he was already taller than she. For once, she appreciated the too long hair, combed bang fashion on his forehead, that kept him a boy. The face with a hint of down about the upper lip, was the male variety of her own, except for the sullen lips that came straight from Van.

"Son, how are you doing with tennis?"

"Okay. Billy showed me a couple of things."

"Did you check around for a teacher?"

"Not really. Mom, I don't want lessons. I just want to play like I play, knock a few balls around with the guys. Teachers make you learn all this stuff."

"If you learned to play properly, you could get really good at it."

"Maybe, but I don't want to yet. Do I have to?"

"Of course not. It's just that I thought you wanted to take lessons. When we first moved in, I mean."

"Changed my mind. Everybody else is always changing their mind. Guess I can change mine sometimes, too."

"Changing your mind's no crime, but what are you trying to say?"

"Nothing."

"What is it, son?"

"Well, I don't think I like this set up much, I guess."

"Oh? I thought you liked it fine."

"I did at first."

"What happened, Jamey?"

"Nothing, Mom, truly. I just miss the neighborhood where we used to live and our old house."

"But you have twice the friends here, and you know what a problem we had keeping the house up. It took all day on Saturday just mowing the grass. Here, you have the pool and tennis courts. At your age, I would have given anything for a swimming pool."

"Sure, it's nice, but we lived in the old place so long, and everything's changed. It's all so different."

"I know, darling," she said, and wondered if the echo of bad judgment about marrying would ever stop. "Son, we only took a six months lease and we just rented the house out. When our lease here runs out, if you aren't happy, we can always move back."

"Do you like it here, Mom?"

"So far, so good. It's still too soon to know."

"Do... do you think you might get married again?"

"Uh, I don't know. I guess so... someday. Why?"

"Nothing, I was just wondering."

"Well, I really haven't been single very long. At lease not long enough to be thinking about getting married again."

"I know but guys are always asking about my dad."

"Kids can be very cruel, sometimes, Jamey."

"Oh, I know, but it isn't that. They just ask. It's like natural they should ask. If I say my dad's dead, they look funny or look away. You know what I mean, Mom."

"Yes, I know."

"I know how Dad made you cry sometimes. Made me cry sometimes, too. He was gone too much and mostly grumpy when he was home. Still Dad was good to me a lot. Especially when he wasn't dru— well, when he was himself."

"Your father could be very good to you and to me when he was home and sober. I know you loved him and that's okay."

Van had been getting progressively worse, still, since things turned out as they had, she was glad, for her son's sake, the divorce had not gone through. It was easier for Jamey to still think of them as a family. Time was already recalling fond memories for him and leaving the bad ones behind.

"I promised Billy I'd meet him for a swim. Really, Mom, is there a possibility you might marry again?"

"There's always a possibility but, darling, I don't have anyone in mind at the moment."

"That's okay. Just as long as there's hope," he said smiling. "Guess, I'd better get dressed now and meet Billy."

Except for buying a Queen Ann sofa, Reeda had found little time to shop for the apartment but she and Jamey had wrestled moving mayhem into good order. Then she hired a cleaning lady who left the place sparkling. Reeda loved the open floor plan of their new home. On her last Sunday of leave, she had Cynthia in for the day.

After the three of them lunched together, Jamey left to play in a basketball game at the club house. Reeda and Cynthia chatted awhile on the deck of the apartment. Then they dressed for swimming and strolled down to the pool with paper cups and a tote jug of iced tea. They found lounge chairs in the shade of a table umbrella at pool side on a perfect high eighty's afternoon.

Stretched out on her chair, Cynthia said, "After that big lunch you fed me, I won't be doing much swimming for awhile."

"You're not fooling me. You aren't about to get your hair wet."

"Not if I can help it. Besides, what I'm after is some sun."

"It does feel good to be out in the sun for a change," Reeda said.

"And looks good on you."

"The pool's been a great place to be with Jamey without him being so painfully aware of it. Thought you were bringing your boys."

"Another time, thank you. I took them to Six Flags last weekend. Except for the office, I haven't had any time away from them in three weeks. Today, I need a little break from my boys. I wouldn't enjoy watching the water near as much if I was having to watch them. And Mom and Dad wanted to entertain them today. Thank God."

"You're a trip, Cyn. You do tell it like it is."

"I try. You mentioned the other day your Jamey seems depressed. He was in a big way at lunch."

"Yeah, we had this talk and Jamey has been a different kid."

"What did you do, promise him the moon? With sons of my own, I'm subject to need your secret."

"Just a new dad."

"A what?"

"A new dad."

"Well, who is the lucky fellow?"

"There is no lucky fellow. I only told him, maybe someday, but it seemed to put Jamey's mind at rest."

"Just goes to show, kids do worry about the damnedest things. Say, when have you heard from Howard?"

"Cynthia, Howard isn't a fit father for anything."

"I didn't mean that. I just mean, have you heard from him?"

"Not since that night we had our talk. Guess he got the message."

"And you haven't been with him since the night Van..."

"Died, Cyn. Died! It's all right to say it. No, I haven't been with Howard. Haven't talked or heard from him, since I told him how I felt. He knows I don't intend to see him again. Ever!"

"Sounds like you tried to put him in the know. Keeps mentioning you at the office though. Even called me at home one night to talk about you. I think Howard really cares for you."

"Ha! Howard doesn't know how to really care for anybody."

"Well, he mentioned getting a divorce, like it might make some difference to you."

"It wouldn't. Besides, his wife couldn't run him off."

"I don't know, he's sure got me convinced."

"If he's thinking of getting a divorce for me, he can forget it."

"Well, I guess, when the lady's through, she's through."

"Don't sound surprised, your advice did it. And by the way, thanks."

"You're welcome, but what did I say?"

"You told me, if I didn't enjoy seeing Howard to stop seeing him. It had gotten to where I didn't, so I did."

"Damn, that's the trouble with giving advice. Never know when somebody's gonna take it. Reeda, honey, remind me to watch my mouth in front of you from now on."

"Fire away if you have anymore more gems like that one," Reeda said, as she nodded and smiled at a tall, dark woman passing by.

"Where did that tall package floating by come from?" Cynthia asked, her jade eyes inspecting the woman as if studying for a test.

"She's just another resident."

"Just another resident nothing! It isn't who she is, it's what she is."

"What then," Reeda said.

"You really don't know?"

"No. We talked here at pool side a time or two. Should I?"

"Probably, since you two are neighbors and it's pretty common knowledge to anybody who has been in trucking awhile."

"They say everyone eats a peck of dirt in a lifetime. I can tell by the gleam in your eyes, this is a big cup full of mine. What is she?"

"A very high priced call girl."

"Are you serious?"

"Serious as sin," Cynthia assured.
"A paid prostitute?"
"Alive and kicking and expensive."
"I can't believe it. She has so much class."
"You ever noticed her leaving for work?"
"No, but I know very little about any of my neighbors."
"Well, how does she manage to eat and hang out in a snazzy apartment complex like this?"
"She could be rich. I understand some people are, Cyn."
"I hear that, and she could be, but she ain't. That woman was raised on the north side of town by two of the plainest, nicest, parents you ever saw. But they were dirt poor. Her daddy was illiterate, couldn't even sign his name. Worked in a foundry all his life, for never more than minimum wage, till he finally coughed up his lungs."
"Cyn, she's too beautiful to have to live off men."
"Surely you don't think an ugly woman could."
"You know what I mean. A woman so beautiful could be a movie star, or marry well. She could have anybody she wants. Can't imagine anyone that lovely being passed from man to man."
"The way I get it, she ain't passed. She goes.
"Ugh! I can't imagine anything more horrible."
"It's a cold world out there."
"And I thought you had some news," Reeda said, wearily.
"I'll quit editorializing and get down to facts. That woman has been all the way from the bottom to the top. Picture it, two kids, just out of high school get married. She, because he doesn't paw at her and she wants to get away from home. He, because she's so beautiful he can't believe she's real. He's a good boy, but not much above minimum wage material, like her dad. He's weak like her dad, but he isn't as lucky. He needs a mouse of a wife, a girl few other men would be interested in, like her mother.
"Melinda is wild, gorgeous, passionate and gutsy. She needs a rich, gentle bull of a husband. It's a horrible miss-match and their marriage is doomed from the get go.
"They start out in two rented rooms in somebody's basement and work at jobs that pay peanuts. They buy furniture and a new car with a high-jack finance joint backing the lot. Combined, they have a hundred dollars a month above their loan and living expenses. They really don't even have gas money for their new car.

"In six months, she hates him. In six more months, she's five months pregnant, hates him more. They're taking pinto bean sandwiches to work for lunch. Six months with child, she has to take maternity leave with no pay since she hasn't worked long enough to earn any benefits. When the baby comes, his folks scrape up a few bucks to help them get through.

"The atmosphere is better till she goes back to work. With the added expense of child care, they are taking mustard and mayonnaise sandwiches for lunch. When the baby is six months old, she decides being pawed over is better that being buried alive."

"Oh, no, Cynthia!"

"Oh, yes. Now here comes the nitty gritty. The horny asses eventually get brave enough to deliver her to her front door. One three-o'clock-in-the-morning, she comes wiggling in to a loaded husband, holding a loaded shotgun and their crying baby in the baby crib. Her husband's eyes are more horrible than the gun. Too scared to say a word, she starts crying and inching along the wall to the crib with the barrel of the gun following her, till she comes to the crib and climbs in with the crying baby."

"Well, don't stop there! What happened?"

"He killed her!" Cynthia exclaimed, in a low voice, then giggled.

"She's over there taking a sun bath. What happened?"

"Seriously, he stands the shotgun in the corner, then sits down in the floor beside it and weeps. Melinda slips back out before daylight, left him and the baby. I understand she has been living high on the hog ever since."

"Proving crime does pay?"

"I guess, Reeda, when you got what she's got."

"She is stacked."

"Melinda is gorgeous and knows it. She also knows there's always some drooling sugar-daddy just begging to pay."

"The drooling sugar-daddy is the part I couldn't stomach."

"Hey, you went for the true love, broke as hell, faithful as a dog, little wife bit, once. Didn't you learn a damn thing, Reeda?"

"Yeah! In the gutter is in the gutter, whether it's with a rich bastard or somebody's bastard of a husband."

"Ain't that the truth. Course, we have to keep our amateur status and give it away. I ain't sure that makes us better than a woman who up-front gets paid for getting laid."

"To each her own," Reeda said.

"Hell, we never have been exposed to real money. Neither had Melinda, back then," Cynthia said, stealing a look at the woman lying on a chaise lounge across the pool.

"What's her last name?"

"At the moment, I don't know her last name. She's had two or three husbands. She was born Melinda Fox. Everybody on the north side of town knows about the Fox sisters. Her sister, Vivian, isn't as tall as Melinda, but she is as beautiful and in the same profession."

"What happened after she left her first husband and the baby?"

"They say, at that point, she was still trying to be legit and took a job as a waitress at Hilda's truck stop where the tips were good. Hilda's was two blocks from Renfro Transport and most everybody at Renfro ate lunch and hung out there. At that time, Renfro was the biggest family owned common carrier south of the Mason Dixon."

"They aren't even in business now, are they?"

"No, they went broke," Cynthia said.

"How could anybody build something that big, then go broke?"

"I guess you can womanize, booze and kickback yourself out of any business. They say Chase Renfro was in with the teamster's like a son, and the parties he threw in the best hotels were unreal."

"I think we came in trucking after the wild west days were over."

"They say Chase's parties were like a Roman orgy. Wine flowed like water. Women flowed on their backs, knees, upside down, crossways, backwards or hind-part-before. Anything his guests wanted or could dream up— so the story goes. Had a call girl in the men's room giving blow jobs to any guy who wanted one while he dried his hands."

"God! How gross!"

"Rumor has it that Chase paid the bill to get politicians and union officials laid, from governors to congressional and presidential candidates. They say he had public officials and the teamster's local in his hip pocket. Made truckloads of money for years."

"That is so wild, Cyn."

"Tell me about it. I don't know how he got his start. I've heard from his first wife's money, but he was a dock worker at one point in time. Somehow he got control of a three point line and snowballed it into a Goliath sized operation. Some think Chase got his backing from the teamsters from the start. They say he's the smartest, most crooked, most high energy SOB. that ever lived, with a face like a big mouth bass and ten times as hard to catch.

"Anyway, one night he rolls his red El Dorado Cadillac in for supper at the truck stop where Melinda is waiting tables. She's twisting around in her brief little pirate uniform and old Chase just totally flips. He treats her like a princess and he leaves her a fifty dollar tip. Comes back six nights in a row and leaves her a fifty dollar tip every night. He was too old, too married and running to fat from high living, but that is how he got her."

"Guess the price of a soul comes to three hundred dollars."

"I guess," Cynthia agreed, "if you wanna look at it like that."

"I always wondered what a soul was worth."

"When you live on mustard and mayonnaise sandwiches, you can't afford a soul. And that was only the beginning. He married her."

"That's rare."

"There was a delay till the legal-eagles got him loose from a wife of twenty-five years and Melinda loose from her husband."

"Bet it was the best break she ever had. Maybe we all would do better to forget love and go for the money."

"Melinda did sit on a satin pillow, for awhile. The marriage lasted several years; till Renfro went broke. After that she dumped Chase. They say Melinda said, she'd had all the financial hard times she could stand. I kind of have an aversion to them myself."

"Yeah, it's what keeps us all clocking in at Alpha. I just can't see how anybody with such a fortune could wind up broke."

"I don't understand all that stuff. It's all I can do to remember to pay the light bill and put a dollar or two in the credit union. Hell, balancing my little checkbook is a major operation. Oh, yeah, Renfro also got in a bunch of legal troubles."

"What kind of legal troubles?"

"His divorce first. Then he got involved in a huge kickback scandal over state contracts. There was labor trouble, strikes and some sin concerning the Taft-Hartley Act. Then good old Internal Revenue jumped him. Those bastards could bankrupt Fort Knox. Chase fell in red financial waters. Before he could swim out, the sharks moved in and his friends moved out. The man wound up serving time in the penitentiary. Word is he came out broke and broken."

"That's an amazing story, Cyn."

"It blows my mind. Which, reminds me, I'm glad you're coming back to work tomorrow. You need to be there."

"What's going on?"

"I don't know, but I know what it smells like. The home office was in a stew all last week. They been cawing on the Watts line worse than a bunch of crows. All the brass will be coming in, tomorrow."

"What do you think it is, Cyn?"

"If I was a betting woman, I'd bet they are on to Carter and Sara. I'd say we've seen just about the last of that loving, little duo."

"Lord, you get the story before it happens."

"You don't believe me?"

"My dear, wonderful friend, I've learned to never, never doubt that you have the facts in spades."

"Reeda, It's easy working on a switchboard, if you pay any attention at all. One more thing, Matt Fletcher's been talking a lot on the q.t. about organizing the office." Cynthia looked around and lowered her voice before saying, "Plus Mat has started getting some calls from the local brotherhood."

"You mean the teamsters?" Reeda whispered.

"Right. Now don't quote me, cause this is just my very own personal opinion. Okay?"

"Okay. What?" Reeda said, feeling like a conspirator.

"I think the natives are restless enough for a serious attempt to try and unionize the office."

"God! Cyn, are you for it?"

"Yeah, I think so. Matt says we'd get a raise, job security, a good pension plan. What really got my attention, Matt says sexual harassment will be a thing of the past. So, are you for it, Reeda?"

"Subject to all that, sure. It's a God sent for anybody who has to work for a living. Especially if they have kids to raise."

"I hear that. By the way, what do you actually know about Hoffa?"

"You mean Jimmy Hoffa, Cyn?"

"Of course Jimmy Hoffa. Who else?"

"Only what my Dad and brothers say. They worked in freight when Hoffa ran the Teamsters before he went to federal prison. After he got out he disappeared."

"Was he really a gangster?"

"Bobby Kennedy made Jimmy Hoffa out to be some kind of gangster. Bobby was instrumental in getting him put in prison. My daddy and brothers think of Hoffa as the savior of working people. They say he did more than any one individual in history for labor. Dad says Hoffa is a hero should have had a medal instead of incarceration. My kin believe he fought in a labor revolution and soldiers in war are not criminals. Dad is as honest as folks get but he doubts anyone could have stayed strictly on the straight and narrow and gotten anywhere when Hoffa was organizing for the teamsters."

"Reeda, I think it's high time we started asking questions and doing some independent research."

"Yeah, but where? You know union people are going to be pro union. Management people are going to be against it and a bunch of uninvolved folks could care less."

"When all else fails, there's always the library."

"I already know Hoffa raised freight people out of poverty. He is the main one who negotiated with management to get a decent day's pay for a decent day's work. I'm already convinced if Jimmy Hoffa hadn't come along we wouldn't be making minimum wage right now."

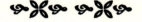

CHAPTER 9

The office was as charged as a hospital waiting room during major surgery. As she and Cynthia exchanged another keep your chin up glance, Reeda decided it was major surgery job wise

Nathaniel Vance, Alpha owner and president, Chief of Operations Winston Briley and Chief of Labor relations Able Golden all visited the Manchester terminal on occasion— but never all together. As a group, they all stopped and visited briefly at each employee's desk, making the plastic conversation management utters to hirelings.

Hank Carter tagged along behind with a sick grin, as nervous as a bleeding shark swimming with his brothers.

Last they visited very briefly at Sara Major's desk before retiring to Carter's office. It seemed to Reeda that Sara smiled with more sincerity and was more at ease than anyone.

Vance confiscated Hank's desk, Briley and Golden parked in the remaining chairs. Hank stood fidgeting like a Chihuahua finding a Saint Bernard at his feeding dish. Ultimately he decided to haul in another chair from the outer office. A few minutes later Hank emerged again to ask Mona to bring coffee.

On her way to the big coffee urn in the break room, Mona clicked past Reeda's desk muttering, "I'm supposed to be a secretary not a damn waitress."

In spite of Mona's resentment, Reeda noticed the woman managed a convincing smile as she carried coffee, two cups at a time, to the men in the terminal manager's office. When Mona had all their coffee requirements met, she came out of Carter's office. She closed the door and as she sat down at her desk rolled her eyes at Reeda.

A computer started printing out freight bills and cut the tense silence in the outer office. Sitting at his desk, Stanley attempted to joke but his voice almost whispered, "Reeda, maybe they just wanted to see our sweet, smiling faces."

In a normal voice, she answered, "Yeah, we can always hope." As her phone rang, she added, "But, to be honest, I could do just as well without having to look at their sphinx faces."

Reeda kept an eye on the management men through the window of Carter's office. The four men seemed to finally have their nests made in the proper pecking order. It was obvious the conversation did not include Hank Carter.

When Hank's phone rang, he had to pick his way around the other men and there was no lag in their conversation. Subsequently, he was reduced to a state of sitting with his chin propped in his palm. When that eventually became unbearable, he started a steady route from his office to the dock and back to his office on the pretext of checking on freight or whatever..

Behind their thick glasses, Sara's weak eyes glanced with sympathy each time Hank passed her desk. The other people working in the outer office, hourly or salaried, kept their eyes down and worked as if Armageddon was eminent.

Since Reeda's job involved working between the phone and the computer, she could see what was happening without being obvious. Men could be so cold and cruel when they coped that "looking-out-for-the-company" attitude. Vance, Briley and Golden watched the sweating terminal manager, as he darted in and out of their presence, like patient crocodiles waiting for just the right time to pounce. It was just awful. Three against one was a sick situation in the school yard with kids or the work place with men.

At lunch Cynthia was as happy as a girl with a new doll, as she spent their entire lunch break speculating about how long they would be enjoying the company of Hank and Sara.

Weary of the miserable mess, Reeda tried to change the subject with, "How are your boys doing?"

"Fine, for once, since they got over the damn chicken pox. It nearly killed Brad, his skin is so fair."

"Brad's sure is his Mama's son. Got his blond hair and fair skin from you," Reeda continued, trying to keep Cyn into one of her favorite subjects, her sons.

But Cynthia was only momentarily detoured as she said, "Yeah, his dad's hair was dark. Listen, I predict we've worked our last day with old Hank and Sara and I say amen to that."

Reeda was relieved when lunch time was almost over and she could say, "We better get on back to work. With Patsy out sick, I've got to post all her receivables."

"You're right. I need to get back to the switchboard on time. You know Fay has a doctor's appointment."

"Yeah. Maybe he can settle her down. Fay has looked like she's just looking for a chance to tune up and bawl all morning long."

"When you're pregnant, bawling just goes along with the territory. At least it did for me. We still have nearly six minutes, Reeda. Let's not give sweet Alpha a minute we don't have to."

"Okay, we won't give Alpha anything. You know we have to brush our teeth and primp up a little."

"I wish you wouldn't say primp. It sounds so country."

"It is country, my grandma used to say primp all the time. Grandma was one of the sharpest women I've ever known and I like country. Come on, Cyn, let's get going. I really do have to brush my teeth and primp up some."

"You can do that on evening break."

"Hey, I love fresh baloney but I don't want my breath smelling like baloney for the next three hours. I'm gone," Reeda said, getting up from the table. "The last thing we want right now is to give those conniving bastards a chance to get on our case.. Come on, Cyn."

When they went back to work, the rest of the office force was at lunch. Vance left with Carter in tow, after telling Cynthia at the switchboard, if an emergency came up they could be reached at The Cherokee Steak House.

When they were out the door, Cynthia caught Reeda's eye and formed her lips into a silent whistle and rolling her eyes toward the door the men had just closed behind them.

Reeda rang Cynthia and asked, "Will Vance fire Carter now?"

"I don't think so without Briley. He's still in there with Golden. Vance is an old hand at leaving the distasteful things to Briley. Don't look like they're tired of making Hank sweat— yet."

"Maybe they won't fire him."

"Trust me, Reeda girl, Hank Carter is out of here."

"Could be. You have been around longer than I have," Reeda conceded and hung up.

Trace calls were seldom heavy at lunch time, she searched in her purse for a nail file. Doing Patsy's daily paperwork filing had her nails in a mess and she had to do something about the one she had broken.

Filing her nails with most of the office at lunch and no printer noise to cover conversation, Reeda became conscious of Briley's voice in Carter's office. "You know, Able, the most obnoxious part of this mess, I knew it was going to happen. You just don't put that many attractive women to work in one office and nothing come of it."

"Not with a fool like Carter," Golden said.

"That's what's wrong with his hiring techniques. There has been a complete turn-over in female personnel since he's managed here."

"Yes, I'm aware of that."

"That, in itself, doesn't distress me. Most terminal managers like to fire and hire their own help but Carter hired nothing but lookers. Too many lookers have no place in a freight office."

Golden said, "You have to admit I rather enjoy looking at the pretty girls here in the Manchester office. Briley, are you saying terminal managers need to hire ugly women?"

"No, but it might be a good idea. Even if local management has some control, which I don't think for one minute Carter has, every road driver in the world comes off the road horny as a horny toad."

"He wasn't thinking about road drivers when he hired these girls."

"With all his faults, Carter isn't a total fool. Every girl he hired falls in the twenty-five to forty bracket. That's the years when a married woman is most likely to know discontent and a single woman gets worried about her biological clock. I advised Nathaniel against hiring Carter, but he owed somebody a favor who owed Carter a favor. The ape has a history of plugging office help. He caused havoc and left a legacy of trouble with every carrier he's worked for the last several years. That's what got him fired from his last terminal."

"It's a blessing we all weren't judged by our past, Winston," Able said. "Because of women and... other things, quite a few of us wouldn't be working for Alpha if Nathaniel hadn't been extenuating."

For the moment, Winston Briley had forgotten Able had drawn some time while serving as a union business agent, years ago. Winston hadn't meant to step on any toes.

"Hell, Able, working in labor keeps a man standing on the edge but labor trouble and woman trouble are two different things. Women are on earth, like a lot of other pestilence. A terminal manager has to be able to be above to hire and work around women without trying to mount his entire female staff. In checking back, with some discreet phone calls, I found out Carter has never been able to leave women alone. It's a wonder we hadn't found them screwing on the desk tops."

"I know, I did some checking on my own."

"He misjudged most of the girls he hired. Most of them have some morals and enough self-respect to be discreet. I got it straight, Hank tried to put the make on every female here till he got mixed with this Sara bitch. If Hank hadn't fired the Luna woman, to make room for her the other girls would probably have been glad for the relief."

"An aging stud can be a pathetic thing. What will you do if he doesn't—"

Lost in listening in on Briley and Golden, Reeda was startled by the watts line that rang in direct on her phone. But she automatically answered, "Customer service."

"This is Leonetti in the Chicago terminal. Is Winston Briley there?"

"Yes, sir, just one moment." Reeda rang in Carter's office. The watts line, in all Alpha's terminals, was like an enormous party line stretching from Canada to the Keys and from New York to San Francisco.

"Yeah?" Briley answered rudely.

"Winston, Leonetti here, returning your call."

"Leonetti, why in the hell did you pile these last two trailers in here a day late? What do you think the Manchester terminal can do with the son-of-a-bitches in the middle of the morning."

"Sir, I—"

"Sir, shit! You know damn well all you're doing is throwing the burden of trace calls on this terminal. Plus, it's all late freight!"

"I know, sir, but it was just one of those things. We have had every kind of set-back here you can imagine."

"Crap! Leonetti, you have been running that terminal long enough to have it straightened out. That's what you said you could do when you were dogging me for the job like a whore coming on to a trick."

"Sir, I'm sorry—"

"Don't be! How much longer am I going to have to chew on your ass about this kind of screw up?"

"I... I'll get right on it."

"Do that! Get on it and stay on it till you get to running right."

"Yes, sir, I will."

"Leonetti, fire who you have to, hire who you need to, but I want your freight moved and moved on time. You have a couple of foremen up there you need to bore a new one for or terminate. The last time I was there, about all they contributed was a turn around the dock once in a while to scratch their ass in private, then pile up in the dispatch office with their number twelve shoes hiked up on a desk."

"I know, but good foremen are hard to find up here."

"Good foremen are hard to find, Leonetti, but there's no room in this organization for loafers. I don't want to have to tell you that again. Do you understand me?"

"I understand, Winston. I've been meaning to crack down but you can't find experienced dock foremen up here. You're in worse shape than ever if you make them mad and they quit."

Reeda loved the way Winston's drawl subdued Leonetti's excuses. "Look, I don't give a damn if they do quit. Hire some new personnel if you can't make your present staff work worth a shit. Stay on at night and train them yourself if you have to, but stop babying what you have. They won't ever be worth a damn if you have to keep on babying them. And stop dispatching freight with a beard on it. Late freight ain't what this company is about. You hear me?"

"I'll take care of it. You still coming in tomorrow?"

"Yeah, but it'll be late— my flight is due in at six ten."

"Okay, I'll be there to meet you."

"Hell, get your freight straight. I can find your damn terminal."

"I know... I want to talk with you before you get here."

"All right. I'm on Universal Flight six forty-two."

"I'll be there, Winston. Bye, bye."

Reeda winced as Briley slammed the phone down, then growled, "A man who ends a phone conversation with another man with bye, bye has got to be some kind of queer."

Golden's chuckle was his answer.

"I wonder," Briley continued, "what Leonetti wants to whine about now. I can't wet nurse him forever."

"Sounds like you might have to let him go."

"If I keep him on, he is going to have to run with the ball himself. I never should have hired a college boy. College boys want job security, a conference on every decision and an eight hour day."

"Then he should have got a union job."

"There again, Nathaniel grew up with Leonetti's father. That's one more family favor I have to work around."

"Winston, Nathaniel likes college degrees," Able said. "He believes it helps trucking's image. Maybe it does. Hell, the industry needs all the help it can get."

"The problem is, a college background hardly ever produces the work attitude that makes a competent terminal manager. College gets them hung up on job benefits."

"You don't like job benefits?"

"Of course, but it isn't the first thing I think about. Managers need to know what it's like to shimmy across an icy log on your behind to cross the creek to get to school, with the old man long gone and four brothers at home hungry to appreciate a decent job. The well bred, well fed boys from the frat houses don't usually work out."

"I agree, but Nathaniel wants college boys and it's his freight line."

"And he wants me to keep it his and making money and operating. Like Leonetti, he's too soft. Hell, an eight hour day in trucking is a joke where supervision is concerned."

"Then Leonetti doesn't have the balls to be a terminal manager?"

"I really doubt it, but like old Carter, he has done a great job with his terminal. Since Carter took Manchester over tonnage has tripled. Manchester had operated in the red for three solid years before Carter came and he gets along with the brotherhood like family. Carter has reduced grievances here right at fifty percent. Hell, he worked on the President's staff with the last carrier he worked for."

"I know. Did a fine job till he got caught with a secretary."

"This terminal was losing so much money, before Carter came, if it wasn't for its huge break bulk dock, we'd have shut it down."

"I'm well aware of that, Winston."

"Tell me something then, Able. You're the labor expert. You know any legal way to have the bastard castrated."

"Not literally, but there are ways of getting similar results."

"Let's have it. If possible, I'd like to keep Carter, at least awhile. He will be hard as hell to replace, right now. I don't know of an experienced, available manager anywhere. I sure don't want to turn this facility over to Summers. We would be worse off. From what I can hear, Summers is hot as Carter after women and he's younger."

"Let me close the door. Nathaniel and Carter should be back from lunch any time and I don't like surprises. You know, Winston, some time ago I saw—" The door closed and Reeda could hear no more.

That evening when Reeda and Cynthia clocked out together, the anticipated climax had not come. As they walked to the parking lot, Reeda said, "Cyn, you think this is all subject to just blow over."

"Not on your life. You can bet your boobies all that brass didn't come all the way to Manchester for the scenery."

The next morning, Sara Majors did not report to work. It was late morning before the hourly employees realized Sara had been sacked and Hank was staying.

It took several more hours for them to comprehend that Alpha had one set of rules for management and another set for hourly. No one felt Sara had been mistreated, but the injustice of firing one employee for a transgression and retaining another equally guilty, maybe more so, deeply shook the security of the entire office force.

Fred Griffin divided the remainder of the week between his duties as office manager and those of Sara's vacated cashier desk. After lunch on Monday, he asked Reeda to join him in Carter's office.

Though the home office brass had left the building, Hank's forced heartiness failed to erase the strain of pressure from his eyes. Rumor had it that Mrs. Carter had left him. Reeda didn't blame the woman for that. She noticed, and not for the first time, Carter had probably some years ago been an attractive man. Time, hard drinking, hard work, unbelievable hours and steady bed hopping had taken their toll.

Cynthia's spying in the personnel files had revealed Hank was fifty-eight years old. He was a really old fifty-eight, Reeda thought. She felt a twinge of pity for the aging womanizer. He had squandered the respect of his employees, not to mention the love and respect of his wife. You would think that by the time a man lived over a half century, he'd have some common sense about sex. Hank was worse than a teenager.

"Sit down, Reeda," Hank invited. "You too, Fred. By the way, Reeda, how is your new apartment working out?"

"Just fine, sir."

"Good. Glad to hear it. Relieves you of the upkeep that goes with living in a house. You should have let me send the truck and two men I offered to move you. It would have made moving easier and cheaper for you."

"Thanks but like I told you, Mr. Carter, I already had the movers booked. But I appreciated your offer."

"I like to try and help. Reeda, as you know," Carter said, then was interrupted by his phone. "Carter speaking... Well, sir, my damn trace clerk happens to be in my damn office, at the moment. That's the reason you can't reach her." Hank winked at Reeda.

Again, she was reminded of how supportive he had always been to her and the rest of the girls. His support had strings, like his offer to move her. Hank always got around to trying to coerce his female clerks into bed. He had never been demanding about it with her, only suggestive, with his let's do it look burning up his eyes.

Half the time she pretended she didn't know what he was talking about. The other half she pretended she thought he was kidding.

Then she heard him say, "Could I have the trace clerk call you shortly?... Sir, have you considered she will call you back when she has an answer on your tracer?... All right, hold on and I'll ask her. What was your name again?... Okay." Carter put his phone on hold and said, "Reeda, a Mr. Johnson is hot about a shipment of steel. Know anything about it?"

"Yes, I spoke with his secretary right before I came in here. Mr. Johnson was out. Crammer Express gave it to Samson Lines at Chicago yesterday. Mr. Carter, we're not even involved. Alpha hasn't touched the man's freight."

"I'll be damned!" Hank said, then punched back in on the phone, "Johnson, you got a secretary?... Would you please ask her about the message she took from my trace clerk, about ten minutes ago, while you were out. Alpha isn't carrying your shipment." Carter hung up, then muttered, "Son-of-a-bitch! Pardon my French, honey, but these idiots refuse to route their freight, then start tracing every line in town. God! how unprofessional can a traffic manager get?"

"It's unreal," Reeda said.

"Looks like this is a good time to ask the question I had Fred bring you in here for. Reeda, without a doubt, you are one of the finest trace clerks I have ever worked with."

"Thank you."

"You're welcome. As quick as your mind is, I wonder if you might want to learn something about the freight business besides tracing?"

"I would like to learn all I can."

"Good. As you know we are short a cashier. It pays a quarter more on the hour, and you would learn another facet of the trucking industry. Interested?"

"Yes, sir, but I'm inexperienced at handling money."

"You won't have any trouble learning to handle money or anything else on the cashier desk. You're very capable, Reeda. In the not too distant future, I'd like to see you in management. It is obvious you like working in trucking."

"Yes, sir, I really do."

"Would you like to learn the cashier desk?"

"Yes, Mr. Carter, I would."

"Good. I was hoping you would. Fred, find us a new girl for the trace desk and start Reeda on cashier. Reeda, Fred will work with you a couple of weeks until you get the hang of things. The cashier desk is a good job— and you will learn more about rates. Once you know what you're doing, I think it will be a breeze after that tracing desk wringer."

"Thank you, sir. I'll do the best I can."

"I know you will, that's all we can ask of anyone."

In four weeks, Cynthia said, "Reeda, you're as comfortable in the cashier job as last year's girdle".

"It's easier in a way than tracing, but there's a ton of clerical boredom and I hate that."

"Better bored than run to death and it pays a quarter more on the hour. Count your blessings, girl."

After another two weeks, Reeda realized the repetitive clerical work was offset by the small revenge she enjoyed getting to legitimately hound some of the customers for payment who had hounded her on the trace desk for freight. At last she had confirmed her theory that the shoe-string business was the most demanding about delivery and the least concerned about paying freight charges.

For the most part, established firms allowed for operational variances in motor freight. She wondered what was profitable about cultivating customers who cost the company money at every turn. When every shipment, mostly minimum weight, was hot, rush and requiring expeditious handling from pick-up to delivery, there was no way a trucking company could realize a profit from such a customer. When that same customer required rigorous collection efforts before payment of freight bills, Alpha had to eat the loss.

It seemed feasible, if they were coordinated closely together, tracing and past due accounts could work for one another. It was a point to think about. Of course there were folks around, more experienced than she, who apparently didn't see any reason to connect the two. Maybe she failed to understand the big picture yet, but a fresh viewpoint was sometimes—

Reeda's phone interrupted her thoughts, and she answered, "Cashier".

"Ma'am, I'm Mort Morgan, the owner of City Tool and Die. Your driver is standing here with a C.O.D. shipment and refuses to take my company check."

"Didn't the C.O.D. clerk call before delivery and explain that I.C.C. requires cash or certified check, Mr. Morgan?"

"Lady, everybody takes my company checks. I pay my damn bills."

"Yes, sir, I'm sure you do but it is an I.C.C. ruling. C.O.D. shipments require payment by cash or certified checks."

"Well, if you people are too good to accept my check, you all can kiss my business goodbye. You tell your boss, Alpha will never haul another pound of freight for me."

"I'm sorry you feel that way, sir, but any carrier will collect C.O.D. shipments in the same manner. If you will consider our position, I'm sure you can see we have no choice."

Morgan apparently wearied of the conversation because he hung up.

"Bastard!" Reeda hissed to the dial tone before hanging up. Immediately her phone rang again. "Cashier."

In an excited hush of conspiracy, Cynthia whispered, "Wait a few minutes, but after I hang up; slip around and tell Fay to break with us. I need to talk with you both, but not on the phones. Matt says they just may be bugged."

"Bugged? Our phones?"

"Yes, of course our phones! Think I would be talking about the office next door?"

"No, it's just weird, Cyn."

"I hear that! Gotta go. This damn switchboard's been ringing off the wall all day. Break's in ten minutes. Tell Fay."

At the start of their break, Cynthia said, "We better go on in the john. I don't trust these walls. We can flush the toilets and run the water in there to cover our voices."

The three women moved to have lunch in the ladies room. Reeda and Fay sat down. Cynthia checked all three toilet booths to satisfy herself they were alone.

"Lord, Cynthia, have you got the secret of the atom?"

"I don't know about the atom, Reeda, but what I know will sure as hell blow the roof off when it comes out."

"Well, hurry up and tell it before you kill me. The anticipation's making my heartburn worse," Fay said.

"Okay, just settle down little mother. Let me get me a filter king lit up. It won't make you nauseous will it?"

"No, I finally got over that."

Cynthia lit a cigarette, then asked, "Want one, Reeda?'

"No, but I'm gonna take Fay's heartburn if you don't get on with it.."

"Y'all remember Hank had me relieving in billing this morning?"

"Yeah," Fay said, "I had to relieve you on the board."

"God, I hate billing! Always have, always will. It's unreal what a girl will do to stay off her back, in a professional way at least, and to keep food on the table. Anyway, all week, Matt has been acting like he wanted to say something. This morning he came out with it." Cynthia took a deep draw from her cigarette.

"You always stop to smoke at the good parts," Fay said, impatiently. "What'd he say?"

"There is union talk."

"Not again," Fay said.

"Naw, this is serious union talk. I mean it really is."

"There's been serious union talk forever," Reeda said.

"But this time, Matt is taking an office poll. He wants to know for sure and certain, how all the hourly people feel in the office. This time, Matt is dead serious about it. For all our sake he needs to know who else is."

"Cyn, you know I was raised on union and that my Dad and my three brothers are all union electricians. I told you when they fired Molly, we are in bad need of the union."

"I know, Reeda, I told Matt you'd be for it. Bill Crawford and Sara got about the same deal as Molly, not to mention the fired clerks we were hired to replace. Also, you may as well know this now. The men in the billing department didn't like it when Carter gave you the cashier desk. There are people with more seniority who think they should have been offered the job first."

"I never thought about that," Reeda said.

"I know, you couldn't have helped it if you had. But in a union office, job vacancies are awarded by seniority and qualifications. Matt says it's the only fair way to do it."

"Matt is right," Reeda agreed.

"I told him you'd feel that way. Fay, how do you feel about it? Matt says now is the time to speak up and no hard feelings either way."

"You ought to know how I feel. Starting my maternity leave in seven weeks. I might have a job after the baby and I might not. Carter doesn't like pregnant women."

Cynthia quipped, "Yeah, I know. He takes it as a sign they get along with their husbands."

"Well, I certainly hope so," Reeda said, noticing Fay's sick smile.

Fay said, "I want to come back to my job so you all can surely count me in."

"You're not staying home with the baby?"

"No, Reeda, I... I changed my mind."

Cynthia put in, "Now you're getting smart. Raising kids is a bore, hard work, and a thankless job. Listen, I have to find out about the other girls. If everyone agrees, we're having a meeting tonight at Matt's house with a union business agent."

"You mean this night?" Fay said.

"Yeah, Matt says the more it's discussed before signing sanction cards, the more likely it is to get to the wrong ears. That could change some of our minds and get some of us fired. Once we sign the cards, they can't fire anyone till after the election."

"Can they fire us after the election?" Reeda said.

"If the vote doesn't go union, they can and most likely will."

"How can they do that?" Fay said.

"Matt says, maybe not right away, but when an attempt to organize an office flops, they eventually fire everyone involved. Reeda, would you say something to Patsy when we go back from break?"

"Sure."

"Fay, since you sit the closest, would you ask Helen?"

"Of course. Cyn, I'm just pregnant, not an invalid."

"Okay, good. I'll talk to the others."

"When do you need to know?" Reeda asked.

"This afternoon before clocking out time. Y'all just be sure nobody that doesn't need to know doesn't hear. If we go union, there's another immediate benefit besides bid rights and job security. We work fifty cents an hour below scale."

"You mean if the union gets in we get a raise?"

"We sure do, Fay, honey. The office over at Jones Truck is hard nose union. Has been for years. Everybody there makes at least fifty cents on the hour more than we do. Also, this is a contract year. After the new contract is negotiated, Matt says the Teamsters will get another across the board raise. Maybe as much as a dollar an hour."

Fay grinned and said, "That does it for me! Obviously I'll be having another dependent soon. Where do I sign?" The women shared a nervous laugh.

Cynthia checked her watch and said, "Girls, we better get back to work. Reeda, let me know what Patsy says. The meeting's set for seven-thirty at Matt's house. Pass the word. And tell everybody, whatever they do, to keep their mouths shut if they want to win this thing!"

CHAPTER 10

"Hey, Stanley, come on in," Matt said, holding the door open." An empty chair's over there by Reeda."

Stanley sat down smiling and nodding greetings to his co-workers. Feeling vaguely guilty, he said, "Hi, Reeda, you doing okay?"

"Yeah. Just a little nervous."

"Am I the last one here?"

"Yes, but we haven't started. Looks like Matt is starting now."

Standing in the middle of the room, Matt said, "With Stanley here that makes everybody." He asked his wife, "Mary, if you would get Stanley some coffee we'll get started."

They sat in the living-dining room combination of a mid-size, classic ranch house build all over the southeastern states in the seventies. Seating was arranged in a U shape around the walls with a dining table placed across the top of the U.

Standing behind the table next to a seated man, heavy set with ice-blue eyes, Matt said, "Welcome and thanks for coming. The word is out that I want the office to join the Teamsters Union. As we speak, company rats may be circling the block. Company spies may be in this very room. I hope not. Because if the company hears about our meeting tonight, none of us might work another full week. Especially if the vote doesn't carry for the union. I respect you all too much to pretend otherwise.

"As for me, I'm sick of pay below scale, meager benefits, and no job security or retirement. My gray hair shows I've worked long enough for non union truck lines. The Teamsters have the best pay and benefits for hourly workers known to man or woman. That's why I'm all for joining.

"My friend sitting here at the table is Rob Sands, ex over the road driver, now business agent with the Teamsters Local. We go way back. He's honest, smart and will answer all your questions. Let's turn the meeting over to Mr. Rob Sands."

Flashing a smile, Sands stood and said, "Thank you, Matt, for the very kind words."

He took a moment to make eye contact with each worker present. Then as he picked up his coffee cup and drained it, Reeda and Cynthia exchanged a knowing look. The very confident Mr. Sands came off looking remarkably like the union thugs portrayed in the photographs in their library research.

Sands went on, "Nice to see all you folks. It's good luck to have a fine turnout at a first organizational meeting. Matt says the office is present a hundred percent— that's as good as it gets.

"Hear you folks are tired of getting jacked around, seeing your co-workers get run off, so you want to check out joining the Teamsters Union. If you want to know about the Teamsters, you're talking to the right man. I'm happy telling about the union as a preacher is telling about the Bible.

"Know this— I believe in the union with all my heart. I'm blessed and proud to be part of it. And I won't care who knows that I love Jimmy Hoffa for lifting up workers in the trucking industry. Nobody ever fought harder or won more for working folks.

"Also, I hate how Bobby Kennedy harassed and railroaded Mr. Hoffa, my personal hero, into a federal pen when he deserved a medal. Shows how much a millionaire's son knows about working for a pittance.

"That's why we have to put more working class people in congress. Talk about affirmative action. The house and senate are bad hurting for some serious affirmative action in there. A majority of the wealthy are making laws to rob from the poor and give to the rich.

"Course, that's another story, but keep it in mind. We got all our hands full tonight getting y'all started toward getting in the union.

"People, I gotta admit, till I got a dock job and joined the Teamsters, I couldn't make a living for my wife and kids. Always was more month than paycheck. The Teamsters have picked up millions of workers down on their luck and helped them get started with a decent job.

"Nobody thinks he's a thug or stupid when a rich man joins his Rotary Club. Nobody should think a working person is a thug or stupid when they join the Teamsters Union. Every worker needs to join a union representing their job craft.

"Yeah, management volunteering to pay making-a-living-wages is scarce as hen's teeth. They mostly work folks like slaves when they can get away with it. Like all those old Egyptian pyramids— built on the blood, sweat and tears of trillions of workers. A Pharaoh never paid a worker a cent. Hell, they owned the workers. Too bad Jimmy wasn't around then.

"That reminds me of my pet project. It's to help found a Labor Union Hall of Fame to honor those who fought and still fight for the American working class. Our first inductee will be Mr. James R. Hoffa. Fighting for decent jobs is as patriotic as anything anybody can do for the country. Working men and women are the backbone of our nation, the very spirit of democracy and they deserve respect.

"Folks, if you plan on voting pro union, expect a fight for sure. When your bosses hear about it, they won't be thrilled. They'll try to talk you out of joining any way they can. They'll bad mouth the union and all it stands for with half truths and lies. They'll damn Jimmy Hoffa like he was a gangster. But don't you believe it.

"But let me level with you. There is no perfect union, employer or employee. My Mama's the only perfect person I know— at times I doubt her.

"But I ain't selling perfect. All I'm selling is decent pay for decent work. That's good for us and for management. It creates stability, cuts cost on training new help, promotes experienced employees on the job. Experienced employees are better employees. Course the management boys ain't about to admit that. They're too incompetent to admit they have dedicated, competent, hourly people around.

"In the labor struggle, over the last sixty years or so, heads have been knocked together. Folks got hurt on both sides. Some lost their lives. When it came to knocking heads, management gave union organizers a light to go by. They were first to use hired thugs to break strikes.

"Just goes to show you can't peacefully negotiate decent labor contracts with greedy guts. It was tried for centuries. So for centuries a middle class was nonexistent.. It was Lords and serfs till organized labor started fighting for decent wages and benefits and finally won.

That's how our strong middle class got started. Atrocities like serfdom and slavery can't survive where strong labor unions live.

"These days we don't have much head knocking, but management loves playing games. Now they use brainwashing to kill union bids. They love fouling up a worker's mind— the media's as well. They want everybody to think union's a dirty word. They connive to fool folks into believing joining a labor union is weak and worse and they have no shame.

"They'll manipulate anybody, any way they can for profit. Down in Mississippi last year, they broke a bid to organize an office by telling the girls if they joined the Teamsters, they'd be called Hoffa's women. Those girls never saw the man, but that slur made them back down.

"Then, one by one everybody got fired. It took management ten months getting it done, but it slowly happened. Every office worker involved was fired and replaced with new people just for trying to join the Teamsters..

"Another trick is saying truck drivers, dock workers and such are ignorant and need help. They say office people are educated and can do their own talking. Don't fall for that! Right this minute, y'all are working under scale over fifty cents an hour. Effective the day your office is officially declared union, you get raised that fifty-odd cents.

"Yeah. they love tempting the bit of snob in us all. They love saying y'all don't want to associate with the low class in a labor union. Lord, every labor executive Alpha hires is a former union employee. The Teamster Union is the training ground for trucking's labor relations people.

"Be wary of management offers. If they haven't offered before it's a trick. Any promise the union makes to you has to be kept. If not the federal government is hot on our case.

"Friends, now I'm about to pass out the union sanction cards. If the vote goes pro union say nothing to your bosses. Let me do your talking. That's what I get paid for. Management wants to intimidate you, split your vote and defeat your union bid. So they will be wanting to talk to you all. I know it sounds bazaar. God, they are bazaar. With just fifteen people involved, one or two scared turncoats can torpedo your effort to organize and get you all fired.

"Seriously consider your vote It's kind of like marrying. Ain't no going back to the way things are. If you like the way things are, vote no and best of luck left on your own.

"Besides the sanction cards, you get copies of the currant office labor contract. All the crafts in trucking such as dock, road, mechanic and janitor have separate contracts. We'll read the office contract and answer all your questions. Any questions?"

Cynthia elbowed Reeda and whispered, "Ask him, Reeda!"

"You ask him," Reeda whispered back.

"Excuse me, do you girls have a question?"

Cynthia hissed, "Do it Reeda. Ask him!"

"Yeah, Reeda," Sands said, "ask me, honey. No matter what you may have heard, business agents don't bite."

"Well, we are just wondering, if women make the same as men under the Teamster contract. Is it equal pay for equal work?"

"Yes, ma'am. And you can bet on that. Pay rate is based on the job classification. Sex, color, race and so on have no say. For example, rate of pay for bill clerk is the same if a St. Bernard holds the job."

"Thank you," Reeda said, "we just wanted to be sure."

"You're welcome. Anymore questions?" Rob waited but no hand went up. Taking a stack of papers from his briefcase, he said, "Matt, pass these contracts out on the left side of the room, I'll get the right."

"Sure thing," Matt said, taking half the stack.

With contracts in everyone's hands, Rob sat behind the table and continued, "Let me explain something before reading the contract. When the union goes in, there will be no job bumping. Voting in the union secures your job as long as you want it. Bids are posted only for vacancies. Vacancies will be filled by seniority and qualifications.

"Now, listen close. This concerns the living you will earn and still raise your hands for questions. I got all night. Okay, here we go."

"'Alpha Trucking Co. Inc., herein called the employer and Teamster Freight Local 7777, affiliated with Trans-American Freight Handlers Association, herein called the union, mutually agree — '"

As Rob read the contract, stopping for questions when hands were raised, Reeda became impressed. Some questions seemed stupid, but the man avoided no one and gave sound answers. The contract was long with much legal language but he kept on reading and answering questions patient as a proud, old grandfather.

When the contract reading was done and all questions answered, Rob said, "Now, the moment of truth. We pass out sanction cards. If you will, Matt, help me with the cards."

When every one had a card, Rob said, "Again, read your card carefully. If you don't want the union, turn your card in blank. If you do check yes and sign on the dotted line. If the vote goes union, until such time as the National Labor Relations Board holds your final election, you are dependent on each other for your jobs. Be strong, be loyal if the union bid wins."

Deliberation was minimal. In minutes the cards came back to the table. After Rob and Matt counted and witnessed the vote, Rob stood and said with a big smile, "Congratulations, my brothers and sisters. Be proud of yourselves! You have voted one hundred percent to join the Teamsters Union.

"In the morning, I'll notify the proper people. Stay united like you are tonight and you got it made. And I solemnly vow, you never will be sorry about becoming a Teamster."

☙❈❧

"Reeda, this is Murphy. I'm at this place called Bargain Carpet with a C.O.D. That new trace clerk says we can only take cash or a certified check. The man had a cashier's check. I thought that was like cash money. The new trace clerk says only certified or cash."

"The check's good. It's okay to take it, Murphy."

"Reeda, it don't say certified anywhere. Lord, I sure don't need another warning letter."

"It's all right, Murphy. Take the check and just write, okayed by Reeda Davis on the bill."

"Okay, since you say so. But somebody needs to set that girl in your old job straight."

"I will. Just take the check, Murphy, and don't worry about it," Reeda said and hung up.

Rob Sands had breezed in first thing, walking from desk to desk grinning and speaking to all the clerks, happy as heaven. Now, he had been in with Carter over an hour. Reeda could see through the window to Carter's office how his face was burning tomato red.

All the girls were nervous like herself. The office was as tight as a ten months pregnancy. Patsy's naturally pop eyes looked like twin moons. Cynthia was smoking like the Midnight Special and it seemed like Fay might have to move her desk into the ladies room.

Reeda managed apathy and a fake smile now and then. Helen Beach had worked under a union contract before. She was the only hourly person even halfway composed.

Fred Griffin and Mona Burns were classed as confidential employees and therefore not union candidates. Fred was out of the office on an errand. Mona, though really uninvolved, was still about as tense as everyone else.

Past experience, plus the fact one was too active on the trace desk to do much thinking had rendered Helen into a sort of Gibraltar. The women kept looking at her and drawing strength. Helen just kept answering trace calls.

Remembering how tracing made you forget what went on around you, made Reeda wish she was still tracing.

When Sands emerged from Carter's office, he made a spectacle of visiting the office force. At Reeda's desk, he crowed, "Hank couldn't believe y'all signed up a hundred percent till I showed him the cards. I sure thought he'd bust a gut." Sands enjoyed a horse laugh before adding, "The brass will be in here full force tomorrow, Reeda. Make sure you girls all stick together now."

"Don't worry, we will. Our minds are totally made up."

"Good. The National Labor Relations Board will send a team to hold your election in a couple of weeks. Then you'll all be home-free. Reeda, pass the word on to the rest of the women and tell them, not to be afraid and not to back up cause they got it made."

When Sands left, Carter appeared in his office door and took a long look at each employee in the outer office. Finally, as if failing to understand what he saw, he shook his head sadly and returned to his desk. Reeda couldn't help feeling sorry for him.

In the afternoon, Fred ushered the eight-to-five shift into Carter's office, then took over the trace phone, while Mona took over the switchboard. Chairs were provided for everyone, the women eyed each other uncertainly. Since Stanley was the only male on the shift, they looked to him. He smiled a thin smile and shrugged.

Cyn whispered, "Damn, Reeda, his wife must keep him on an oatmeal diet."

"Don't get me tickled," Reeda whispered, stifling a nervous giggle.

For the first time anyone could remember, Carter dialed the switchboard and instructed Mona to hold all his calls, except from the corporate office. Then, pondering each individual like a male Joan of Ark, Carter cleared his throat as if about to speak, then looked at Reeda and said, "Davis, you got a cigarette?"

Laying her pack and lighter on his desk, Reeda said, "Thought you quit smoking."

"Yeah, right. Thought you were quitting, too."

"Well, I am still trying."

"How, by buying cigarettes?" Hank Carter managed a weak grin, lit up and then gave Reeda her lighter and pack of cigarettes.

"Yes, sir, I guess you could say that."

Watching Reeda walk to her seat, Carter drew on the cigarette and inhaled deeply. With smoke erupting from his mouth, he said, "If the tobacco don't get you, the job will."

As Reeda sat down and faced him, he caught her eyes obviously expecting a comment. For once in her life, she was silent. She really hated this whole mess and wondered why somebody always had to be hung on a cross before anybody else could be saved.

"Understand you folks want a union. If that's what you want it's your right. I just can't believe it. Not one of you hinted such to me. Most bill clerks clock in after I leave, but I thought you eight to five folks and I were close. I thought if you were dissatisfied you would tell me and we could work it out. Apparently, I was wrong. The main reason I wanted this talk with you all was to be sure you know what you're getting yourselves into.

"As I said, if you want a union, the company has no objection. Several offices in our company are union already. But I care about you all. You need to realize what the big picture is. I doubt you want to associate with the class of people that constitute the Teamsters Union. They're crude, mostly uneducated and often unwashed.

"In a union shop, things will not be like they have been. Working under a contract has repercussions you can't imagine. Y'all are too smart to need a job steward or a business agent to express yourselves. I know, I hired most of you. It's like a man buying three shoes when he can only wear a pair." Again he waited for comments.

The group eyed each other, but no one spoke. Sands had cautioned them, the best thing to say was nothing. No need to tell a man his indiscretion had betrayed them all, when he already knew it.

Finally, Carter asked, "Have I offended any of you?" Again eyes shifted from face to face but no utterance came. "Surely, you can answer that. Have I offended any of you personally?" Still there was no comment for his question or his searching eyes. "All right, let's take it one on one. Stanley, you have been employed the longest. In fact, you were here when I came. Have I offended you personally?"

Every ear in the room was waiting to hear what Stanley would say. He had asked for the cashier desk several times. Carter always refused. Like Stanley said, nobody wanted to work OS&D. Carter kept him stuck on the worst job in any freight office. Now, Stanley had a chance to give Carter what for. Stanley blandly said, "No, sir."

"Cynthia?" Carter went on.

"No, sir."

"Fay?"

"No, Mr. Carter."

"Reeda?"

"No, sir."

"Patsy?"

"No, sir."

"Helen?"

"No, sir."

"Didn't think I had. Some corporate folks think I treated y'all badly. We'll have visitors from the corporate office tomorrow. When they ask, I would appreciate it if you would tell them what you have just told me. Can I, at least, count on you for that?"

As a body they all said, "Yes, sir."

"One more thing, if you should decide to change your minds, there is nothing to fear. You have my word on it. I don't know who put you all up to this, but it is a bad move for all of you. And I'm not kidding. That's all, and thank you."

On evening break Cyn said, "We got nothing to fear! Ha! After we vote the Teamsters in, Carter's ass won't stay around long enough to warm a chair. Much less conjure up another lie, Reeda."

"I know. I feel sorry for Hank, don't you?"

"Yeah, right, like I feel sorry for a snake! How many times has he tried to coerce every woman here into the sack?"

"I know, Cyn, but he never tried to force us."

"Stop it! Of course, he tried to force us. Don't shed any sympathy for that crocodile around me. I... you know I got kids to feed and he damn well knew it too!"

"Oh, Cyn! Honey, I never even thought about you and... Darling, I am truly so very sorry!"

"Don't be, I'm a big girl. I'm ashamed to say, it ain't the first time I let myself get pecker thrashed. Anyway, I am gonna be still clocking in here and that bastard is gonna be long gone."

"I hope so. Cyn, you really think they will fire him?"

"Does an eighteen wheeler have eighteen wheels?"

❧✖❧

Morning brought Able Golden. Reeda and Cynthia exchanged a knowing look. The man had never before walked up to each desk and cordially greet each employee. His manner implied some ungodly creature had scared the sheep, but he would have things back to normal shortly. Behind Golden's back, Cynthia briefly poked a stiff middle finger message up for him from her switchboard. Reeda had to look away to hide her grin.

After lunch, Mona took over the switchboard, Fred took trace calls and again the clerks were assembled in Hank's office. Golden, as usual, occupied Hank's desk. Hank was excused from the meeting. One more time, they were informed how intelligent they were, how much the company valued them and how utterly useless a union would be. Again, Golden explained, there was a certain stigma in being a member of a union, despite the fact that Golden had been a card carrying Teamster, then a union business agent.

Due to the total silence to his commentary, it was not long before like a wind-up-toy, Able Golden had run down with "Would anyone like to say anything?" He looked expectantly at each employee. Their total silence left him no choice but to excuse them.

The next day, Winston Briley swaggered in for reinforcement. One more wonderful time the office force was assembled like school kids for health shots. Reeda and Cyn exchanged resentful glances.

Cyn whispered, "This damned routine is getting real boring."

"You sure got that right," Reeda said.

After everyone was seated, Briley began, "I must say, I was surprised, but if you all want a union that is your prerogative."

Cynthia whispered, "Reeda, he's spinning the same old record."

"Lord, I gave him more credit."

"Several Alpha offices are in the brotherhood," Briley said. "We manage. Not as well, and not with the latitude you people enjoy. If we can settle things without going to that extent, I believe we all will be better off. I won't lie to you, we had rather run Alpha without outside interference.

"Folks can get real petty working under a union contract. In one of our offices, they squabbled over who sat in which chair until we had to assign chairs on the basis of seniority. Clerks who were friends and worked side by side for years stopped speaking. That can't make for the best working conditions for anyone.

"Beyond that, a union is primarily a collective bargaining agent. You are all educated people, unlike most of our dock workers, and quite capable of bargaining for yourselves. If you want something, you have the intelligence and verbosity to present your case. And these office doors are always open to you.

"Let me remind you again, that you are put on an unsavory, if not illegal level, when you join the Teamsters. I believe you should all be aware of that."

Hardly realizing she was going to speak, Reeda heard herself say, "They said you all would say that. And you have said everything they said you would say, almost word for word."

Briley's face registered surprise and was slightly flushed as he said, "Well, just because they predicted the fact doesn't make it untrue or any less valid." He waited for Reeda to answer.

Hush! Just hush, she told herself. Rob Sands plainly said to say nothing. And she had truly meant to heed his advise.

In a sympathetic tone, Briley went on, "Sincerely, Reeda, you should have let Alpha know if you were dissatisfied. It would have been no more than fair."

The man's hypocrisy goaded her into snapping, "Alpha had to know things weren't right here. Employees get run in and out almost as often as the trucks."

"I agree with you, but such things are sometimes hard to notice in a corporate office with thirty-odd terminals to manage."

Reeda and Cynthia were seated on a couch side by side. Cynthia's elbow pressing in her rib was saying shut up! But Reeda had to say, "Isn't it odd then, how quickly the corporate office notices if one of those thirty-odd terminals isn't showing a profit or gets out of step enough to decide to vote in the Teamsters Union?"

Briley poured himself a glass of water from Carter's desk carafe.

Cynthia hissed, "Hush, Reeda. You're gonna get in trouble."

"Can't help it— leave me alone." Cyn knew her too well to press.

After having some water, Briley recovered his tongue enough to say, "However it looks, Reeda, we do value our employees. I can assure you, if you people had let us know things weren't right, it never would have gone this far."

"If the corporate office is so almighty benevolent, why did they fire Sara Majors and retain Hank Carter?"

"That shouldn't be too hard for a professional person to understand, Reeda. The situation couldn't continue as it was and terminal managers aren't easy to hire every day. That's why Mrs. Majors went first. What possible difference can a little more time make? Believe me, Hank Carter's days are numbered."

"Really? Hank was assuring us of our job security less than forty-eight hours ago. I wouldn't say he is in a position to assure anyone of anything. Would you, Mr. Briley?"

"Reeda, no one in or out of a union has any job security if they can't keep their nose clean. Though it grieves me to say it, things sometimes do have a way of failing to be as they should be."

"When they do, if I understand Alpha's policy correctly, if you're easy to replace you are tersely fired. If you are a rung or two higher and harder to replace, your sins may be over looked."

"I've explained, it wasn't a matter of overlooking, but a matter of finding a replacement."

"With all due respect, I doubt that, Mr. Briley. I don't think Carter would have been in any jeopardy if there hadn't been any union talk."

"I won't argue the point. I've explained the company's position. Now, let's just get down to the bottom line. What is it you all want? More money?"

"Guess we all can use more money, but we make decent salaries."

"Fringe benefits?"

"Fringe benefits aren't the true issue."

"Suppose we fire Carter immediately. Will that do it?"

"Hank Carter isn't the true issue now, either. He has played the fool but personally he's been good to me. He always backed all of us with the customers," Reeda said, looking around at her fellow employees, who nodded their heads in agreement.

"Level with me, Reeda, what is the real issue."

"As far as I'm concerned, he lost his head over a skirt and fired someone he shouldn't have. But his indiscretion was with another consenting adult. He isn't the first man to do it, he won't be the last."

"Or woman," Briley said, smiling at Reeda's confusion.

"Of course," she said uncertainly, her composure ruffled.

"By your own admission," he went on, his face serious, "you have good pay and benefits and no complaints about your terminal manager. What more could you want?"

Reeda looked around for someone else to speak. They all looked at her. Having ventured this far, she decided to go all the way. If the union came in, it wouldn't matter. If not they'd all be fired anyway.

"Sir, don't you recognize people who have seen so much negative happen they're running scared?"

"No. I don't know what there is to be scared of."

"I doubt you can be that dense and hold your job, but for the record, it's Alpha's corporate policy. The way y'all excuse or don't excuse things isn't based on right or wrong but on who you are. All of us have families to support and bills to pay. We must have jobs that are as secure as possible to live with any of peace of mind. Anymore, we don't feel we can have peace of mind at Alpha Truck Lines without the Teamsters Union."

"I know there has been turnover. Still, I don't believe you can hold the company responsible for what happens on the local level."

"Believe it! The local level is where the hourly person lives or dies. Alpha is known for hiring and firing system wide. We can't keep up with who is manager of what terminal even for message purposes. Only the union offices have any stability."

Everyone recognized Briley's final shot, as he barked, "If I couldn't hold my job on my own merit, I wouldn't want it."

"Sir, with all due respect, if merit kept folks working, labor unions never would have happened. Frankly, I could use some help keeping my job. All too often I feel like a sheep posing in wolf's clothing and I'm tired of it. I tired of being worried one dark day or night, I might need my job badly enough to get on my back to keep it. Too many working women get forced into that crap. A long time ago, I made up my mind not to live by the mattress."

"Reeda, I think you are vastly over simplifying."

"I hope you're right, Mr. Briley, but I honestly don't think so. With the company fighting so hard and dirty to keep the union out, by joining we must stand to gain more than we know."

"What makes you surmise that?"

"Maybe the fact that company brass is gracing us with their presence, for the first time, seems to add up to the other two."

"What other two?"

"The other two, as in two and two always makes four. Joining the Teamsters must be really good for us and bad for y'all. Seems like your team believes in winning at any cost. Even as a kid, I never liked to play, even hop-scotch, with kids who cheat and chalk up cheating as just another way to win. I don't cheat and can't stand cheaters."

"Lord, a woman with your spunk couldn't begin to like being tagged one of Hoffa's women."

"Actually, I take it as high praise and I'd be proud to be in his union. The truth is, I never wanted to be a card, carrying Teamster more than this very minute!"

Knowing he had lost, swallowing his vexation, Briley asked, "Tell me, Reeda, how do you know Hoffa?"

Looking Winston Briley right in the eye, she said, "I never met him... I never saw him... but if it wasn't for his legacy, working people never would have gained their right to a decent day's work for a decent day's pay."

Reeda got up and walked out with the balance of the office force right on her dress tail.

CHAPTER 11

On Monday the corporate brass was gone and the office was miles calmer. Reeda still found it disturbing. And now Howard just had to pick this particular day to ask her to lunch. Her black eyes were on fire as she snapped, "You know, good and well, we settled all that."

"I don't want to rehash old news, hon. A lot's been happening around here. I need to talk to you in private. For both our sakes."

Seeing his green eyes were sad and uncommonly serious, she still said, "I'm sorry, Cynthia and I have already made plans for lunch."

"Okay, how about after work this afternoon?"

"Can't. I have plans after work."

"Well, then, Reeda, how about lunch tomorrow?"

"I've already requested an extended lunch period tomorrow for a conference with one of Jamey's teachers."

"God, give me a little slack. What about day after tomorrow?"

"Okay, but I don't know why I should."

"Cause I'm cute." He grinned and sauntered back to city dispatch.

In the afternoon, Rob Sands dropped in to make his rounds. He stopped a few minutes at each potential union member's desk offering words of support and encouragement.

As he was leaving, he said, "Now, you all, stick together and stand pat. That's all you have to do, it's going your way. Nathaniel Vance hates taking this laying down, so don't take no wooden nickels. Listen to me, he don't have any choice but to take it."

"It just seems impossible for a hand full of people to win against a corporation like, Alpha," Stanley said.

"Stanley, if you will just stand strong, it ain't a hand full of people. That's the beauty of it. You got the power of the Teamster's behind you and that's the biggest, strongest union in the world. Plus you got the United States government behind you to boot. Man, everybody has a constitutional right to union representation if they so choose."

Rob was still in the office, when Reeda and Cynthia punched out for the day, talking with Matt Fletcher and the billing people on the second shift. After hearing how his prospective union members were being harassed by management, Rob called for another meeting. That night Reeda got a call from Matt telling her about the meeting. As soon as she hung up, the phone rang again. "Hello."

"Hey, Reeda, did Matt call you," Cynthia said.

"Yes, I just hung up from talking with Matt."

"I'm scared to death."

"Me too, Cyn. Guess we all are."

"I'm afraid we might be making a big mistake, Reeda. And Bryan wants me to vote no. He says we're all going to get our butts fired."

"Is Bryan paying your house note?"

"Well... no."

"Is he paying your utility bill or car payment?"

"No, of course not. Come on, Reeda!"

"Naw, you come on. Is smart Bryan paying your phone bill or your doctor bills or buying your groceries?"

"You know he isn't! You know he doesn't make enough money to pay my bills and the bills for his wife and family."

"Then when it involves making your living, you need to make the most you can, the most decent way you possibly can. So, where making your living's concerned, tell married Bryan to mind his own rotten business."

"Married or not, I know Bryan cares about me."

"Maybe so, but he's married. And that's a problem. It's bad enough you're in a limbo relationship. At the absolute least, for the sake of your sons, not to mention your co-workers, don't let Bryan talk you into a limbo job!"

"Reeda, don't be judging me."

"I'm not judging you. I'm worried about you."

"Maybe Bryan is just as worried about me."

"Could be, Cyn, but when it comes to your job and working for Alpha, I'm sorry. Bryan doesn't know shit. And you know it!"

"Maybe he does. Bryan isn't as wrapped up in it as we are."

"Let me tell you something, Cynthia Madden, you were bitching to join the teamsters union the first conversation I ever had with you.

"Let me tell you something, Cynthia Madden, you were bitching to join the teamsters union the first conversation I ever had with you. Don't you dare vote anything but, yes. Don't get all our butts fired! Yours included! Screw this up, girl, and I'll never speak to you again. You hear me?"

After the office people helped themselves to coffee and donuts, Sands ended his small talk and officially took the floor. "Hate to interrupt your Saturday, but I hear you been having your trial by fire. I been getting reports along. Like I warned you, what you have been going through is always a part of becoming union members. Management doesn't give up raises and fringe benefits without a fight, but they live in their mansions and could care less, if you folks have to live in a mud house. Now, that you have been exposed to some of their pressure, do you still favor the union?"

"Yes," they all answered with gusto.

"Good! They're throwing everything but the kitchen sink at you, now. Y'all are holding up fine. I heard Reeda set Briley back ten years at his meeting with y'all." Everyone applauded; Reeda grinned and said nothing. "Reeda, I like what you said about being proud to be one of Hoffa's women. I'm proud to be one of his men. You're a real scrapper, I like a scrapper."

"Thank you— I think," she answered, and everyone chuckled.

Rob went on, "I want y'all to know, once the union's in, where your job's concerned, you're all going to be your own woman and your own man. That's what being a union member's all about.

"Always give an honest day's work for an honest day's pay. Don't sluff off on the job and always punch in on time. If you are caught doping, drinking or stealing on the job, don't call me. I got no time for thieves and drunks.

"If you should be treated in a bad, sub-human way, and think you need to knock the hell out of your supervisor, do it right then. I can defend passion of the moment. Just don't think it over for two or three days, then come in to work and take a poke at your supervisor. Your job might be gone if you do it like that.

"But back to the main issue, I think most of them have said what they have to say. I told them to lay off you folks, told them no more meetings. I figured Nathaniel Vance to be grinding on y'all before now, but they've had their chance. If they start anymore pressure or meetings, let me know. I'll get it stopped, so don't hesitate. So far they have hit you as two groups. The eight to five people, during the day, the billing people at night.

"That's all normal. Be skeptical of them getting you off in singles or pairs. You have met what they have tried so far, solid as a wall. I'm proud of you. Be proud of yourselves, I know this ain't easy. We all grow up being trained to listen to the boss. You all have been taught the boss is always right, so you gotta please the boss. That's a lie. If the boss comes in the form of Mama or Daddy, the teacher, the preacher, the cop or a business agent from the Teamster's Union, the boss ain't always right. Always is a mighty big word— ain't nobody always right. That's the main new thing you have to remember.

"They will try to make you suspect each other so don't let them single you out. You don't want doubt created among yourselves. Distrust of each other can kill your effort, split the vote, make you lose your election and if that should be the case, make no mistake, none of you will be employed by Alpha within a year.

"They've shot their big guns. Briley and Golden, next to Nathaniel Vance, himself, are the biggest guns Alpha's got. They may leave you alone. I've told them to keep Vance in Atlanta, warned them about an unfair labor practice suite. Y'all are supposed to enjoy the privilege of electing to or not to vote on having a union without harassment. I could slap a suite on them for what has already gone on, but the less litigation stirred up the better. As long as they aren't singling you out, we will let well enough alone." Grasping the wisdom of his words, Reeda raised her hand. "You have a question, Reeda?"

"Howard Summers asked me to have lunch with him tomorrow."

"What does that scum want?"

"He just wants to talk to me. When I first started out on the trace desk with Alpha, Howard was pretty nice to me."

"Summers was never nice to a woman in his life, without a reason. Go if you must, but you better watch him. The man's a snake."

"Okay, Rob."

"I know all about Howard, worked with him over three years at Jones Truck. Then, he was in the union, working the dock and relief city driver before he went in supervision. But he belongs in supervision. He's a scab, through and through and nuts to boot.

"When he was still a union member, I've seen him drive a tow-motor through TV cartons on the sly for the hell of it. After he made dock foreman, I've seen him take shirts out of the carton and wear them to work the next day. Unpack fans, plug them in to fan himself all day, then take them home at night. Take radios out of cartons to play in the dock shack. He's created more shortages stealing freight off the dock than you can imagine. He's nobody's friend, not even his own. Ask Matt. He knows who Howard is."

"That's right," Matt said, "Howard Summers would use his own mother. Watch out for him, Reeda."

Wishing she had told Howard no, she answered, "Okay."

Sands said, "One day Howard was driving city pick up, rolled out of his truck and jumped the governor's chauffeur. The union got him out of jail on that occasion and two more I can think of right off. Don't let him snow you the union's done nothing for him— or any of the rest of you. The way Carter's tried to bed all you girls, the brass knows he has no influence. They may think Summers is the one who might can turn some of the women around.

"He has less respect for women than Carter. One day he called in at three, says he's made his deliveries and pick ups. Dispatcher says come on in. Howard shows at six and starts telling some lie about helping at a wreck. Then the cops walk in.

"Seems Summers was really on his way back to the terminal, driving by the girl's dorm at Froman College. Sees this girl undressing in front of a window. He keeps driving around and around the building. The girl keeps teasing him, but she won't give him the come on up sign. He goes up anyway and kicks her door in. She starts screaming, somebody called the cops, he hears the sirens and climbs down the fire escape. The cops don't know his identity, but somebody saw a Jones Truck.

"Don't ask me why but the dispatcher covered for the bastard, or the union covered for the bastard. Anybody else would have been unemployed or in the penitentiary, years ago.

"Once he was making a house delivery and cornered somebody's wife in the basement. Her screaming brought the cops. That time they had sense enough not to turn on the sirens. Caught Summers red-handed, had the woman's cloths just about off. Her husband pressed charges. Took a bunch of money to get him out of that one." Reeda raised her hand. "You got a question, Reeda?"

"Why would the union get him out of attempted rape?"

"Actually, the union told him to forget it. His brother got him out of that one. Howard's brother has money, friends in politics and Jones Truck didn't want a law suit. That's when Jones made him a foreman. It was the only way they could find to keep him on their side.

"Yeah, I know Summers. When he hears about what I've told y'all, he won't beat me up because I can outrun him, but I'm telling you the facts. He's poison. Watch him, Reeda. Don't go thinking he has been mistreated or slighted. The man's had more chances to get straight than a swamp snake to get wet. Are there anymore questions?"

After a silence, Stanley said, "Mr. Sands, according to the morning paper, your union shot up a truck from a milk plant you are trying to organize down state. Is that true?"

Without hesitation or apology, Sands said, "Yes, we shot the truck. The men are on strike as you probably read. But what you didn't read, is that management brought in a gang of goon strike breakers out of Texas. If you wanna see decent, peaceable folks get rough and tough, bring in a bunch of hired trash to bust their heads and rob them of their jobs that keep their kids fed.

"Like old Whitley Sutton, the union business agent down there told the hired goons, every good cowboy gets his horse shot out from under him once in while." Sands laughed and then added, "Made all the Texas boys right mad but come daylight, they were humping it on back down to Texas."

"That sounds like a gangster movie," Stanley said.

"Gangster movies come from real life. I told you folks before, you can't always say please. Sometimes you have to fight fire with fire. We would all still be working for ten cents a day if we didn't. Anymore questions?" Seeing Patsy timidly raise her hand, Rob grinned and said, "Yes, ma'am, what can I do for you?"

"Uh, Mr. Sands, is there any danger we might strike?"

"Little lady, you got nothing to worry about there. Vance knows how far to push. He's smarter than any of the jokers helping him run Alpha. With an office voting a hundred percent union like you folks have, we can strike the city, dock, shop and road. We can tie up his operation from coast to coast and from Canada to the Keys.

"He won't risk that over fifteen employees going into the union. Say the additional pay and benefits increase you all with receive over your average working life comes to an additional million dollars for you. Say maybe even two million. That's a gradual pay out; not a drop in the bucket compared to the several million a strike, he is sure to lose, would cost him. Does that answer your question?"

"Yes, thank you."

"Another thing I want to point out. The union has no discrimination. If you hold the job, you get the pay that job title calls for, be you black, white, male, female or whatever. Anymore questions?" Rob waited a few moments then said, "I want to remind you to keep up your nerve and do like I tell you. Reps from the NLRB will be here within the next ten days to hold the election. All you have to do is hang in there, vote yes and you have it made.

"I must say, this is the easiest office I've organized. I appreciate that. Okay, if no one has a question, let's all go home."

🙠✘🙢

Her first warning wiggled when he took her to the best restaurant in town. Howard never kept that kind of money and wouldn't have spent it on the best restaurant in town if he did. Reeda listened as he talked all around it before he finally made his pitch with the, not the first time she had heard it, statement, "Reeda, you don't want to associate with the class of people that make up the Teamsters Union. I know what I'm talking about. Hell, I used to be in it."

"If they are any more dog than you and me, I sure don't."

"Damn, girl, screwing is just a normal sin. Don't hurt nobody if you don't get caught and we didn't. Anyway, that ain't what I mean."

"Just what do you mean?"

"That whole local is a low-life bunch. Everybody knows that."

"And we're not?"

"Reeda, you're not. I ain't talking about me."

"Explain the difference."

"I don't have to explain. You know."

"You mean because they wear overalls sometimes and don't always know which fork to use, that makes them low class?"

"That and lots more. Anyway, the damn union won't help you. It's a sucker deal. All they want's your twenty-five dollars a month."

"I hear they rescued you several times in your dock working days."

"No such thing."

"Hear they got you out of jail. Then they say your brother bought off your charge of attempted rape."

"That was a trumped up deal. I never tried to rape any woman in my life. Her neighbor walked in, she got scared and started hollering rape. That's the God's truth. That's all there was to it. If it hadn't been for the neighbor, another five minutes and it would have all been over but the afterglow. Hell, I can finesse me a piece anytime I want one. I don't have to rape nobody."

"But the union got you out of it."

"Naw, not that time. It was my brother and Jones Truck that time."

"What about the college girl?"

"What college girl?"

"The one at the window. You went up and broke down her door."

"Oh, hell, I was just teaching her a lesson."

"Breaking down a college dorm door is teaching a lesson?"

"I was teaching her not to wave her boobs out the window." Howard chuckled and said, "I'll bet she don't no more, either. Reeda, you know I wouldn't touch a kid like that." She knew he was telling the truth. In Howard's world his actions made perfect sense.

"I guess everybody spreads it on a little thick when they're selling something. But, Howard, I sure never figured you for this."

"Figured me for what?"

"For playing rat fink. I didn't think anybody ran you."

"Nobody does! Never have! Never will!"

"Then who put you up to trying to con me?"

"Listen, I love my job, told you that sometime back. I'm a bastard, told you that, too. But don't nobody run me, Reeda, including you."

"Man, I can hardly run me. I sure don't want to run you."

"Hell, I know it. Wish you did. Still, nobody makes me do a damn thing I don't really want to do."

"Then you wanted to take me to lunch and try to break the vote?"

"Hell, yes! What do I care about any union?"

"And what the hell do you care about me or my job?"

"You got nothing to worry about."

"Ha! You know what they do when a union bid gets busted."

"Reeda, you belong in management, like me, not in the union. Hon, they're figuring on setting you up when this thing blows over."

"Now, Howard, they're who-doing you!"

"Naw, they ain't, I got assurance on that."

"Lord, man, you and Hank are two of a kind! Let's get out of here. It's real got deep and I didn't bring a paddle."

After lunch Howard worked like hell but the frenzied activity of the dock failed to clear the bile from his gut. Briley had told him,

"Talk to any of the hourly people you think you might carry any weight with. We want this union bid squashed. If there's anything you can do, any pressure you can bring to bear, the company would be grateful. Plans for the Alaska terminal are complete. One big thing we look for in our terminal managers is the ability to deal with the union. We like to beat them at their own game. They try to get our people and we try to keep them. Go about it anyway you choose. At this point I don't think it can be made any worse. They are quietly solid, that's the toughest kind of people to break."

So he tried. But he wasn't prepared for the disgust in Reeda's eyes. She never loved him, but she had respected him. He had known that without knowing exactly why. Now, that was gone. Damn, he always had thrown away everything that meant anything.

Shoulda stayed on the dock. Wasn't cut out to be a scab. This was the first thing in his life that had made him feel this cheap. He'd let Briley put it to him and it was his own fault. People would fuck you to death if you didn't stay on guard. It was a shame what a man had to do at times to make a living.

He was looking forward to meeting Fay about like a knee in the groin. But, she owed him. Big as a barn now with a young'un.

They had no problem meeting at the airport the first and only time he had been with her so she agreed to meet him there again. He was driving a borrowed a car, just in case some union asshole was tailing him. An unfair labor practice law suit was the last thing he needed. When he parked, Fay didn't recognize him till he rolled down the glass and shoved opened the door.

As Fay got into his car and sat down, he said, "Thanks for coming, hon. No chance of Bob following you here is there?"

"No, he's out of town. I just have to be home by ten when he calls. What was it you wanted to talk to me about, Howard?"

"Hear you office people want a labor union."

"Yeah. Our election's next week."

"Fay, you don't really dig this union crap, do you?"

"I guess, Howard. I sure signed the card."

"I know but I think you mostly went along with your buddies. I know how close you are with Reeda and Cyn but it don't amount to you much, personally, does it, honey?"

"Well, it seems like a pretty good thing after the way Carter ran Molly off for Sara. Then here they come in with hardly a howdy-doody and fire Sara."

"Still, you were pretty much influenced by the other girls, and, well, most of the other girls are single or divorced. A girl like you, I figure don't care much one way or the other about unions, hon."

"What do you mean, a girl like me, Howard?"

"Well, you being the wifely type. I can see you in a frilly apron setting supper on the table with your old man holding the baby. And knowing how far you went to give him one. When it's born, you'll probably just mind the baby, keep house and forget Alpha."

"I wish," Fay said. "Nothing would suit me better."

Looking at her swollen stomach, He said, "Here awhile back, I done you a big favor and put a smile on your face to boot. Remember?"

Fay's burning cheeks made her grateful for the darkness of the car, as she stammered, "Oh, uh, yeah, I remember."

"Hon, Uncle Howard sure could use a favor right now. Wonder if you might help me out a little bit this time?"

"Sure... if I can. What is it you need?"

"To make points with my boss, like you needed to make points with your husband. You might be glad to know, I've had it with Manchester. I'm sick of this town. Want to get out and move up while I'm doing it, if there's any way. If I play my cards right, I think there is. You'd probably just as soon see me go. Don't spread it around, it was told to me in confidence. Alpha's opening a terminal in Alaska. I want up there as terminal manager."

"Really?"

"Yep. If I had a hand in putting down the office vote for the union, it would put the job right in my lap." He waited for her comment. Fay turned her head and looked silently out her window. Thinking she needed to think it over, he went on, "You don't really care, since you'll be resigning to be a full time mom. If you vote no at the election, along with whoever else will vote no, it might kill the union and get me out of Manchester."

"But no one will vote no, we're all for the union."

"They all say that. Some still vote no, law of averages tells you that. And in another few weeks, you'll be home rocking Junior there."

"Don't be so sure, Howard. I may be hitting the clock every morning, after my maternity leave, like always."

"Your husband won't ever let you leave that baby with a sitter. Bad as he wants a baby, there ain't no way."

"My husband might not be around. Bob doubts the baby is his."

"Shit, Fay! How did he get an idea like that?"

"I have no idea. He was delighted till I started showing. Now, every night when he comes home from work, he starts. He's accused me of everything in the book. I didn't know it was in my Bob to be so suspicious."

"Girl, you haven't admitted anything have you?"

"No, of course not."

"Good. After Bob sees the baby he'll be fine. It's a boy ain't it?"

"That's what the ultrasound said."

Howard grinned proudly and said, "Some things your old Uncle Howard does right."

"We were just trying to save my marriage."

"Yeah, of course, I know that. Now, you just relax, hon. I know what I'm talking about. When your Bob sees that baby, he'll be so proud, he'll forget he ever had any doubt."

"Hope you're right. But he's threatening to have a blood test."

"Ooops," Howard said.

"Ooops, nothing, if Bob learns the truth!" Fay started crying till she heard Howard laughing. "It isn't funny! Bob's really nice, and hardly ever gets mad, but he was a college line backer. He's taller than you, weighs more and has a black belt in karate. He could kill us both, if he made up his mind to."

"Probably so, honey, cause I'm a lover not a fighter. But all the times I was guilty and now, the one time I'm innocent as new snow, a husband may kill me. That's a hoot," he said, laughing again.

"Innocent? What do you mean innocent?"

"Uh, well, I'm sorry. I don't know how you'll take this. I mean... hon, I never thought it'd come to this."

"What are you saying, Howard?"

"Guess, you shoulda just gone to a sperm bank, or maybe you did."

"No. There might have been a record. What is it, Howard?"

"Hon, I'm sorry but I had a vasectomy after my third young'un was born. That boy's seven years old now."

"You mean you can't have any more children?"

"No. And don't want any more. Three is plenty."

"Why didn't you tell me that?"

"Girl, you came on at a time when I was blue over breaking up with someone I really cared about. And, well, most anytime I can't hardly pass up a chance at good loving."

"Lord, Howard, all this time I've been worrying and worrying. It never even crossed my mind, it could be Bob's own baby."

"Sure is, hon. Well, if you ain't been with nobody but him and me."

"Oh, I'm so happy," she said and gave him a hug. "Everybody says you're terrible but I think you're wonderful. Every thing is going to work out just fine. I can just feel it!"

"Then you'll help me on this union thing?" Despite the dark in the car but he could see her determined look. He waited, wary of the seriousness she had taken on. This little powder puff of a woman was nobody's fool.

"Howard, I truly appreciate how you have helped me. I... I really so want to help you, but my friends and their jobs are counting on me. I simply can't let them down."

"But what about me? I want that job in Alaska."

"Howard, you'll get it, if you really want it. You're just like Bob—you both always get what you want. One way or another."

CHAPTER 12

"Ralph, we have big problems at the Manchester terminal. I suppose you have heard, we also have a new union office."

"Yes, Nathaniel, afraid I have."

"You know Hank Carter, the terminal manager, up there?"

"I've never met the man, but I've talked with him on the watts line."

"I'm sure you've heard by now, he hired his mistress in his office and brought on havoc."

"Yes. I'm sorry, Nathaniel."

"Hank's crap caused the natives to get restless, so the Manchester office is organized and the teamsters win again. Needless to say, that was Hank's fatal mistake. I'm firing the bastard. Picked him up off the trash pile and this is the thanks I get for my trouble."

"In your place, I would most certainly fire him."

"Ralph, I need you to take Manchester over and get it straightened out. I need you there within two weeks. You can move your family whenever it's convenient."

"Nathaniel, I—" Ralph Stevens started, then stopped. He covered his hesitancy with a cough. Nathaniel waited until Ralph had no choice but to continue, "My son loves school. All his friends are here and he is doing really well. Especially in football."

"Kids hot rod the road with some long haired bunch in one city as well as another. In six weeks max, he won't know he moved."

"But it would mean selling my house, Nathaniel."

"Not necessarily. You don't need to live in Manchester over a year or so, if you don't care to. Right now, I need someone I know to be competent and trustworthy. A newly organized office is subject to bitch over the wrong color toilet paper. "

"I understand but—"

"Of course, if you should decide to sell, list your house with a real estate agent Alpha will pay the sales commission. If it doesn't sell for what it appraises for, Alpha will reimburse you for the difference. Also, you get a five thousand dollar moving allowance, your salary will be whatever you think is fair."

"Well, Nathaniel, that's most generous but— "

"Say ten thousand a year raise and ten thousand in Alpha stock."

"That's all very tempting but I don't know, Nathaniel."

"I'm not greedy, I'm demanding. It's the nature of hauling freight."

"You know, but Eve is pretty fond of our house and she has been through some rough years, moving around to hell and back with me."

"Don't stall me, Ralph. I need you or I wouldn't be calling. I remember some ten years ago, you were paroled out of the pen on a Taft-Hartley infraction and needed a job."

"Yes, Nathaniel and I appreci—"

"Ralph, you didn't need a job because it was convenient for me. You needed a job to breath free air again, as I recall."

"I— I can be ready, whenever you say."

"Good. Leave tomorrow to meet with Briley at Manchester to appraise things. Your flight's booked. Five nineteen departs at noon."

Nathaniel hung up, leaving Stevens to think, working for Vance was as bad as being in the damn army. Maybe it was time to resign. Being ordered to different places was why he got his discharge after ten years in the motor pool. Course, if the army had paid as well as Vance, he probably would have stayed in and made a career of it.

✥

In less than ten weeks from the start of the union movement, Alpha's Manchester office was working under a union contract with Ralph Stevens as terminal manager.

Federal representatives from the labor board came in and set up shop in the sales office to hold the office worker's election. Everyone was terribly nervous as they filed in to cast their ballots. But, as Cynthia said later, "Reeda, it came off without a hitch, like it was no big deal. I can't believe it."

"I can't either. We changed our whole working lives by just marking a piece of paper."

"I thought the union or somebody would at least throw a celebration party."

Reeda said, "I haven't heard anything about a party. I think maybe our bunch is too stunned. We are all creeping around like refugees in a new country. Happy to be gone from what we left behind and insecure about what might lay ahead. But we are all tired of hearing about it and dealing with it."

After lunch, on Monday week after the election and Alpha's office employees had unanimously voted pro union, Winston Briley and a stranger briskly walked in. Without speaking to a soul they both walked on into the terminal manager's office. Before he closed the door and they sat down, Reeda could tell Briley was making an introduction to a surprised and then strained faced Hank Carter.

That evening, like most evenings, Reeda and Cynthia clocked out, then walked out of the office together. Briley and the stranger were still with Carter in his office and none of the three had come out for so much as a trip to the men's room.

The next morning Hank had vanished and Briley introduced the stranger as their new terminal manager, Ralph Stevens. Hank had not even been permitted the small dignity of saying goodbye. It was as thought the gods had swept him off to oblivion.

It reminded Reeda of getting married and in a way, she supposed they had. Almost over night their whole world had changed, the office had settled into working under the teamster contract, a new terminal manager and their immediate interest had shifted.

Now, rumors were flying that the Alaska terminal was finally opening and some of Manchester's management was being transferred to Anchorage. It was also rumored there would be a chance for the hourly people to transfer, dock, road, maintenance and office personnel, if they cared to.

Cynthia's car was in the shop, so she rode into work with Reeda the day the Alaska rumors were intensified by a road driver. The driver said he had run a load of office furniture up to the new Alpha facility in Anchorage.

On their way home that evening, Cynthia said, "Anyone who goes to Alaska will get a three thousand dollar sign on bonus. Some folks were talking about it on the watts line."

"Who?" Reeda asked.

"Don't know for sure who they all were, except for Nathaniel Vance."

"Whoops! Guess it's true then."

"You think you might go, if you get a chance?"

"I don't think I would like living in Alaska. How about you, Cyn?"

"Hell, Reeda, as cold natured as I am, I'd freeze to death. Thanks, but no thanks. If I ever move again, it's going to be further south."

༄༅༄

Less than an hour before punch out time, Summers had simply insisted on a meeting. Reeda insisted on declining until he said, "Look, hon, I'm not going to be around much longer. I need to talk to you right away." She had never witnessed such seriousness in his green eyes. The grin that always seemed to be there was gone. So was the subdued anger. It was a bit overwhelming to see Howard's eyes without their usual mockery.

That evening, waiting in a booth, he sat nervously craning his head. The neighborhood restaurant was familiar to Reeda. She had entered by a side door and stood out of his view, taking petty pleasure in knowing he was anxious for her coming. After a moment, realizing there had been a time it had not been necessary to feed her ego with such triviality, she walked to his table.

"Reeda!" he said, smiling with relief.

"Hey, Howard." She smiled as he stood, mentally approving of his politeness. When they were seated, he looked at her sitting across from him rather like Moses might have beheld the tablets of stone until she said, "What?"

"I don't remember ever seriously telling a woman before, but you really are so beautiful. And you know that ain't easy for me to say, not being after anything."

"Yes, and thanks. The way you appreciate women, I don't know why it's hard for you to compliment one."

"It ain't— when I'm finessing."

A waitress came and said, "Good evening," placing glasses of ice water before them.

"What'll you have, Reeda?"

"Just coffee."

"Two black coffees," he ordered, then offered her a cigarette.

"No, thanks."

"You used to like to smoke with me— especially after."

"That was a long time ago."

"Hell, hon, not that long."

"In my mind, it was before The Flood." He was disappointed to see she wasn't kidding. For her, it was a simple truth.

"Have you heard, Alpha's finally opening the Anchorage terminal?"

"Yes, but that rumor has been circulating for years."

"This time it's true. Briley offered me the terminal manager job."

"Howard, that's wonderful!"

"Is it?" The question in his eyes was profound.

"God, yes. It's a golden opportunity for you. You're a natural and Anchorage will give you a fresh start. It's just what you have been wanting and the challenge you need."

"What if I get up there and fall flat on my ass?"

"You know how to run a terminal. You ran Manchester the last year Carter worked."

"I know, but having the title puts the pressure on."

"There are no guarantees. You and I know that very well."

"Yeah, that's always the hell of it."

Reeda realized she was offering truth to a man looking for reassurance and said, "Just think of the fun of it, Howard. You and I are people who need a challenge."

"You need a challenge. I don't know about me."

"But that's why you're so hot after women. If you turn that drive to your career, you could wind up Nathaniel's right hand man."

"Hell, I doubt that."

"I don't. You've been in freight all your life. You know the business from start to finish. You'll do a super job, Howard Summers!"

"Do you promise?" he said and chuckled.

"Yes, I do promise. You're going to make the best possible terminal manager for Anchorage and don't you forget it."

He smiled, "I knew you'd have enough confidence for both of us."

"After all that's happened, it's a wonder I have any confidence."

"Reeda, you were born confident and independent. It's easy for folks born that way. Briley was— so was Vance."

"How can you tell?"

"It's always in the eyes and the walk of folks like y'all. You make other folks think they can do a job just talking it up."

"Hey, don't hold me responsible for the way I was born."

"When it's the other way around people sure do."

"You're the last person, I would accuse of caring about the opinions of other people," she shot with a raised eyebrow.

Summers laughed a you're-getting-too-close-to-the-quick laugh, then said, "I don't. At least I didn't. A hayseed like me? No education, no background— anyway I went was up. But these last few years, since I been knowing you and being operations manager, folks have started looking up to me and treating me with respect. And... well, hon, I like it."

"We all like respect."

"But at times, it hits me like wine hits a wino, that pisses me off."

"But why when it's so normal?"

"Hell, when something gets to meaning too much that's when you can be whipped and really beat down. But I do like feeling like I'm somebody, and I loved having a woman like you. The ones I knew before hardly knew which fork to use. Then— I couldn't have cared less. I was just making it through the night. A man could really be somebody with a truly smart woman like you, girl."

"Thanks. That's nice to hear," Reeda said, not exactly believing him but loving his words.

"I know women like I know freight. But I wasn't able to hold on to you with the best in me. Maybe, I can't hold on to Anchorage. The challenge scares the hell out of me."

"It won't once you get up there and go to work."

"If I had you with me, I wouldn't have any trouble at all. You would keep me straight. You'd be my reason to want to be straight. What I'm trying to say is, I want you to go with me. It will mean a big bonus and a nice raise for me. Even with my child support payment, we could have a good living and you wouldn't have to work."

Alarm spread through Reeda like ink on a blotter. Were they all this way? By all outward signs Howard was most certainly a man, in every sense of the word. He possessed as much raw strength; as much raw potential as anybody needed. Still, strip him down where he lives... you find an oversized boy looking for a mother. Maybe, it was her luck to have an attraction for oversized boys. Maybe, somewhere in her subconscious, it was her choice.

"Hey, baby, don't just sit there gazing off in space. How about it?"

"Howard, when we were... together, I was looking for someone to support me. Now, I'm doing that on my own."

"I mean marriage, all on the up and up. I never thought I'd say this again to anybody, but I love you, Reeda. That's why I finally when through with my divorce. You're everything I always needed."

She couldn't relate to what the man was saying. He could pulverize men twice his size, mentally or physically. He took no lip off no one and could get outbound freight on the road and city delivery to the customer's dock in record time, against all odds. At will, he could pull eight hours work from his dock workers in four. Yet, here he was, wanting her to make him believe in himself. He wanted a cheerleader, not a wife. Lord, talk about the blind leading the blind!

"Did you hear me? Hon, I want you to marry me."

Softly but surely, she said, "No. I can't."

"I'll take care of you, make you a good husband. You won't ever want for nothing."

"Howard, that's a wonderful thought. God knows, I'm tired of taking care of myself."

"Then let's do it. Let's just get married."

"Thanks for asking me but... I really can't."

"Why not?"

"I... I don't love you. If I did, the other reasons wouldn't matter."

"Hon, if you don't love me, what was all that in the motel?"

"I guess, like I told you then, revenge and—" She felt the heat from her blush and hated it. She hated her feelings of overexposure as well, but she made herself explain. He deserved that much. "I was attracted to you. You are a handsome man, a real hunk and you are a fantastic lover. I may have good glands, but it wasn't love."

"The way you quiver and come alive in my arms is close enough to love for me."

"No, if it was close enough to love for either of us, I wouldn't have felt so cheap after."

He shook his head, then growled, "I've had women trying to marry me, threaten me with guns, knives and the law. Now, I'm begging one to marry me and she's telling me to flake off. Ain't that a trip!" He chuckled bitterly.

"I'm sorry, Howard, and I mean that."

"It's okay. Things that matter never have come to me easy. Anything I ever really wanted... well, it's always been this way. Hell, I should have known." Suddenly he was feeling caged and restless. "Hon, you mind if I leave? They don't serve hard stuff in here and I have a bad thirst for a good big slug of vodka, all of a sudden."

"Of course not," Reeda said and touched his shoulder, "put Alaska on the map for Alpha. You're just the man who can do it."

"I don't know," he said getting to his feet. "They may beat this ole boy yet."

"Howard, trust me. They— never beat us. We beat ourselves."

"Yeah, right. But look out for those damned union people."

"You management people just have to keep on damning the teamsters. I've never been treated any better in my life. The union officials have been as nice as I could ask."

"They got some fine folks, and they got some goons. Like I said, look out for yourself."

The next few weeks, Howard seemed unable to focus his eyes anywhere except on Reeda, as if silently imploring her to reconsider. She was terribly uncomfortable until finally, Winston Briley arrived and started training Howard for the Anchorage job. Then he was too occupied to cause Reeda further discomfort.

As usual, Briley took over the terminal manager's office that now belonged to Ralph Stevens. Like his predecessors, Stevens made a nuisance of himself poaching for space at Mona's desk and in Griffin's office. Reeda knew she would never get used to corporate brass dispossessing the terminal manager of his office. The salesmen's office was empty from ten in the morning till four in the afternoon ninety-nine percent of the time.

That week, Briley spent Monday through Wednesday with Howard, Thursday with Fred and took both men to lunch on Friday. After lunch, Briley called Reeda in Stevens' office. Flashing his broad Irish smile under a pelt of auburn hair, Briley resembled a lumber jack cramped into his blue business suit. The monstrous paw he extended was freckled and powerful, but his handshake was amazingly warm.

"Reeda, you probably know, one can't gauge the grapevine, but to make it official, Alpha Truck has immediate plans to open a terminal in Anchorage, Alaska."

"Yes, sir, I have heard."

"Two men from here are transferring up there as well as several dock men and road drivers. Howard Summers will be terminal manager, Fred Griffin will be operations manager. That leaves some holes here. I want you to take Fred's place as office manager." Reeda tried to look suave, but she was staring in disbelief as Briley went on, "While you've been with Alpha, you've worked several jobs; tracing, cashier and billing. You have an excellent background, the girls look to you as their leader; some of the men as well. There isn't a clerk in the office you can't direct." Briley paused, Reeda swallowed, knowing she was supposed to speak. She still couldn't find her tongue. "My dear, are you interested?" Briley's tone of slight irritation activated her voice.

"Look, if you want to fire me, don't beat around the bush. Do it!"

"Fire you? Reeda, I just offered you a promotion."

"That's standard when management wants rid of an undesirable. You entice her away from union protection, then boot her out!"

"Union! Union! All I hear in this terminal is union. It's an obsession. That's why I hate to see an office go union. The distrust it breeds is unreal. No one can go to the can without hollering, union. To hell with the union! This is a legitimate offer. Fred's going to Anchorage, that creates a vacancy. You can do the job, it as simple as that."

"What about Matt Fletcher? He's been with Alpha a long time and he is very capable."

"Matt is a good man and an excellent employee. He was my first choice. He turned me down. Like he said, it is too late. He has too many years, the union picked up toward his retirement, to give up. Alpha won't follow suit. The supervisory breaks didn't fall right for Matt, years ago, but I wanted him to have his chance, if he still wanted it."

"Stanley and Cynthia both have been with Alpha longer than me."

"Supervisory positions aren't tied to seniority, thank God. Matt and you are the only people in the Manchester terminal I would consider. If you refuse, I'll look elsewhere. Besides, Reeda, that day you sat in here and fought their union battle with me, Stanley and Cynthia's seniority didn't help them open their mouths."

"Rob Sands told us to be quiet. I was too dumb to listen."

"Too dumb to listen and knowing when to speak are two different things. A good supervisor acts on his or her own initiative. During that ordeal, besides Matt, you were the only one who displayed that kind of intelligence and self-confidence. When I spot those traits, I try to get anyone on the company team at my first opportunity. Reeda, you may have initial problems with some of the men. You might with some of the girls."

"But why?"

"It's human nature, especially human male nature. To a point, they all might resent your new authority. For several reasons and in several ways, it will be your greatest challenge since coming to work at Alpha. Can you handle it?"

"Yes," she said evenly, meeting his eyes.

"Obviously," he said, his voice warm, "You will make a great office manager, and it's an opportunity for you to start your move up in the industry. And high time you did. Don't you agree?" Briley smiled so confident of her answer, she was tempted to say, no.

Instead she purred, "Yes, and thank you." Returning his smile, it occurred to her that he was not the kind of man she called a hunk, but in his sure Irish way, he was so appealing.

❧❧❧ CHAPTER 13 ❧❧❧

"Reeda, you're taking to being office manager like money to mink."
"I hope so. I doubt the union will take me back, if I screw it up."
"Hey, the office is running smoother than it ever has."
"Thanks, Cyn. I appreciate the kind words. Just in case I've never said it, having you for a friend means the world to me. You're one of the few people I know, who won't blow smoke up my izzard."
"Real friends don't blow smoke at each other."

While Fred Griffin trained Reeda, Howard trained his replacement, a man hired from another line. Reeda found the office manager job kin to the cashier desk with a healthy share of tracing, and whatever else might come up. Her natural ability to relate to people, to place herself in their shoes, understand their problems, transmit her sincere interest was her strongest asset and tremendously improved the office climate and public relations.

Seeing her way with employees and customers, inspired Briley to create a new slogan that Cynthia had to answer the phone with it.

"God knows I love you, Reeda," Cynthia said, "but I hate saying 'Alpha the line that freightfully cares.' Ugh! What a funky way to answer the phone."

"I couldn't agree more, but it pays good. Winston coined it, Winston likes it, Winston's the boss. If it's a problem bitch to him."

"Hey, forget I mentioned it. If need be, I'll recite the ingredients on a cereal box for thirteen bucks an hour."

Patsy had said. "I like you being our office manager, Reeda. For once, I don't have to hint around about what's wrong when I have a bad case of cramps."

Reeda feel great that her former union brothers and sisters liked her being their supervisor. And her superiors seemed please. Especially Winston Briley who was the main man she wanted to keep happy.

On the day of the Alaska departure, Briley walked in her office and said, "Got a minute, Reeda?"

"Sure. Sit down, Winston."

He closed her door then took a seat and said, "Before I leave and forget it, I want you to know you're making a fine office manager."

"Thanks, I'll do my best to see that you're never sorry for giving me the opportunity."

"I appreciate that, let's shake on it." As her hand was lost in his, Reeda saw how warm his blue eyes were. When people wound up on the same team many things looked different. Up to now, she had always seen Winston's eyes as cold and intimidating.

That evening as she took her purse from her desk drawer to leave for home, she remembered Howard had not been in to say goodbye. Apparently, he had no intention of doing so. She thought, "Well, if the mountain won't come to Mohammed."

He was alone in the city dispatch office, feet on top of the desk, eating his favorite snack— bananas, potato chips and buttermilk.

"Howard, I wanted to say goodbye."

"Why?" he said, sullenly.

"It's the polite thing to do," she said, just as sullenly.

"You always do the polite thing?"

"I usually try."

"Hon, don't worry about me." His mocking grin failed to make him look happy as he went on, "Got all kinds of things up there in Alaska. Might even get me an Eskimo girl to keep me warm on cold nights. Ain't never had no Eskimo stuff or slept in no igloo. Have you?"

"No, on both counts."

"Might be a real treat." Howard took a two inch bite of banana, chewed it thoughtfully, then washed it down with a gulp of buttermilk from the quart cardboard carton.

"Knowing you, Stud, I don't doubt you'll find out in record time."

"Imagine you're right. Knowing you, hon," he said, cutting her with his eyes, "you won't even give a dog's damn."

"Howard, seriously, I like you and I will miss you."

"Ain't much I ain't covered," he went on, as if he hadn't heard her. "Thought I don't remember any Eskimo."

"You aren't talking much like a terminal manager. They usually hide their seamy side."

"That's right," he said, peeling another banana. He took a healthy bite and went on with his mouth full, "That's where I been wrong. I was Howard Summers before I got the hots for you, or a terminal manager's job. I'm always gonna be Howard Summers."

"I don't see that as exactly the acme of achievement."

"For me, it is. That's what I gotta remember from now on. It's the only way I know what the hell I am. That's why I got so screwed up over you and let you lead me way down the Yellow Brick Road."

"Howard, I never led you on."

"Damn it, girl, you did! You made me think I was something besides just what I am. A man starts turning himself inside out over a woman, he's screwed. Even had me playing easy listening music. Last night I set all the stations on my car radio back to my country music where they belong. It's time I got back to being me. Same thing applies to a job of work."

"Meaning?"

"Meaning, from now on, hon, the world can take me like I am, or it can leave my redneck ass alone."

"It doesn't hurt any of us to grow a little."

"Sweets, I'm just a good old boy. I operate on work, feed on women, whiskey, country music and a good time. You made me forget that. Without even trying, that's how you broke me in two. Won't forget again. From now on, it's back to work, women and whiskey. That's what I thrive on, ain't even gonna think about it twice. Now that I got me back together, I'll be all right. But, hon," he stopped to put several potato chips in his mouth, chew thoughtfully and take another pull from his buttermilk carton. He went on, "I don't really know about you. Getting that promotion might not be such a good thing for you."

"You don't think I can handle the job?"

"Nope, that ain't no problem. You can handle the job and a dozen more like it. But it's such a shame and a real waste."

"Shame and waste?"

"You're too much woman to be mated to a desk the rest of your life. There's always that danger with a woman like you."

"A woman like me? I'm like a million other women just like me."

"Nope, you ain't. Hon, for one thing, most women ain't gorgeous."

"Give me a break!"

"Reeda, you are gorgeous and you don't even know it. That makes you even more gorgeous. You're built like a calendar girl and them black eyes, depending on what mood you're in, can flash like a gypsy hussy or glow like an angel. You're smart and you ain't afraid."

"Wrong! I'm scared to death of the dark. I have to have some light to even sleep."

"But you ain't afraid of yourself. You ain't afraid to try yourself or to trust yourself. Maybe brave is a better word. Anyway, for yourself, you need a bull of a man with a spine like a ramrod."

"You make me sound like some kind of freak."

"Naw, you ain't no freak but you are one hell of a female and I told you that, lots of times before. But I just lately figured out, you're the damnation of a weak man and I'm lucky you turned me down."

"That's not very complimentary."

"Don't know why not. Offered to marry you. No woman but my ex-wife has ever heard me say that. None probably won't ever hear me say it again. And I'm not taking it back. My offer's still good. I don't have the guts to refuse if you wanted me. I think I always knew you never really did."

"Howard, I— "

"I'm lucky, you don't." He sincerely grinned and said, "We both know, I got the bull part, right now. But married to you, I can see me waking up, not too far down the road, and feeling the slick place where they used to be and wondering what happened to my—."

"Thanks a lot!"

"Calls it like I sees it. You know that."

"Just because you're still a little miffed at me, you wouldn't exaggerate would you?"

"Maybe, a little."

"Listen, I have to get home. I promised to take Jamey to the mall. Best of luck in Anchorage. I mean that. Howard, you do a good job as terminal manager up there and I'll work on my black widow ways."

"Black widow?"

"Spider. After mating, they always kill the male."

The front office was deserted except for Ralph with Briley in his office. She waved goodbye and Briley called, "Wait a minute, Reeda," and came walking out to her. "I meant to spend more time with you today, but there were so many things to go over with Ralph, the day got away from me. We have an early flight in the morning. I know it's an imposition but could you have dinner with me? That way we will have time for review."

"Didn't think the brass had any after hours association with the hired help," she kidded.

"My dear, you aren't hired help anymore. Office managers are management. You had better remember that before you pull your union card on me," he said and smiled.

"Couldn't if I wanted to. The brotherhood took it away from me. They're not the best sports in the world."

"I know the feeling, a long time ago, they took mine."

"Winston, I didn't know you were ever in the union."

"More years ago than I can believe. When I turned in my card and took my first dock foreman's job, I was so afraid."

"I can't imagine you being afraid of anything."

"I was terrified, but I've never regretted getting into supervision. I doubt you will either. About dinner, when should I call for you?"

"Why don't I meet you. It will save time and I have something to do with my son, first."

"Whatever you say. Reeda, do you know Raymond's?"

"Yes, that's a right ritzy place."

"One of my compensations for living like a nomad. Raymond's around nine, okay?"

"See you then."

At dinner, they discussed office procedure from past due accounts to the easy acceptance as office manager she had received from her former peers. Discussing business, his brisk manner bordered on bluntness as he threw out questions like a lawyer, sometimes providing his own answers.

He was so into his work, Reeda realized he might not have an identity, apart from trucking. Obviously in love with his career, he was still an inspiration to her. He was totally committed and informed about the trucking industry; she wanted to pick his brain and learn everything he had to teach her.

As long as a supervisor's house was in order, there was nothing to dread from Winston Briley, as a boss. Reeda silently pitied anyone he might suspect of laziness. He would never accept from underlings, any less than his own total commitment to the company.

Even after they covered every aspect of her position, he seemed reluctant to leave their pleasant surroundings with the abundant foliage, spurting fountain and blue and green decor. He cocked his head, listening intently to the piano man at the bar across the room before saying, "*Killing Me Softly* is one of my favorite songs."

"I love it, but the melody's too beautiful to be real."

"Many things don't have to be real to be beautiful."

"No, but it might be less painful if they did."

"You loved him very much," he said gently.

"Who?"

"The man who left you so bitter." His sincerity was disconcerting.

Feeling shaken by his perception, she still managed to smile and say lightly, "Is it that obvious?"

"Probably not. I have a sixth sense about people."

"I suppose we all have our scars."

"That's true, but a scar is one thing and a wound is something else."

"How do you mean?"

"No matter how ugly, a scar signifies healing. A wound may not have even started to heal and bitterness is like an infected wound."

"One is seldom responsible for one's own wounds."

"Of course not, but in affairs of the heart, one is usually responsible for one's own healing."

"Other than time, how does one accomplish that?"

"Love wounds, once properly forgotten, have a way of healing quickly. Therapy helps to forget."

"Such as?"

"The best way for a road driver to forget a wreck is to climb back in a tractor the moment he's able."

"Provided he gets able," Reeda said.

"Right. It isn't always something one can do overnight, but the sooner the better."

"I've had time enough, I guess."

"The deeper the wound— the longer the recovery," he said, gently. "The most terrible thing about death is there is no going back."

"My husband was killed long after the marriage was over."

"You were still living under the same roof and if he had lived, you might have worked things out."

"Not likely. After the other woman bit, we had already been the patch-things-up route. My dear husband was with another, other woman when he died."

"Sorry."

"Don't be. Not for me."

"Playing it tough, huh?"

"Not really. I really didn't love him, anymore. My son is the one to be sorry for. I hope this doesn't sound mean but to be honest, for me, in some ways, it was a relief. But a boy only has one father and he doesn't have to totally know what kind of man he was."

"That's true, but you still have a big load to haul."

"I'd say you haven't had it all wine and roses. Aren't you divorced?"

"Isn't everyone? Or considering it?"

"Just about," she said, smiling back.

"There wasn't any tragedy in my divorce for me, or my ex-wife."

"I think there's always something tragic about a broken dream or a broken marriage."

"Mine just burned itself out. I'm afraid most marriages do. So many people can't or just don't bother doing anything about it. Minna and I were too much alive to live like that. She had money of her own, a career of her own and we had no children."

"Sounds as if you still have a lot of respect for her."

"Minna is a fine woman. But she isn't the kind to sit by forever and wait for a husband with a job that takes him all over the country. I'm not the kind of man to give up a job I love for a nine to five boring position or a pipe and kids. I had to claw my way up to a point not quite to where she was born. People born to money don't realize what it is to be without. But Minna is one of the most beautiful women I have ever seen. She decorates a room just by walking in it."

"She doesn't sound overly bright."

"On the contrary, she has more brains than most of us."

"Well, she let you get away."

"Reeda, in the pond where Minna swims, I was a small fish."

"How did you claw your way up, as you put it. I know Polk county. It's dirt poor. Not many people come so far so fast from anywhere. Did it take talent or guts, Winston?"

"Talent is second to guts, in anything."

"How do you mean?"

"I never saw a job I didn't think I could do. Never wanted a job that I couldn't talk my way into. That's guts and good to have, it's a long way from talent. I was lucky to come to Nathaniel Vance's attention. I have worked like a mother but he has been damn good to me."

"And you threw away the time clock."

"Yes. Anymore, there isn't a clock connected with my job."

"Do you and Nathaniel Vance get along? You don't come across as a man who likes to take orders."

He grinned and said, "I've never minded taking orders from someone I am hired to, and who is equipped to give them. Nathaniel is both. But I can't take crap. Once, I hit him up the side of his head with a yardstick," he said, laughing.

Reeda rolled her eyes, then said, "You're not serious".

"It kind of happened before I knew it. You see, Reeda, I'm goosey. Let somebody poke me in the ribs, when I'm not expecting it, and I'll jump ten feet. Back then, I was working in central dispatch. Hell, it was late. I'd been at it fourteen hours, and no one to relieve me in sight. Almost everybody was down with the flu."

"I know what that's like."

"Sick or well, freight has to roll. Anyway, it was about three a.m., I was sitting at a printer watching a dispatch print out. I didn't know there was another soul in the world. Nathaniel and Able Golden dropped in and I didn't hear them. Nathaniel slipped up behind me, goosed me with a yardstick; I almost jumped over the damn printer. We all had a big laugh, Nathaniel and I talked awhile, then he and Able went over to the maintenance shop. Nathaniel is prone to show up anywhere, any time.

"I had loads to coordinate, so I picked up the watts line and started calling my terminals. Maybe forty-five minutes later, Nathaniel slipped up behind me and pulled the yardstick trick, again. I jumped sky high, again. He has another bit laugh, but he hacked me off that time. I've never had much patience with horseplay."

"I wouldn't think you would," Reeda said.

"Why?"

"Just an observation. But then, just hearing him on the watts, I wouldn't think Vance would be into horseplay."

"He isn't much. But I was tired and busy and I lost it that time. Before I knew it, I had jumped up, pointed my finger in his face and said, "Dammit, Boss, don't do that again!"

"Ooophs, sounds like you meant it."

"I did. I thought that would end it, or end me working for Alpha. But Nathaniel apologized and said he was going home so I went on back to work. Hell, in less that five minutes, he slipped up and goosed me the third time. I went ape. Before I could catch myself, I jerked his yardstick away and warped him right above his ear. God, it made him mad. I thought he was going to bust a blood vessel, his face turned as red as a pig's heart but he just stood there and looked at me for what seemed like forever. I was getting braced to be fired on the spot. Then, without a word, Nathaniel turned and walked out, mumbling about, a bastard too dumb to take a joke."

"Well, you're obviously still working for him, so he didn't fire you."

"No. He didn't speak to me for three months. Didn't goose me anymore, either," Briley ended, with a chuckle.

"I wouldn't imagine someone as powerful as Mr. Vance would have taken being hit with a yardstick, under any circumstances."

"Most men in his position wouldn't have, but Nathaniel is the fairest man I have ever known. He was wrong, he had gone dead against his own policy and he knew it. That's why he let it pass."

"He didn't start Alpha Truck did he?"

"No. His father, Alex, started Alpha. Alex is ninety something and Alzheimer's has what's left of him. Up until a couple of years ago, he came to work every day. Alex was a huge hulk of a man... pulling freight at seventeen and wound up with a trucking empire."

"I see you have great respect for the father as well as the son."

"Oh, yes. Alex is one of my few true heroes and he pulled off the American dream if anyone ever did."

"I've heard they're Jewish."

"By birth, yes, but Alex fell in love with and married a gentile. Nathaniel told me once that old Alex's dad held his funeral for marrying outside Judaism."

"That's sounds extreme."

"We Native American Rednecks aren't the only ones who can be mega intolerant."

"That's a good thought. I'll keep it in mind, since I'm also a member of the Native American Redneck tribe."

"Since their mother was Baptist, Alex got thrown out of the Jewish faith. Nathaniel and Aaron were raised Baptist."

"Winston, we don't hear much at Manchester about Aaron."

"Aaron is a lush and a womanizer. He would have destroyed the business a long time ago if Nathaniel and Alex hadn't held a tight rein. When the sons first came into the business, everybody thought Aaron would be the big cheese. He's huge and hearty, like the old man, but for brains he got sawdust. Nathaniel is conservative, approaches things in a quiet way that can be deceiving. Some people have made the mistake of thinking he's weak because he's a laid back kind of man but when Nathaniel feels the need, he can come on with the impact of a loaded forty-five foot rig on a rampage."

"Seems to me, you have a fair impact yourself."

"I've done okay for a country boy. Been luckier than most."

"I don't see how you can call it luck when I know, you have worked like a jackhammer over the years and still do."

"My luck was getting into something I liked and could advance in, with a tenth grade education. Trucking is one of the few industries left, where a degree isn't mandatory to advance. It's getting more so. We require a high school diploma, even for a dockhand."

"You're not for that?"

"Yes. One reason we have so many grievances and freight discrepancies, stems from dockhands who barely read. We all need good reading skills. I don't think a college degree is necessary. Most college folks want to sit around think-tanking and philosophizing."

"That's bad?"

"That doesn't get the job done. The first rule in freight is to get the job done within a time frame. In running a truck line, I put love for the industry, common sense and a total lack of laziness at the top of my list. You can't believe how many flop out in management because they can't accept the fact that supervision can't leave the terminal when the dock is covered up with freight or when there's a wreck out on the highway with freight scattered over a forty acre field."

"Might I ask how long you expect a supervisor to stay on the job?"

"You have a son. When he was a baby and cried in the night, how long did you stay up with him? How long do you see about him now? How long will you see about him as long as he lives?"

"However long it takes. But there's a difference between a child and a job, or even a career."

"Not much. A man's job is his original nature, like a baby is a woman's original nature."

"There are some who would argue the point, Winston."

"Right! But they're wrong. A man needs his job and then his woman. It doesn't matter if he is wearing an animal skin and carrying a spear or a business suit and carrying an attaché case. If a man's work satisfies his need to prove himself and provide for his family, he will perform well and be reasonably happy."

She grinned, "You sound very sure."

"Anyone can make a mistake, but when a man habitually chases, it's usually from being in a job that fits him like a six fingered glove with no thumb and synonymous with being buried alive."

"Then, you don't believe a man's wife and children mean to him what a woman's husband and children mean to her."

"No. Man could't have accomplished the things he has in this world if they did. Picture a woman leaving her baby for three or four years to go to war, for instance."

"Do you call war an accomplishment?"

"Maybe necessity is a better word. I was giving an example, you supply the word."

"But from what you tell me, your wife wanting to express herself outside of the keep-the-home-fires-burning and baby bearing stereotype, destroyed your marriage. That just doesn't compute."

"I know. But so much of the time what pulls a couple together, in the first place, is usually what breaks them apart in the end."

"That doesn't make sense."

"Love rarely makes sense. If Minna had been happy to stay home, if we had had a couple of kids, we would probably still be married."

"But that isn't fair."

"Maybe not. Facts aren't necessarily fair."

"Do you think you married the wrong woman?"

"I don't know, I was attracted to Minna because she was different. I was worn out with women who kept trying to marry me and have a bunch of brats. Minna was so aloof and independent and that was my big mistake in judging myself and her. It took nearly ten years to come out, but she really wanted the kids and me home in the cave every night. Silly as it sounds, if we had kids, I would have been."

"And that would have been wrong?"

"Not in the higher sense. Just wrong for me, at that time. No matter how hard one tries to pretend, a square peg has corners. Corners aren't compatible with round holes."

"But family life is based on being, as you put it, in the cave with the kids every night."

"I agree. And what you're actually saying is that if you can't lick them join them. The trouble is, you have to be emotionally in tune to join anything. A proselyte never joins. A proselyte merely attaches himself and muddles his own idea of what he truly is."

"Whoa! You're getting too deep for me. But talking about kids, I have one of my own I need to get home to. I didn't think I would be late, so I let my housekeeper go home."

"Your son is a pretty big boy isn't he?"

"Almost fourteen and too old for a sitter. Just hates it when I hire one, but he's still too young to be alone late at night. Thanks for dinner."

"You're welcome. Let me get the bill, then I'll walk you to your car."

"That isn't necessary. I'm glad we agree on how I run the office."

"Just keep those account receivables current."

"Yes, I will. Thanks again. I have enjoyed the evening, even if I haven't quite understood all the conversation."

"So have I," he said, returning her smile and rising with her.

"Good night."

"Good night, Reeda." He sat back down and watched her until she walked behind the green plants and he lost her to the lobby.

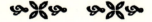

ஒ❊ஒ CHAPTER 14 ஒ❊ஒ

Three months passed before Winston returned to Manchester. By then, Reeda had conceded that from the magnitude of his six foot three inch frame to his dynamic personality, he was the acme of maleness. The morning he returned, Winston spoke cordially, but made no further attempt at conversation. He was in conference with Ralph till noon when they left to attend a freight carriers luncheon.

It was an hour after quitting time before Reeda left the office but they had not returned. Driving home, she felt vaguely provoked.

The next morning when she walked in the terminal, the tingle she felt seeing Winston standing out on the dock talking to Mike Osborn, Howard's replacement, put her on the defensive. Consequently, when Briley stopped by her office, her manner was pointedly polite.

There was no way of knowing whether her cool attitude prompted his inquiry or whether he had entered the room to say, "I don't mean to pick, but I feel your office people are into too much idle chatter."

"Really?"

"Yes. I think you should put a stop to it," he said, companionably, taking the chair across from her desk.

"Have you seen my cost report?"

"Yes, of course."

"Have you checked the cost of hours worked to get the cost factor for work accomplished in this office?"

"Yes, it's excellent. Your people really put out for you."

"Then why should I correct my people for talking?"

"For one thing, it's inappropriate. A stream of conversation among employees isn't becoming in a business office. Besides, your hourly cost for work ratio might increase even more if you cracked down."

"And... it might decrease."

"Why would you think that?"

"Winston, have you ever worked hourly in an office?"

"No, but I have worked hourly loading and unloading trailers. It didn't give me time for much conversation."

"As you know, I have worked hourly here. Contrary to popular opinion, office work isn't manual labor and office workers aren't mules."

"I know that but— "

"One of the common faults of management is not acknowledging when enough is enough. My people clearly earn their pay. Secretly sluffing off on the job costs much more than a bit of sluffing off openly. If... that's how you see my people's human side."

"How do you mean?"

"Hank Carter, with all his sins, had his good points. He didn't care if we talked, were silent as the sphinx, or had a party if the work was kept up. Till he let sex warp his brain, working for Hank made me feel valued. He gave me credit for being a responsible adult. In response, I gave him a hundred and ten percent. Ralph goes along with that precedent for me and my clerks. I believe it is wise and if you have the right kind of people, it works. I do and it does."

"But you have more conversation than any office in my division."

"And the best hour-work ratio cost. I see no reason for change or concern," she said, returning his insistent look, just as insistently"

"Employees aren't supposed to chatter like a flock of crows."

"God! This isn't a classroom and my girls aren't school children, irresponsible or dumb. They don't need to pretend that silence is indicative of concentration. They aren't housewives taking time away from the kids, but career employees with a living to earn. If they were out for fun, or taking a break from home, they wouldn't be caught dead working in a truck line office."

"Why not? We pay union scale. For comparable job skills, that translates to truck lines paying the highest wages in town."

"The profit margin more than compensates Alpha for paying union scale and higher wages is all that's positive about working in freight."

"Is Alpha that hard to work for?"

"At least! Alpha and any other trucking firm."

"Seems to me, Alpha has been damn good to you."

"Yes, but plush offices in the high rent district and long lunch breaks aren't part of the picture for hourly employees. Sausage and biscuit breakfasts, baloney parties in the afternoon aren't part of our deal either. We pay well but we don't have the amenities that can make getting out of the house very pleasant. We offer great pay for good work and entertain yourself after hours."

"That doesn't wash with how your girls can talk so much if the work is so demanding."

"Volume and pressure make it demanding. It has to be done today, tomorrow's too late. You have tomorrow's work tomorrow. Other than tracing, which requires a thick skin, diplomacy and sensitivity to the needs of our customers, the rest is simple work. It requires basic office skills such as computer literacy, typing and operating figuring machines. But it is about as fulfilling as dusting and washing dishes."

"Then you agree it doesn't take a doctorate degree."

"Of course, I could teach my sophomore son any job here. He couldn't support the volume or the boredom from repetition but he would know the routine. Once a clerk is trained our clerical work requires about the same intelligence as stringing beads. The hard part? It requires the constitution of a mule and the guts of Godzilla."

"Maybe we are paying too much," Briley said.

"Our clerks are dedicated, hard working and worth every penny they make. Given the choice, I wouldn't want us to operate like most non-union companies. It's cheaper our way."

"How do you mean?"

"It would take two ordinary clerks to do the work our folks do. Clerical jobs go all over town for six to eight dollars an hour. Shallow minds think that is a savings next to our pay scale. They pay two clerks more money, in double the work space, pay benefits on two employees with five times the job turnover. Even within our company, my folks save money in overtime hours and very little casual help to keep the backlog caught up."

"All our offices have overtime and the backlog is never caught up."

"Mine doesn't. Our office people keep the backlog caught up with an average of twenty casual hours a week."

"Let me get this straight. You're saying your work stays caught up with forty hours per regular employee and twenty casual hours?"

"I thought you read my cost report."

"I did, Reeda, but maybe not as close as I should have. No overtime and no ongoing backlog is unusual."

"Yes, because my clerks are on my side and I'm on theirs."

"You sound more like one of Hoffa's women than a supervisor."

"In some ways, I hope so. Say what you will about Hoffa but the man knew how to win and how to share. That was the reason for his success."

"How do you know that?"

"He demanded decent wages for his members. Left up to most owners of trucking companies or most any other business, all they are concerned with is building themselves a bigger mansion, paying employees fifty cents a day and whining about that being too much for working people to make. I reckon they want working people to live with the hogs."

"I don't know that I agree with that."

"Then read your history. It's a matter of record. Hoffa got his folks into the hourly rate you're always bitching about. Whatever else he did or didn't do, I love that about the man. Where the office is concerned, I've been there. Conversation relieves the monotony and increases the rapport. All our office work is related, we need good communication among our clerks."

"I'd say you have that," Briley said sardonically.

"If you really listened to what is being said, you would be surprised at how much of it is work related. A donkey pulling a turnstile loses little motion if he brays. He doesn't even have to stop pulling."

"You obviously don't think much of our industry."

"Actually, I think trucking is a tremendous industry. It doesn't put enough value on it's employees. Freight is the lifeblood of the nation. It bothers me how few people outside of trucking realize how vital it is to their lives. But that's the industry's fault. If GE didn't advertise, who would know they manufacture fantastic refrigerators? And who would want to buy one in a grease covered carton, delivered by a dirty delivery man?"

"You do have a point," he said and grinned.

"What I don't care for is what's been dubbed the "feminine mystic.""

"Then you object to career women?"

"I object to the destruction that's been rained on the idea of Mom and apple pie. I hate the coercion that has put women to work. I'm not talking about the financially deprived or the truly career motivated. Still, when it comes to very young children, I doubt there's any true justification except for the financially deprived."

"You don't believe in surrogate child care?"

"It's the lack of child care I don't believe in. Mom offers the best child care in creation. Latch key kids are a disgrace, all too often, caused by the move to make wives feel dumb if they aren't hot-footing it to some penny-anti job. The kids are left on their own, with the house going to hell and the husband loosing what the very word, husband denotes for a few extra dollars. Then those dollars buying cars for sixteen year old boys to get killed in and bleached blond hair for fifteen year old girls to get pregnant in is criminal Bottom line, a child is a huge responsibility."

Briley said, "You have put a lot of thought into working women."

"That's my life and I've been lucky. You gave me a chance at a job without someone looking over my shoulder every minute. I can't bear to force people who must work to limit phone calls to weekends, or to watch every word when their work is most commendable. Hell, I never could bear to be the hall monitor."

"Then how do you propose to supervise them?"

"Results. I believe if we hire the right people in the first place, and train them properly in the second place, we won't have many problems."

"What if you do?"

"After a warning or two, if they can't or won't get with the program, get rid of them."

"Well, you know what you're after, but you sound more like a union business agent than an office manager."

"I hope I sound like a caring, competent office manager."

"You do, maybe too much so. I still believe you allow too much gossip in your office," he insisted.

"Winston, more gossip goes on at management meetings than in this office. Why must the haves always give the have nots a bad rap? Why do they want to keep that invisible line drawn between hourly and salaried?"

"Why not? It gives an employee something to work toward."

"I think it's too expensive in more ways than one."

After a pensive silence he said, "I don't mean to be hard nosed. And my main reason for wanting a female office manager is because we employee mostly women in this office. Reeda as long as your cost report stays up, you have the say on office conduct. Should it slip, then I'll ask you to do some revamping. Fair enough?"

"More than fair and thank you," Reeda said and smiled.

"You're very welcome," he smiled back. "Now, to something pleasant. Will you have dinner with me tonight?"

"Hope I'm not doing anything else, work wise, that displeases you."

"Other than the gossip, I am delighted. I want you to have dinner with me, strictly on a personal level."

"That might get us problems with the company."

"I've explained before, that rule applies to management mixing socially with hourly employees. Because of the union."

"But that seems ridiculous."

"It won't when you've been around longer, as a supervisor, and learn the mechanics of grievance hearings. There it's survival of the fittest, period. No trick's too low if it means winning."

"You make it sound like war."

"Darling, it's sure no ladies' tea party. But enough business. Are we on for dinner?"

Reeda smiled and said, "Where and what time shall I meet you?"

"I'll come for you."

"It's simpler if I just meet you."

"I said, I'll come for you," he repeated.

Once he had the car rolling, Briley said, "You have a fine son and he looks a lot like you— same dark eyes and hair."

"Thank you. I won't pretend I'm not proud of Jamey."

"You have the right. Kids take a lot of work. Very few teenagers I have been around are that cordial."

"He misses his Dad. He's pleased when a man comes around."

"Is he pleased often?"

"Not nearly enough for his likes. Jamey wants another father."

"And how about you, Reeda? Do you want another husband."

"Maybe, someday."

"You don't sound overly enthusiastic."

She said softly, "Marriage lasts a long time."

"Amen to that and divorce lasts even longer. By the way, where would you like to eat."

"Wherever."

"You mean I've come up with a subject that I'm not going to get an argument out of you?" Briley said with a grin.

"Not about eating," she said, smiling, "I'm easy to feed."

"Does going back to Raymond's stretch the point?"

"Of course not."

As usual, Raymond's food and drinks were fantastic. After dinner, she accepted Briley's invitation to inspect the company apartment.

"Alpha maintains similar quarters in all our terminal cities," he said, showing her through the suite of rooms.

"It's very nice. Looks expensive."

"It's deductible. It relieves the branch terminals from the responsibility of making reservations for company visitors."

"And it helps you guys appear on the local scene unannounced."

"Well, yes." Winston smiled and said, "You do have a knack for dispensing with the trimmings."

"I was kidding. It really is beautiful."

"Thanks. Make yourself at home. I'll put some music on. You do like good music?"

"Love it. The company thinks of everything."

"The tapes are mine. Manchester's central location puts me in here quite often. Many times I don't visit your terminal. At least," he said, looking meaningfully at her, "I haven't in the past. There is coffee, but I make terrible coffee."

"I think I hear a hint," Reeda said, smiling.

"You are most perceptive. Step into my kitchen."

Making the coffee, she said, "Where is home?"

"Company apartments mostly— my personal things are scattered all over. Right now, here more than anywhere else."

"You don't have your own place?"

"I used my house so seldom, I'm leasing it out."

"That must be a terrible way to live."

"Actually, Reeda, it feels marvelous."

"You are a rare bird, Mr. Briley."

"I've had the home and roots bit. The roots got around my neck. Come on, let's listen to the music while the coffee's running through."

She followed him into the long living room with mauve carpet and drapes. There were four beige lounge chairs. Two were placed at each end of an extra long floral sofa, mostly country blue with mauve and beige scattered in the background.

"Love the colors in here," she said, looking around.
"Sink in that sofa and kick off your shoes."
"Thanks, but I can make myself at home with my shoes on."
"I love walking on a plush carpet in my sock feet. Do you mind?"
"Of course not."
"Good girl," he said, slipping out of his shoes.
"What did you mean about roots around your neck?"
"Think I told you how my ex-wife started despising the traveling my job requires. Didn't blame her, but I couldn't give up my job. It got to the point that long distance or face to face, we argued about it constantly. Minna finally told me she would rather be a widow than married to me. She said, a widow at least could be honorably looking. That was the final shot."
"You didn't love her enough to give it up?"
"Reeda, could you love anyone enough to give up, Jamey?"
"Never. That isn't the same thing."
"It is to me, my job is my life. It's who I am. I gave my love, my faithfulness, my earthly goods. I couldn't give my soul. Funny, but she isn't the kind of woman that I thought would ever demand it."
"She probably didn't think of it like that."
"Probably not. But she started wanting one thing out of life, and I wanted another. In spite of her poise, Minna never got over being raised by a governess and house staff while her parents ran all over the globe. At the end, she literally craved the closeness of a family. I never got over being poor along with four brothers and too many people in a four room house. When Minna got to obsessing over my physical presence, it felt like a noose around my neck. I wonder if it's possible for two people to get along, who need opposite ways of life and both be right."
"Only if they aren't married."
"Right. It's a pity couples can't discuss all the no's before marriage."
"It would probably take all the fun out of fighting."
"It's remarkable that you have retained your sense of humor after being through the hell side of marriage yourself."
"Winston, it's more than remarkable. It's a necessity. When I get problems I can't joke about, I'm real close to the funny farm. And... I didn't learn to joke about my marital foul up overnight."
"I know. Even when you laugh all the hurt doesn't leave your eyes."

"The laugh is a front. Possibly cushioning is a better word. If a joint loses its cushioning, it doesn't work properly. It can't take any punishment at all."

Briley said, "There is nothing wrong with your joints."

"Thank you, kindly, but emotional joints are my point."

"They are the easiest ones to fix." He smiled and moved closer to her on the sofa.

"They haven't been for me."

"You haven't had the proper therapy. Here, let me show you," he said, then kissed her.

Despite her warm lips, she said, "I didn't say you could do that."

"Asking permission ruins some things," he said, kissed her again, then settled her into his arms.

"You may be right," she said, trying to settle down, thinking maybe it was time to roll with the flow.

"You are a beautiful woman," he said, kissing the top of her head, then tilted her chin back to kiss her again.

"No," she said, turning her head, "we mustn't do this." But she was penned against the sofa by overpowering arms, then thoroughly kissed again by tender but persuading lips.

The confidence on his face, when he released her mouth and smiled into her eyes, brought back that last sick night with Van. His smile hit her like the smirk that had lit Van's face. Reeda's revulsion spurred more strength in her than any hundred and fifteen pounds should be able to exert. "No!" she growled, with the ferocity of swearing, and somehow twisted away from him and got to her feet.

His surprised face flushed with anger. "Surely, in this enlightened day, I haven't run into a prude divorcee." Then he smiled and said, "Hey, relax. You don't need to be running behind that chair. I have no intention of raping you, for God's sake!"

But she clung to the chair, seemingly for support, as she said, "I don't mean to give you a bad time or play the innocent. It seems my Victorian ancestors have an impregnable grip on me. If you will be so kind, I'd appreciate you calling me a cab."

Briley chuckled, and said, "Come on, just because I struck out doesn't mean you have to call the game." As she actually backed away from his advance, he held up his hands in surrender, and pleaded, "Hold on now. I'll behave, I promise." The anger in her eyes told she was not convinced. "Reeda, I can't believe you're running from me like a scared turkey. Lord, relax! I won't ever touch you again if you don't want me to, I just got a little carried away. You're a very desirable woman. Is that so hard to believe?"

"No," she said, returning his smile, beginning to relax. "I took one detour and got lost. I don't want to take another."

"Enough said. Come on, our coffee should be ready by now."

By their second cup of coffee, Reeda was at ease. She was thinking, while Winston was definitely all male, there was something warm and strong and reassuring about him. Knowing the freight business inside out, gave him much to teach her. Though she felt their mutual attraction, the friendship she felt for him was too special to be wasted on some spur of the moment bedroom romp.

Briley was thinking, what a truly handsome woman she was. But he could wait. He had no intention of turning her off again by rushing. Tonight was out— there was always next week or next month. He said, "I guessed you are one of those women who must have love to have a relationship."

"I've learned the hard way, I certainly don't want to make love without love."

"Why not?"

"Call if personal preference. Course, if I sat down at a computer and gave it some real thought, I could probably enter a thousand good reasons. At the top of the list would be that it's stupid to lose a first rate friendship on a third rate affair. Besides, I really don't care for sex with a governor on it."

"Governor?"

"I don't think either party can truly let go in a mere, so called, relationship. Do you? I mean sincerely, Winston?"

"Maybe not," he smiled. Reeda saw how very tender his blue eyes were as he added, "If we take our time, we just might get lucky. Maybe, one more time might be real love."

CHAPTER 15

In the following months, knowing she wasn't feeling the way she wanted to feel, but hoping she might somehow grow into loving Winston, Reeda continued to see him.

He was a nice man, an attractive man and he was giving her a true master's education in the freight business. There was no reason for her not to care for him. Maybe she just needed more time with him. They had fun together and she liked his affection. But she backed off big time when he became arduous.

Grievance hearings and labor problems in other terminals had kept him away from Manchester too long. Long distance phone calls was the nearest he had been to Reeda in eight weeks. The first night he saw her after his return, the patience of a man who realized patience was a tremendous part of winning was running onion skin thin.

She was especially desirable wearing a melon colored chiffon dress. Her dark hair was styled in a soft roll along her cheeks and shoulders. "You look very chic and as feminine as lace," he said as they sipped wine and ate from the plate of tiny sandwiches she had prepared for a late snack.

"Thank you— and thank you for a lovely evening."

"My pleasure," he said, appreciating her beauty. Like a sculptor scrutinizing a block of fine marble, Briley was thinking of a hundred things he could do to bring her to life. "You know I like spending time with you very much, Reeda."

She thought a moment about being more up front. He had taken her to a fabulous dinner club. She had been royally wined, dined and danced. Lord, she didn't want tonight to end on a sour note. So she simply said, "Thank you, Winston."

"I think we're good for each other. We could be so good together."

She wasn't sure what he meant. She was sure she wasn't ready to discuss whatever he meant. She was also sure he was not a man to let a relationship run long on a platonic basis. Clearly, she was supposed to come back with something personal. But, "Tell me, how were the southern grievance hearings?" came out of her mouth.

"Same old, same old. More money, less work."

"Not much new in that," she said, with an understanding smile.

Briley saw the woman had no idea how beautiful she was. It made her all the more alluring. She watched him carefully place his glass on the coffee table.

Taking her into his arms, he said, "There's not much new in this, but just the thought of holding you is so stimulating."

After he had kissed her, he looked into her eyes a long moment and smiled. Then he kissed her several more times until the slant of her eyes made a liar of the hands she braced against his chest. He smiled tenderly, almost piteously at the small, insignificant hands. "No matter what, you just can't let yourself go. Can you?"

"Oh, I could— very easily."

"Then why not? You know how happy we could make each other?"

"We have been through this before."

"But it doesn't make any sense," he said, harshly.

"Just because one person wants to do something, doesn't make it right for the other person. I'm not ready for that kind of intimacy."

She hated his saying, "I'd marry you in a minute, if I thought it had the slightest possibility of working."

"I don't remember asking you to marry me."

"You act it out every time you set me on fire with your lips, then push me away with your hands. Marriage would screw up both our jobs. Strong people like us don't need marriage, Reeda." Now she realized she had good reasons to be afraid of getting romantically involved with Winston, besides the fact that he was her boss.

"Hey, man, speak for yourself. People like you may not need marriage but people like me need it very much. You need to realize that about me."

"But why? You have a child, a home and you're financially secure. There is nothing I can give you in marriage you don't already have."

"Winston, I'm not ready for another marriage. And as old fashioned as it might sound, I'm not even bidding on being anybody's mistress. Just the word, mistress, sounds so tacky. It would destroy my security and my self-respect."

"Then when you get tired of being my wife, it takes half the country poking into our private affairs to get us single again. Darling, you haven't been in divorce court with a pack of holier than thou strangers rummaging in your life like rats at a garbage dump."

"Please, Winston, I don't want to quarrel with you."

"Hell, just discussing marriage puts us at each other's throats."

"But marriage isn't the problem."

"Okay, you tell me, Reeda, what is the problem?"

"We have different needs, I'm not sure I want to be your mistress or your wife. But I want the possibility of marriage, maybe just the dream of marriage. Every time I start up into my little celestial rise and you make it clear you don't want to even consider marriage, it bursts my bubble. It destroys my sense of well being and my being able to give myself over to you emotionally or physically."

"So that makes me wrong?"

"I don't know but it makes us wrong for each other. I believe when a woman and a man truly care for each other, at some point marriage is their logical goal."

"And I don't," he growled.

"You have made that abundantly clear, and you make me feel like I'm begging for something I haven't even thought about asking for. Under the circumstances, we really should stop seeing each other. Working together just makes it more complicated. And I am well aware you are past the overtures."

"At least we agree on the overture part."

"Winston, no matter how you put it, sex is all you want from me or any other woman."

"What's wrong with that? This isn't fourteen ninety-two and you're no teenager."

She recoiled as if he had struck her. "I don't suppose there's a man alive who could have refrained from that one."

"Reeda, please," he said, trying to embrace her.

"No!" she hissed.

"Forgive me, I didn't mean—"

"Yes, you did. We both know you meant I'm used goods."

"No, Reeda, I—"

"One minute you're spouting off the latest flash from the sexual revolution, the next you're using the oldest manipulative shit around. Hate to tell you, but this ain't no bargaining session and you're right. I wasn't born yesterday. But, mister, when it comes to intimacy, I accept or reject, regardless of my past, present or future. For me, intimacy isn't just bed. It's trust, sharing and growing. It requires a commitment— if not marriage."

"You didn't get all that from marriage before. What makes you think you can get it now?"

"I was dumb enough to imagine I could avoid another nothing like I married. As the saying goes, he could mess up a one car funeral."

"That wasn't my fault," he snapped.

Reeda hated it that suddenly she was angry and not far from tears. She swallowed hard and choked her tears back before saying, "No, and I finally see it wasn't mine either. God! I haven't been this angry since Van died and I don't like it."

"Reeda, I'm sor—"

"Don't be! This side of you needed to come out. I'm so glad it did! I don't ever intend to have to fight again to be me and call it love. We have enough pseudo lovers, mates, politicians and preachers, mouthing about loving and looking after people, to gag a maggot. I hate it and I'm not going to be used by it. To a business, personal or spiritual relationship, individuals have to bring their own character."

"I was trying to be honest. I didn't mean to hurt your feelings or to make you mad."

"Well, without trying, you've done both. But I'm much angrier at me, than you. After Van, I never imagined I would be fool enough to consider a man who let his first wife scare all the faith and security out of him. Minna left him too afraid to trust another woman."

"That isn't true."

"The hell it isn't! But let's just hush. This conversation is demeaning to both of us. Something is broken inside you, Winston. Something a bad time has broken and only you can fix. Getting hurt doesn't give you a license to hurt others. Whether we like it or not, whether we want it or not, with all the heaven and hell, marriage is what a man and woman who truly love each other risk." Her black eyes were blazing as she added "Now, get out! Right now, I can't stand looking at someone as chicken shit as you another minute."

"Don't order me around. I'll get out when I'm good and damn ready. Don't ever think I'm the kind of lowlife you married."

"And don't think I'm the kind of cold, social fish you married. I ain't cold, I ain't social, I ain't rich. I don't want love with a lid on it. And I ain't doing it with anybody who don't want to ever belong to me! When it comes to love, I'm really just another one of Hoffa's women to you. Like I've heard, when it comes to management and hourly, never the twain can meet."

"Hell, woman, you're not in Hoffa's union anymore."

"Union is a state of mind."

"What in God's name are you talking about?"

"I'm talking about I believe in an honest day's work for an honest day's pay and an honest kiss for an honest kiss.

"So do I."

"Actually, Winston, in your heart of hearts, you don't really believe in either. You want to do what you want to do and you want everyone else to do what you want to do. You want everybody to be grateful to you for using them. That's the mind set of trucking management and why workers need unions."

"Is that right?" His sarcastic grin made her feel defeated.

"I'm sorry to say, it is. Also, there's a fatal disease out there called AIDS I'm scared to death of. And I'm worn-out, Winston. Just go before you wake my son with your big mouth spouting sleeping-around-bullshit!"

Her words took the smile off his face like a soapy dishrag takes grease. "I'll go when I'm ready," he snarled, in a lowered voice, but made no move to rise from the sofa.

"Ape! Stay as long as you like. But good night. I've enjoyed all of your male supremacy I can stand. I'm going to bed!" She started from the room then turned to add, "And alone."

Over her shoulder she heard him bark, "Hell, no wonder!"

After the slam of her bedroom door and conclusive click of the lock, he sat alone and pensive. Thinking about how quickly a good deal could go bad, he ate a few more of her good sandwiches and finished the last of the wine bottle, then quietly let himself out.

Walking to his car, he said to the night, "Damn, she has a temper."

Preferring to descend like an eagle from on high, Nathaniel Vance seldom announced his visits to his thirty odd terminals. Manchester was extended no preferential treatment.

For Cynthia, working on the switchboard, it was a normal day until Vance called Stevens and then he was scurrying off like a rabbit to fetch El Presidenta from the airport.

Later, when Stevens walked in Reeda's office with Vance and she officially met Alpha's president, it was rather like preparing to meet God and finding he was running over with sex appeal. She had seen Vance from a distance sometime back and had heard him on the watts numerous times. She had depicted the resonant voice belonging to a kind of straight-laced, modern day Moses.

The man sitting in front of her desk could have posed for Playgirl. His dusted with silver dark hair and tanned face was dominated by engaging, navy-blue eyes.

After he instructed Ralph to continue with whatever it was he was doing before coming to the airport, Nathaniel looked directly at Reeda, took a pack of cigarettes from his pocket and said, "Smoke?"

"No thank you, sir, I quit several months ago. The cancer warning scared me, finally."

"Oh?" lighting his own.

"Aren't you afraid?"

"There are very few things in this life I truly enjoy anymore. This," he said and drew on his cigarette, "happens to be one of them."

"Then you must not believe the reports."

"I'm not equipped to dispute them although cancer strikes non-smokers as well as smokers. Most things of pleasure involve an amount of risk. Are you afraid of risk?"

"I'm afraid of such a statement," she laughed. Her phone rang, she frowned, excused herself and answered, "Reeda Davis... One moment, sir, and I'll give you someone who can help you." She dialed Cynthia on another line, "Cyn, give this call to tracing and hold my calls till I tell you." She hung up and said, "I'm sorry, sir."

"That's all right. You certainly don't handle your job as though you're afraid of risk. Once they get involved in a trace call, most terminal managers are afraid to risk turning it over to the trace clerk."

"There's no risk. I know my clerk and I know what I'm doing."

"Apparently, by all reports, you truly do. And that brings me back to why I'm here. But, if you will pardon my saying so, trace calls have always been allowed to break into most anybody's conference— even mine at times. Shouldn't you have handled that one?"

"Later, maybe, if my trace clerk can't make the customer happy. She is a most competent trace clerk."

"No doubt, if you trained her." She liked his smile and his eyes.

"Mr. Vance, when I assumed this job, everyone was harassed unmercifully by trace calls, big shipper, little shipper, past due account or excellent pay account. Almost daily, some barely literate idiot, with the manners of a pig, would turn this office upside down, demanding service we don't pretend to offer over, in too many cases, a one time minimum shipment. Then, we might have to practically send out the National Guard to collect our freight charges if the driver failed to collect on delivery. It costs the company too much to tolerate that. There is no reason from a profit, customer service, or a human stand point to allow it."

"Your accounts receivable are in excellent shape."

"Thank you, I try and Alpha has the best service from the Lakes to the Keys that money can buy. It needs improvement, still our Atlantic to Pacific service is competitive, to say the least. I don't intend to subject my office personnel to abuse or ridiculous demands as long as I am office manager."

"Has anyone ever accused you of being frank?" he smiled.

She smiled back, and said, "Yes, I'm afraid so, all my life. But at last, I am in a position to use it to advantage. Well, most of the time, anyway."   ??

Nathaniel laughed out loud, then said, "You know that after your first month as office manager. Your receivables have consistently been well above quota."

"Meeting or exceeding collection quota was one of my first goals. I think it's important. I want my money on pay day, so I know you want yours. And I believe that late freight bill payment, besides being hard on cash flow, also makes for bad customer relations."

"Whatever, you must be right. Manchester is our number one terminal consistently collecting above what my cost analyst says we need to stay in business."

"It would be gross hypocrisy for me to deny being aware of that. I set maintaining collection quota as my prime target when I took over the office manager position."

"I wonder, would you be willing to visit our other terminals and show them how to follow your methods?"

"Sir, I can tell you what's wrong without going."

"That is a big statement. I must say, we have had the best and most expensive consulting minds inside and outside the trucking industry to study the problem."

"With all due respect, there is one thing wrong with these best minds, inside the company and out. At least from what I can see, when they come poking their inquisitive little heads around here. They know how to tell to do, but they don't have a clue about what to actually do on a receivables desk."

"Reeda, would you break that down a bit?"

"It's like an old maid telling you how to mind a baby. It's great in theory, but I'm partial to some practical experience. On paper it sounds wonderful, foolproof you might say. In application, it doesn't take into account the spilled milk, the stopped up sink, the knock at the door, the washing machine breaking down, or the baby crying from teething."

"And how do you cope with that?"

"I hire casual help interested in ongoing casual work to make training them worthwhile. I have two clerks on tap at the moment. One is a retired freight office employee who does it all. He can be here in two hours notice. The other is a housewife who has too many kids to work regular. She needs extra money and enjoys getting out of the house now and then. Trucking is the only industry that pays her enough to afford child care. They are both excellent help and I think they will both be around for awhile. Okay?"

"Okay."

"On the cashier desk, instead of company precedent, I have my regular cashier do the follow up work on the old accounts. The casual person does the routine work. That's really the most significant change. When Fred wasn't looking, I did it that way when I was cashier and he gave me casual help."

"Fred didn't do it that way?"

"No. Traditionally casual people are used to call our past due accounts and the regular cashier continues with the daily work. But it's plain as pudding that a regular clerk can do a better job on past due accounts and maintain a better relationship with our clients."

Vance said, "Makes sense and it does sound simple."

"It is but I had to be office manager before I could get it done that way regularly."

"You suggested handling it that way back when you were still on the cashier desk?"

"Yes, and as I said, did when I could get away with it. It was a no no when it came to getting it accepted as ongoing procedure. So it really never amounted to much."

"But any fool can see the advantages."

"Yes, you would think so but it's another matter to get a man who is afraid of losing his job to go against precedent. He had rather let well enough alone. "

"Have we gone that far in destroying incentive, even at the management level?"

"Mr. Vance, it's very common knowledge that truck lines keep their management in such a state of flux, most of the supervisors on any given day are afraid to say good morning in a different tone of voice for fear of getting fired."

"So that's what I keep sensing. It's like conversing with a talking dummy. How can grown men, who are supposed to be leaders, let themselves be intimidated so?"

"Because even leaders have kid's shoes to buy and mortgages to pay. A family man will take a lot to protect his family."

"I suppose, but I don't really understand that. Like this union thing we have in the office. I can't imagine needing a union. I've never needed anyone to do my talking for me." He smiled. "Obviously you don't either."

"With all due respect, Mr. Vance, have you ever been poor?"

"No, but I don't see— "

"Have ever been fired or worked hourly for a living?"

"No, but— "

"Sir, can you possibly imagine raising a family on say... three thousand dollars a year?"

"It must be next to being dead— or buried alive. A man worth his salt would do something about it."

"The smart ones do." It was almost evil the way Reeda smiled and loved saying, "They join a labor union, Mr. Vance."

"Touché. You led me into that one, Mrs. Davis. And... if I did work hourly, perhaps I would join a labor union."

She smiled, "I have no doubt you would. There's also one concrete benefit to management in being a union company. I don't know the figures, but I wouldn't be surprised if it offsets the higher pay-scale."

"I'm most interested in knowing what that is."

"Employee stabilization. Training new hires is the most expensive waste the trucking industry's guilty of."

"You may be right. Maybe sometimes we can't see the expense for the trucks. Which reminds me, I came to Manchester to ask you for a huge favor. I need you to visit the other terminals, and set up the same procedure for handling receivables you have here."

"I will, if you insist, but I had rather not." Jerking management people from terminal to terminal like they were in the French Foreign Legion was another thing she intended to work on. But one thing at a time. She had to show Vance what her ideas would do. Still she might as well let him know, starting now, there was one thing in her life that meant more than her job! And should!

"Why not?"

"I have a teen-age son. He doesn't see enough of me as it is. I'm all he has since his father died. I need to be home at night."

"I was aware of that, but it had slipped my mind. I'm sorry. Of course, it would be most difficult for you to be away from him for any length of time."

Apparently considering her situation, Vance lit another cigarette. His tobacco smoked taunted Reeda unmercifully. Thinking it might as well come out now as later, she said, "If my responsibility for my son is a put off, you might as well know about it now."

Vance thought a moment before saying, "Not at all. Actually I appreciate your remarkable candor. We will just have to work it out. I have two bright boys in the corporate office you could instruct. Perhaps they could make the rounds in the system terminals and incorporate your program."

"Yes, sir, I think that would work."

"Of course, the central computer system isn't here. And there is not enough real privacy here."

"Sir, I wouldn't know how to use the central computer system."

"But my boys do. How about this? How about a weekend at the corporate office. If it's simple as you say, a Saturday and Sunday, perhaps a Monday thrown in would give you time to get the message across to them. Could you manage that?"

"Well, I don't know. You do go full steam ahead."

"Always," he said and smiled.

"I would still be away from Jamey three, maybe four days. I'm away from him too much as it is working forty-five to fifty hours a week. Perhaps, I could just explain to you in detail, and you could pass it along."

"I'm afraid I have no patience with detail. In fact, I hate clerical work about as much as you hate being away from your son. The clerical desks are where my dad started me out. Made me learn every job in a terminal— even OS&D. Ugh!" Vance smiled, "By the way, how much do you love your job?"

"My job means the world, but it isn't in the same world as my son."

"Obviously not. So let's include your son."

"Excuse me?"

"We'll set things up at my home. We can tap into the central system from my place. There's a pool and horses and the flight down. He should enjoy that and there's my sister's boy, Roland, for company. How old is your son?"

"Fourteen."

"Roland just turned fifteen and he doesn't have enough friends his age. They'll make great companions. Say weekend after next? We do need to get this thing rolling."

"Well, I don't know— "

"If you have plans that weekend, we can make it the next."

"No, I don't have plans it's just that—"

"Mrs. Davis— Reeda, if I may, I truly do need your help. Please don't be coy with me. And rest assured there will be extra pay."

He did not miss her blush, as she said, "I'll come, but for your information, I've never been coy in my life."

He smiled and said, "I thought not."

"You just said that to goad me into accepting."

"There's a saying in the freight business, whatever works— works."

"I suppose it's my turn to say touché."

"I think so," Vance said, obviously enjoying himself.

"Please, if you will just handle the expenses. That's all the extra pay that will be involved."

"I never take anything without paying for it."

"Then I won't be going." Her level gaze told him she still wasn't being coy. It also told him the reason why Winston had promoted her.

But clearly this was not the proper time to further fan the fire in her midnight eyes.

He decided it was actually time to smile and say, "All right, Miss Reeda Davis, if you insist. No extra pay. My hand on it."

"Thank you," she said, smiling and shaking his hand.

"This has been a most worthwhile and rewarding trip. In more ways than one, the Manchester office is in very good hands. And very warm hands, I might add." Vance gave her hand a little extra squeeze and then released it.

CHAPTER 16

The white column house, the magnificent old magnolias, the towering oaks hung with moss as if done by a decorator, the pink azaleas, manicured boxwoods, scent of gardenias— all struck Reeda as the music of money and the lyrics of luxury. As she stepped out of the new smelling Cadillac into the scent of flowers and the shade of giant magnolias and old money, she was prompted to breath, "Merciful God!"

"Do you approve?" Nathaniel asked, as he closed her door.

"Approve? I'm overwhelmed. Outside the movies, I didn't know there were any homes left like this. It's— beyond beautiful "

"Thank you. The house is one more thing we agree on." He turned to the two boys already out of the back seat, "Roland, this is a good time to show Jamey around."

"Yes, sir. Come on, Jamey, I want to show you my horse Uncle Nathaniel bought for me. He's a golden palomino." Jamey cast his don't-be-acting-like-a-mom look into Reeda's anxious eyes and rendered her silent.

As the boys walked off through the trees, Nathaniel said, "There aren't many of the original old homes left— this one was a wreck when I bought it. I had wanted it for two years but my wife, now my ex-wife, wouldn't hear of living in it. Eden," he said with a sweep of his arm, "is a fringe benefit of divorce."

"Eden," Reeda repeated, looking around. "Yes, the name fits."

"It's the original name but when I bought the place, Hell would have been a more accurate name or maybe Vance's Folly."

"How could anyone let a home like this go to ruin?"

"Money. The former owner went broke in the freight business."

"Another accounts receivable problem?" Reeda joked.

"In spades. That's why I want to incorporate your system," Vance said, returning her smile. "Broken windows, hanging doors, the roof sagging and the grounds raped by weeds made it a real horror. Like a haunted house in a Stephen King novel."

"You put a lot of work in reclaiming it."

"Yes, but it was worth it. I never mind working for something I really want. I was looking for a new name for the place, but after the face lift, the original name seemed right. Perhaps a little flowery but I was stuck with it. Please come on in, I mustn't keep you standing out in this heat any longer."

She was shown into a canyon size foyer with a winding staircase a confederate belle could have walked down any moment as Vance called, "Grayson? Amanda?"

Getting no response, he said with a touch of humor, "What good is a butler and housekeeper if neither answers the door?"

Reeda smiled, "Mister, you're way out of my league."

A tall young man appeared in the doorway of an adjoining room. He leaned against the door-facing to inspect her with insolent eyes as coldly as a kennel keeper might evaluate a new brood bitch.

"They are in the back, Dad," he called to Vance, down the hall searching for his help. "They're having tea in the garden. You know they always have their tea this time of day."

"Oh, yes, I forgot," Vance said, walking back to them. "Son, this is Mrs. Reeda Davis, office manager at Manchester. I told you about the excellent job she does up there. Reeda, this is my son, Talton."

"How do you do, Talton."

"I do fine, thank you, Ma'am," the young man drawled, his insolence veiled, somewhat, in front of his father.

"Oh, Grayson, Amanda, there you two are," Vance said, rather impatiently, to the graying couple entering from the rear of the foyer that ran front to back of the house.

"Yes, sir," Grayson answered. "We were in the garden having our tea. We didn't expect you, sir, for another ten minutes. I've very sorry, if you were inconvenienced."

"No problem, the flight was early. If you will, get the luggage from the car, and I'd like Amanda to show Mrs. Davis her rooms."

"Yes, sir, right away, sir."

To Reeda, Vance said, "I imagine you want to rest a little while. Tidwell and Claxton, from corporate, are due here at three-thirty. That gives you over an hour to yourself. Will that be long enough?"

"That will be ample."

"Good. We'll meet in the study across the hall," he said, indicating the room Talton had come from. "If you need anything at all, ring Amanda. And don't worry, I'll check on Roland and Jamey. They might want to take a short ride— think I'd like one myself."

※

At three-thirty, wearing a flattering white suit with brass buttons down the blazer and white heels, Reeda walked into the study to join Nathaniel and the two men he introduced as Fred Tidwell and Peter Claxton from the corporate office.

Seated at the conference table, that would have roofed a cottage, she explained to Fred and Peter and a silent Nathaniel, the system she had initiated at Manchester. Then she began answering questions, arguments and suggestions from Tidwell and Claxton.

It was evident Nathaniel was most interested, though he kept silence and occasionally left the room to take phone calls Grayson summoned him to with a hand to his ear.

The meeting had been in session over three hours when Amanda and Grayson rolled in two carts laden with food they spread on the lower end of the table. When they had everything laid out and ready, the president of Alpha said his first words since the discussion had started. "I think that's enough work for today. Let's indulge in some food and drink. After that much talk, anybody ought to be hungry."

When they had eaten their fill, Amanda poured everyone another cup of coffee and Nathaniel said, "I'm having a cigarette. Anyone else who smokes feel free. Anyone who doesn't want to be in tobacco smoke, feel free to step out back to the garden."

Fred Tidwell said, "Actually, sir, there's really nothing new about Reeda's system."

"No?"

"No, sir. It was there all the time."

"That's where you are dead wrong, Fred."

"Excuse me?"

"It was never there. Mrs. Davis has a system that works."

"Oh, yes, sir. Of course, sir."

"Also, if her system was there all the time, why have none of you, so-called, experts sucking on my payroll never thought of it?"

"Sir, there was no thinking of it— it was there all the time."

"Then why didn't you apply it, Tidwell?"

"Frankly, sir, I never thought it was important. What difference does it make who calls a past due account or who mails out current freight bills, so long as the job gets done?"

Vance's eyes held Tidwell's like blue vise grips as he said, "The difference is, Reeda gets my money where I can reinvest it. Hell, you know as well as I do, everything else we've tried drags it's tail."

"Oh, yes, I see."

"Do you also see how much the difference in what you have set up and what she has set up is costing me?"

"Yes, sir. I do see that, sir."

"Good! Results are the issue here. Didn't your Ph.D. teach you how delinquent receivables has broken many a business?"

"Yes, of course, Mr. Vance."

"And in our case, delinquent accounts can get the Interstate Commerce Commission breathing down our necks. And Fred?"

"Yes, sir?"

"Don't ever forget that," Vance warned.

"No, sir. I won't, sir."

"Very well. We'll meet here tomorrow at two o'clock for review. You two think about Mrs. Davis' system tonight and see if you can come up with any further improvements. Then a new collection system, based on her plan, is to be set up. In five weeks, six at the most, I want new manuals, new soft ware and Mrs. Davis' system in operation in all our terminals. And don't plan on any time off or any vacations till it is. I appreciate your coming out, I'll be expecting you at two tomorrow afternoon. Any questions?"

"No, sir," Tidwell and Claxton said as one voice.

"Good. Now, you boys go on and have a good night."

After the two collections experts said their good evenings and took their leave, hurrying out like dismissed army privates, Reeda couldn't suppress her grin.

"What?" Vance said.

"You come on pretty strong."

He grinned back and said, "Sugar, you're no shrinking violet yourself. You're real spunky, articulate very well and you obviously love the freight hauling industry."

"Yes, I find it an exciting business. No two days are alike. Moving freight is like working with a living thing."

"Always has been to me. Wish more of my employees shared our feelings. Nothing keeps one as alert as genuine enthusiasm. But it's rare. Almost as rare as a union employee coming out of the union to make a fine supervisor, with the potential to make an administrator. It is a feather in Winston's cap that he recognized your capabilities."

"Thank you. I try to do a good job."

"You do that."

"Thanks. Listen, Mr. Vance, I'm minus a boy. I haven't seen Jamey since we got here."

"Don't worry, I'm looking after Jamey and Roland and they are having a great time. They came in a while ago from the horses and had a late lunch. Then they went to the pool. About an hour ago they were having dinner and planning another swim before bedtime. I imagine we can find them in the pool by now. Let's go see."

When they approached the garden in back of the house, the sound of water being punished assured they had found Jamey and Roland. The boys called greetings and invited the adults to join the fun. Reeda answered it was too late, Vance agreed and they settled at a pool side table and chairs while the boys continued their swim.

Reeda said, "Jamey will probably resent my sitting here. Says I'm bad to hover. He may think I'm trying to lifeguard. He might be right."

"Nonsense. The night is too lovely to stay indoors. I've found when children get old enough to question parental motives, the best course is to do what you think is proper with a minimum of conversation about it."

"You don't believe in taking them into your confidence?"

"I believe in it, but most of the time it doesn't work. At least it didn't with either of mine. At Jamey's age, unless you were agreeing with Dawn and Talton, all the explaining and confiding in the world reaped more argument."

"But it has gotten better since they have gotten older?"

"It's improved but not like it needs to. Roland is a pleasant exception, we understand each other. He trusts me— always has. I believe if I asked Roland to hold a hot coal in his hand for five minutes, he would try. For me, he might somehow manage to do it and he knows I would try for him."

"You would do the same for your own children."

"Yes, but they don't know it— or don't give a damn if they do."

"Roland is a beautiful young man."

"He is a delight and it's strange. No one ever taught Roland to be nice. All his life he's been beautiful— physically and mentally."

"He looks more like you than your own son."

"Thank you, I'm taking that as a compliment."

"You're welcome, I meant it as one."

"It must be difficult for you, rearing a son alone. When Talton was Jamey's age, his mother had to turn him over to me completely."

"In our case, I doubt it would have been easier if Van had lived."

"This afternoon, while you were resting, Jamey told me he misses his father."

"I think he misses another male around more than he actually misses Van. My late husband rarely had a kind word for his son."

"Why was that?"

"I doubt I should be going into all this with my boss, but Van was born a complainer and a cry baby. He is probably in hell right now, complaining to the devil about the heat and asking for ice water."

When they all called it a night, Vance suggested, "Let's start the morning with a swim."

"I'm afraid I didn't bring a suit," Reeda said.

"We have swim suits and caps, if you like. Most women hate getting their hair wet."

"I'm no different but you have satisfied my objections. I'd love a swim. What time in the morning?"

"Around nine too early?"

"Not at all."

"Good, let's meet here. Amanda will bring the things you'll need for the pool."

❧✖❧

Reeda woke early and lay relishing the comfort of Vance's fine old home. Then a knock brought Amanda with coffee, some unbelievable biscuits, strawberry preserves and a stock of swim wear.

After eating, she chose a swim suit, not quite as scandalous as the others, an attractive beach robe and sandals. Evidently, Vance was prepared for whatever and whoever.

At the foot of the stairs she met Talton again. "Dad will be right with you. As always, he's on the watts."

"There's a watts line here in the house?"

"Yes, and amplified in most of the house. The king never naps. Dad listens to the watts like some folks watch television. He's all connected up now in his study." She found the young man's stare, with the eyes of his father, disconcerting.

"Talton, have you seen the boys this morning? Their bedroom door was open but their room was empty."

"They ate breakfast, then headed for the stables."

"Lord, Jamey doesn't really know how to manage a horse."

"Don't worry. Roland is more at home in a saddle than on his feet. He will take very good care of your son."

"I hope so."

"He worships Dad, or Dad's money and horses. Roland wouldn't dare let anything happen to Jamey. Dad might take the horses away from him. For Roland, that would be a fate worse than death."

"Oh?"

"Trust me. Cousin Roland is very dependent on Dad for things like horses. The boy is almost poor. His dear mother made a ridiculous marriage to a road driver, of all people."

"Really."

"Yes, but several years ago, he was killed trying to conquer a road grader with a tractor and trailer." During his rambling conversation, Talton continued his appraisal of Reeda.

She meant to ignore his rudeness until he drawled, "So, you're my old man's new toy."

"I beg your pardon?"

"Toy, play thing! There are specific words. Are they necessary?"

"Toy is specific enough and you don't have to be anymore specific in showing you don't like me. You made it clear you weren't going to like me the moment I arrived."

"Why should I like you?"

"Why not?"

Talton said, "You're not that much older than I am."

"I'd say my generation's halfway between yours and your Dad's."

"He's been known to favor mine."

"I just work for your father. That's it. What your father does, may not be any of your business. For sure, it's none of mine."

"Honey, I could care less what my old man does."

"He is an attractive man. It's quite understandable he would draw women of all ages."

"And his money makes him all the more attractive?"

Reeda smiled, determined to ignore his insult. "I doubt you find it a disadvantage in your own relationships."

Less belligerence was in Talton's voice as he said, "You are intelligent. That's a cut above the bimbos he usually favors."

"Don't be intimidated by me. I'm your father's employee, nothing more. If I have offended you in some way, I am certainly sor—"

Her kindness showered coals of fire on his head, "Of course you haven't offended me! It's him! It's always been him!"

"Talton, what is it we parents do? My son is sprouting a hot crop of resentment that you seem to have in full harvest."

"Lady, I don't know about you. He threw my mother out."

"I'm sorry you feel badly. Divorce is hard on children, of any age, to understand."

"It isn't hard to understand that something is discarded just because it gets older. Have you noticed how he keeps replacing trucks?"

"We have a saying at Manchester. Something like, the truck line with the finest eighteen wheelers and worst office equipment in use."

"Office equipment isn't important because that doesn't run up and down the road with Alpha painted on it in big blue letters. And here he comes now. Give me a chance to get gone and then ask him yourself if you can't take my word for it."

Vance's appearance relieved a bad moment. "One more time, I got Anchorage off my neck. Winston's still spending a great deal of time up there with Howard Summers. You knew him didn't you Reeda?"

"Yes. How is Anchorage going, overall?"

"Fine, overall, but they've had time to get the bugs out. Anchorage should be running great by now. But enough business for now. You look marvelous. Did you sleep well?"

"Thank you and yes, I slept very well."

"You and Talton getting acquainted?"

"Yes. Your son is a fine young man." She saw that Nathaniel was as relaxed and self assured with his tanned, well built body in bathing trunks as he was in a business suit.

"Thank you. I think he is too. In a few years, he will be taking over for me. Son, this lady is the best damn office manager in the system. I hope you will like her. You say you want to learn everything about the office end of things. Pick her brain. She has given all of us some pointers on how to keep collections current."

"I already like her," Talton said, looking meaningfully at Reeda.

"Good, son. So do I."

Turning to his father, barely hiding the contempt in his eyes, Talton said, "Reeda might make you a good terminal manager. Like you always say, pay enough to keep the good ones. Withhold raises and hope the competition hires away the bad ones before you're forced to fire them."

Vance laughed before saying, "That's my son. Great sense of humor. Did Amanda bring you coffee?"

"Yes, and some great sweet rolls. I'm not used to such service."

"It's a fringe benefit," Talton said, with an edge in his voice.

"Reeda, I'll have your breakfast served out here."

"No, Nathaniel, please, I've had ample. I'm not big on breakfast."

"All right, more coffee will be here shortly. Well, I'm ready for a swim," Nathaniel said. "Talton, will you join us?"

"No, I have an appointment and I had better get going. Later, Reeda, and watch out for my old man. He never knows when enough is enough. Don't let him work you too hard."

Nathaniel watched his son leave by the side gate and listened as he warmed up the Jaguar. Reeda knew a thousand thoughts were in the man's head but she never expected his question, "Just between us scabs, what do you think of my son?"

"He is a very handsome young man. He has your eyes and build but the blond hair must come from his mother."

"Yes. Elizabeth's blond and very fair. Did Talton speak of it?"

"Of what, Mr. Vance?"

"Mr. Vance? God! We're at my home, in bathing suits by the pool. You can't get more informal than that. Please call me Nathaniel."

"You're the boss. Are you called Nathaniel all the time?"

"Yes. My mother hated the nickname Nat. I have a sister named Nannette and mother hated Nan as badly as she did Nat."

"Back in college, everyone called me Vance except my ex-wife. Like my mother, Elizabeth always preferred Nathaniel. Did Talton mention the divorce?"

"Yes. It was mentioned."

"You would think after three years, he could let it lie."

"He's hurt and a little resentful."

"Resentful, hell. The boy hates my guts."

"But he also loves you."

"I didn't know love and hate were compatible."

"They aren't. That's why Talton's having a rough time of it."

"He's having a rough time? Don't think it hasn't been rough on me."

"In any case, we are still hung with being in the parent position."

"That doesn't make us invincible."

"No, just terribly responsible."

"Reeda, I know now why they used to call you the union spit fire of Manchester. Your mind is too logical to belong to a female."

"Don't think that hasn't cost me," she said, returning his smile.

"Yes, I'll bet. Most men tend to like a healthy measure of stupidity in their women."

"In direct ratio to their own intelligence."

"Of course," he said and joined in her chuckle. He looked at her seriously and said, "I want you to know, I didn't do what he believes."

"You have no obligation to explain to me."

"I know, but I want you to understand. It's funny but you are the first woman I have given a damn whether she understood or not."

"Come now," Reeda said, raising a mocking eyebrow.

"It's true. I have found out one thing for sure. Men generally are the money makers, but women are more efficient at spending it. It gives them a tendency to be eager. That isn't true of you. In fact, other than collecting receivables in an expeditious fashion, money doesn't seem to concern you."

"Don't be deceived. I like to keep the cupboards well stocked."

"But you don't really crave money."

"No."

"What then?"

Reeda smiled, "Have you got about three hours?"

"For you, anytime."

His eyes held hers till she managed to smile and quip, "Just kidding. But you do pay office managers very well. Now I can buy what I want or need as it comes to mind."

"I try not to be stingy. What I covet most is peace of mind."

"Don't we all."

"I believe the tender for peace of mind is love and understanding. That's why I want to explain about my divorce, if you don't mind."

"Of course not."

"It has been circulated, and believed by some, who should know me better, that I lost my head over a girl young enough to be my daughter. I suppose that came from the fact that I have known a number of younger women. That, as a single adult, is my prerogative. It isn't my doing that in our society, it is fairly acceptable for an older man to have a relationship with a younger woman and that up until recent years, it has been ridiculous for an older woman to have a relationship with a younger man. I have never seen that six or seven years either way makes any difference, but I didn't make the rules."

"Reckon who did?" Reeda said.

"I don't know but—"

"Bet a week's pay it was a man," she joked, and loved his chuckle.

"Okay, mark one up for you. Anyway, Elizabeth and I hadn't given a damn about each other in years. I still don't know how that happened. We had a great marriage the first ten years or so. While Talton and Dawn were youngsters, we really counted on each other. Somehow, after the kids got older and we got older the marriage got really old. Elizabeth said I spent too much time with the business. I'm sure I did, probably still do, hauling freight is that kind of business."

"Like a passion."

"Yes, trucking has been one of my passions all my life. Trucking is who I am. Elizabeth knew that from the beginning. I saw to it that she had free access to money for personal enjoyment and to hire all the household help she needed."

"Maybe she needed you, Nathaniel."

"Could be. But a freight line is like a kid that never sleeps or outgrows the need for a sitter. I had always spent too much time with the business. Only she didn't nag about it before— before she understood. I guess with the kids in school, she was lonely."

"That wouldn't be unnatural."

"No, it wouldn't. Gradually a cold war set in between us that lasted five or six years. Then boom! About the time I thought we were getting too old for it to make any difference, the whole thing blew up. Talton thinks I bought her off and threw her out. That isn't so."

He looked expectantly at Reeda until she asked, "What happen?"

"I found out she had a lover— a very young lover."

"Was she justified?" Reeda said, evenly.

"Is one ever justified in adultery?"

"You mean with God?"

"Yes."

"I doubt it, but that wasn't what I meant. You weren't married to God. Did you give her cause? Did you provoke her?"

"I know what you meant. I was trying to wiggle off the hook."

"It was your idea for me to understand. There is no understanding without honesty."

"Ever?"

"You're still trying to wiggle off the hook."

"Maybe, but you really hang out for honesty, don't you?"

"I hope so," she said, her eyes locked on his.

"Yes, I provoked her, I suppose. Just don't ever quote me. God, what a brace of expensive lawyers I hired to keep that out of court."

"We're not in court."

"Lady, you sure can come across that way."

"I'm sorry. I have always been too intense."

"About everything?" he leered.

"I refuse to answer that question on the grounds—"

"Hey, this ain't no grievance hearing either."

They shared a laugh before Reeda said, "But, seriously, why should a man divorce a wife for a sin that he is also guilty of?"

"Seriously, I don't know."

"Maybe you tricked her into something you couldn't forgive."

"Perhaps. But, I thought you might understand."

"I do understand. Such things as need, pressure, loneliness, make us all do things we might not do, otherwise. But I don't condone."

"My part?"

"Nor your wife's— or anyone's in a similar situation. Even with mitigating factors, wrong is wrong."

He was pensive a moment before he confessed, "Actually, we both behaved like idiots. Perhaps, my guilt was greater than Elizabeth's.

But right or wrong— I couldn't live with her after finding her drunk and in another man's bed. God, he was Talton's age."

"What did age have to do with it?"

"A great deal, I'm afraid, if we are being honest. I found it ludicrous and I spared her the indignity of catching me in another woman's bed. I suppose I still had some kind of love or respect for her, up to that point, to have reacted so violently. That one incident broke a twenty year marriage that had weathered some mean times."

※

It was after midnight when Reeda and Nathaniel sat having a nightcap together. After their meeting with Tidwell and Claxton, he had taken her, Jamey and Roland on a tour of the corporate office and local terminal. Nathaniel's love and knowledge of his business had never been more evident than when he introduced Reeda and the two boys to the various departments of the corporate offices and explained their functions.

It was also clear that he expected nothing from an employee he was not capable and willing to handle himself. Reeda had never met anyone who was more congenial or informal or competent. He could sit down and type as well as any typist or run the joint by hand till help arrived. Not once had she seen him take the employer-employee status with anyone. Instead, he had a way of approaching an individual simply as one worker to another, whatever the capacity. Still, the vein of iron in his personality was visible in all he did. It prompted her to say, "You are very sure of yourself."

"Sometimes I wonder."

"No, you are, that was clear today."

"I wasn't rude was I?" he asked. Reeda couldn't believe being the company president the man could care less what she thought but his midnight eyes told her he was sincere.

She said, "Not at all, I think you're lucky to feel sure."

"I do know the business, number one. Number two, I know how to make a decision. Once I've made it, I see it through. My father taught me that, at an early age. Much earlier, I must say, than I've been able to teach Talton. My Dad started Alpha at age twenty with two trucks and three pick up and delivery points. Necessity dictated he knew decision making."

Reeda said, "Talton's loyalty's been divided and in the broad sense, he's still a very young man. As a son, you never had your parents being divorced to cope with."

"My parents married as kids and lived together very happily, as far as I know, until my mother died in her eighties."

"Your father's still living?"

"Yes, though there isn't much left of his mind, most days. When he was himself, Dad would never have put up with a son's disloyalty."

"Maybe Talton needs more time."

"Talton is of age, I don't keep him here by force."

"Feelings can't be put on a time clock."

"By now, he should be man enough to decide if this is where he wants to be and simply go on from there."

"Where is his mother?"

"Florida; he was with her for awhile. Talton would never admit it, but he can't stand what his mother has become."

"And what is that?" Reeda asked softly.

"A silly, middle-aged woman with too much money, too much idle time and too little common sense. She has, I understand taken a shine to bourbon and younger men. It's almost impossible for me to connect the now Elizabeth, with the Elizabeth of thirty years ago. The first time I saw her, she was on a ladder picking peaches in a Georgia peach orchard. The wind was playing in that fair hair. It was long then and so beautiful, She smiled at me and made my heart stand still. I was hers before I knew her name."

"You must have loved her very much."

"As far as women were concerned, she was my life. I loved her more than anything before or since. And so they were married, as the saying goes. Then... they slowly began taking each other for granted."

"Nathaniel, why is it so easy for that to happen?"

"I don't know. But I truly doubt second chance lovers subject each other's ego to the round house blows that can become a matter of course somewhere down the line in first love."

"I sincerely hope not."

"If I should ever be blessed enough to find that breath taking kind of love again, Reeda, I would treat it so very preciously. Like the fragile treasure it is, that can rarely be replaced."

Nathaniel's remark brought tears to her eyes and touched her too personally to comment on. She faltered a moment, then changed the subject with, "Uh, your daughter, where is she?"

"With her mother. As we speak, my daughter doesn't take too seriously what her mother or I either one do."

"Does she come here often?"

"She did until last summer when I caught her with a road driver. She was seventeen but I spanked her bottom as if she was in kindergarten. The road driver found it convenient to resign. Dawn found it convenient to go to her mother. Hasn't been back here since, I'm sorry to say."

"Have you invited her?"

"Of course not."

"Isn't that rather harsh?"

"Look, if my own daughter wants to be a tramp, I can't stop her. I can stop it from happening right under my nose."

"You assume because she was with a road driver she is a tramp? You must know her very well."

"I know road drivers."

"What kind of warning letter do you write a man for dating your daughter?"

"Reeda, any union only goes so far. When a company truly wants to be rid of an employee, there are always ways."

"So I've heard, but I haven't seen it demonstrated. Might I ask how you handled it?"

"There are various ways. In this case, a camera, a detective, a fifty dollar hooker and the cab of an Alpha truck. Do you get the picture?"

"I get it. You went pretty far."

"To survive in trucking, you never stop till you get what you need."

At breakfast, she was greeted by Talton's cheery, "Good morning." He rose, pulled out a chair and invited, "Sit down and have some breakfast with me."

"Thanks." She smiled and sat down. "I could use more coffee."

"Dad asked me to make his apologies. He flew to Detroit about three this morning. A train derailed with sixteen Alpha piggy back loads on board."

"Good Lord!"

Pouring her coffee, young Vance said, "We have freight scattered over half of Michigan. Pillage has become the past time of a good percentage of the local population the last few hours. They say it's as wild as Indians attacking a wagon train."

"You mean people are stealing the cargo?"

"Yes. We try to keep it quiet, but it always happens. Color TVs lying along a railroad track seem to be irresistibly tempting."

"Aren't the police there?"

"Yes, and probably the FBI, by now, but Dad had to go."

"Shouldn't you have gone with him, Talton?"

"He didn't invite me."

"Should he have to?"

"Everybody should have to do a few things. In all honesty, he might have, if you hadn't been here. I have to make his excuses and see you off."

"I'm sorry."

"That's okay. I suppose you know if you had been anyone else, in an emergency situation, Amanda and Grayson would have been totally fine to handle getting you back to the airport."

"I truly am sorry if I have inconvenienced you, Talton. It seems like you may be inferring something further."

"I'm not inferring, I'm telling you. There's not another human being alive, including me and my sister, Dad doesn't think Grayson and Amanda can take care of."

"Again, I'm sorry, Talton."

"There's nothing really to be sorry about."

"If it wasn't for me, you'd be with your Dad on a plane to Detroit."

"That's okay and that's not what has me bugged."

"What then?"

"Oh, something to do with why he couldn't have trusted me to handle things up there and stayed here with you himself when he so obviously was enjoying himself."

"Knowing how your father loves the freight business, maybe, your attitude is adolescent, Talton."

"How can wanting to take my place as a man in a company I've been involved with since I was fourteen and slated to manage since I was born, be adolescent?"

"I don't think anyone doubts your ability or that you're a man. It's your attitude that's immature, not your competence."

"How so?"

"With a mature attitude, you would appreciate how your father has made a place for you in Alpha right in the front seat with him."

"Reeda, maybe I want the driver's side."

"Talton, you know your father, like your grandfather, runs off the fuel of his involvement with Alpha like a road unit runs off diesel. Given good health, like Alex, it will be years before Nathaniel will climb out of the driver's seat and let you or anyone else, chauffeur him around. Surely, you know him well enough to know that."

"I'll never let him railroad me out of my birthright like my mother."

"There isn't the slightest chance of that. Nathaniel may never forgive me, but it's time you knew he didn't railroad your mother."

"What makes you say that, Reeda?"

"Because he told me he didn't."

"My mother told me he did. Are you calling my mother a liar?"

"I'm not calling your mother anything. But, in my opinion, when she told you things to wreck your love for your dad, she was wrong."

"What makes you an authority? And have some bacon and eggs."

"Because I was married to one of the lowest forms of human life. And, no, I don't want any bacon and eggs. Thank God, he killed his silly self in a car wreck before his rottenness became so obvious it killed our son's love for him. Jamey doesn't know how abominable his father was. I hope and pray he never does. Unless Van was still around to tell Jamey lies about me, I wouldn't tell him for anything what a creep his Daddy really was. He badly needs to love the memory of his father. Every child is perfectly capable of loving both parents without loving either any less."

"You may be right but it still doesn't erase the fact that my father is here, in this lovely house. My Mother is living in a rented apartment in Florida, making a fool of herself."

"And that's Nathaniel's fault?"

"I don't know. He's so sure, so damn good at everything. Why couldn't he have held their marriage together?"

"We are all only half of any relationship, romantic or otherwise. And you have no right to judge your father. He isn't God."

"For years I thought he was."

"And now you see he's human just like the rest of us."

"Yes, and it breaks my heart."

"Talton, you can't imagine what kind of terrain you're running when a marriage goes sour. You may see it coming for years but when it actually hits, it's like a blow-out at ninety miles an hour. Nothing you do helps. You can only ride it out and hope."

"I don't know."

"I do. Trust me, Talton."

The young man smiled sadly. Even with his mother's complexion and hair color, Reeda saw his eyes talked like his father's, as he said softly, "Okay."

On impulse, she added, "And trust me about something else. Take the initiative and join Nathaniel up in Michigan."

"He didn't ask me."

"But you are doing what he did ask you to do. After seeing me off, why not put yourself on the next flight to Detroit?"

"If Dad had wanted me there, he would have asked."

"Like sons and daughters, dads and moms aren't perfect. Besides, does he always have to ask before you to do all the things you do?"

Talton grinned and said, "You know he doesn't."

"Then take the bull by the horns, call the airport. I'll bet a flight is due out not too far from the time mine leaves."

"I see why Dad likes you. You are so real. I— I like you too."

CHAPTER 17

Four weeks had passed since the Atlanta meetings. Reeda hadn't heard directly from Nathaniel or Winston. From time to time, she heard them talking on the watts line. Earlier that morning on hold with Kansas City, she overheard a conversation that told her Winston was back in Manchester. She was glad for the warning.

She was working up her cost report and hoping never to hear from Winston again when Willard Brown, one of the road drivers, knocked on her open office door.

"Miss Reeda, if you ain't too busy, I need a new log book."

"Sure thing, Willard. The log books are here in my supply cabinet. By the way, I saw that new gold Cadillac of yours parked outside."

"You like it?" he asked shyly.

"Yes. It's beautiful. You must really be getting rich."

Willard grinned all over his six foot five inch frame before saying, "There's two things I promised myself a long time ago, Miss Reeda. One was someday I was gonna drive a Caddy. The other was someday I was gonna buy me a diamond ring for my pinkie finger. The Caddy's setting outside."

"And the diamond?"

"I'm still working and studying on the ring. Been pricing diamonds. Guess I'm gonna have to settle on one of them clusters. Want something big enough to see without a spy glass. When you got a hand big as mine, it takes a good size stone to show up. Don't guess a road driver could ever make enough money, extra, to buy a single diamond that wouldn't look too little on a big man's hand."

"You road drivers must make more money than I thought."

"Can't complain, I take every run I can get. I remember too many cornbread breakfasts to complain too much."

"Cornbread breakfasts?" Reeda said.

"Yes'm. A back woods kid raised on a red dirt farm has to eat what he can get. Sometimes cornbread and potatoes was all we had. Sometimes not even the potatoes."

"Surviving childhood may be the roughest test some of us are subjected to, Willard."

"Was kinda rough, but we never stole, never begged, never was on the street or on welfare. My kids won't either. Not as long as I'm able to work a union job in freight hauling."

"I guess our kids keep us all punching in."

"Miss Reeda, You can't believe how in debt I was when I got on here at Alpha. No steady work for a long time. The wife bad sick, then me sick."

"Y'all okay now?"

"Yes'm. Since I got me a union job, where they can't fire you over how you part your hair, we're doing fine. Got all them old debts paid off. Bought the Cadillac, on notes of course. The credit union give me a good interest rate. I'll pay back ever penny. The good Lord willing and the credit union giving me time. And they helped me set up a good savings program with them."

"Willard, doesn't being on the road get old."

"Not to me. Me and my family got a chance now. The best we ever had it. So, I don't mind the road. I love being out there where I can see the world happening. Beats the fire out of being cooped up in some factory job. I like blue skies and green grass. Don't wanna ever do nothing but over-the-road driving."

"Wouldn't driving city pick up keep you home more?"

"Done tried that. City driving has too many bosses and red lights and too little money. And ain't nothing hotter than a truck cab in downtown traffic come summer. Plumb boils your brains. I ain't strong enough for that."

"Pulling forty-five thousand pounds of freight on over a hundred thousand dollars worth of equipment would scare me to death."

"Don't scare me half as much as pushing that pencil you got there would, Miss Reeda. Hell, I know I'm a good road driver."

"Do you ever worry about someone running into you?"

"Not too much. Worry more about keeping the rig smooth on the road, so it don't jack-knife. Last winter, I was coming over Mount Eagle Mountain. Drove that road, I don't know how many times before— least a hundred. When a highway's a sheet of ice, that steering wheel don't mean much if forty tons starts a slipping and a sliding. Miss Reeda, it was two degrees below zero. Cold as it was, the sweat was running down in my socks."

"Would have been running down in mine, too."

"Knew if I got past Horseshoe Bend I'd be fine. Hit ice coming off the hill before the Bend. That was all she wrote. Next thing I know, the last third of the trailer was hanging off the highway out in mid air. The cab was jack-knifed and I was out flagging down a car, trying to get to a phone for help before the head load of booze shifted."

"Good Lord! And after that, you're still driving."

"A man has to make a living."

"Does your wife work?"

"Shucks no. No wife of mine's gonna work. My wife looks after my young'uns and drags the vacuum around when the house needs cleaning. Puts good home cooking on the table and," Willard grinned, "does one or two more little chores when I'm at home."

"The male in you is talking now, Willard."

"That's the best part about being a man, Miss Reeda, over Cadillacs, or diamonds or anything." Willard's grin resembled the dying-to-please aura of a hound wagging it's tail.

Reeda ignored the insinuation and said, "With you away so much, it's a wonder she doesn't work just to get out of the house."

"I don't want her out of the house. That's how come I bought the house so she'd have a place to be. Might not have time for me when I get home working public work. Might get too tired, or go to having headaches. No, ma'am. No working for my little woman."

"You don't believe in working women?"

"Every case is separate. We just got a good thing going that works for us. My wife does the woman part, I do the man part. That way we don't have no trouble knowing who's supposed to do what. Well, I gotta get going. Thank you kindly for the log book."

ೞ✖ೞ

That afternoon when she returned from having lunch with Cyn and making the company bank deposit, Reeda was surprised to find Nathaniel, Winston and Ralph waiting in her office.

Nathaniel's warm, "Hello, Reeda. How are you?" followed by Winston's questioning eyes gave her a small victory.

Winston did not miss her gracious smile, as she replied, "I'm just fine, thank you. Nice to see you again. I trust you have Detroit recovered by now."

"Talton and I together mended things up there the best we could. Thanks for advising him to take that flight."

"You're very welcome."

Nathaniel went on, "Now, let's all sit down. We have a few things to discuss."

Reeda was pleased that Nathaniel, Winston and Ralph took the guest chairs and left her desk for her. At times being a woman did have an advantage or two.

"Reeda, I have come to ask another favor to ask of you."

"I'll be glad to do anything I can," she said returning his smile.

"Your system for collection follow up isn't working in the other terminals as well as I had hoped. I believe it lost something in the translation. There was an almost immediate difference when you initiated your methods here in Manchester. I have reviewed those figures again— we badly need to utilize the source. I want you, personally, to follow up on what Tidwell and Claxton have started, if you would be so kind."

"But I have explained about Jamey," she said. If she got on the road too much, her fate would be like most of the company executives. There would be no end to it. Nathaniel himself, then and now, stayed gone from home too much running from terminal to terminal. He had picked his priority.

"No need for concern. I have worked it out. We will charter a plane and take Jamey with us. We will also take Roland to keep him company. My nephew could use a vacation and they like each other. We can all stay in company quarters in each city."

"But Jamey's school work—"

"Has Jamey been to New York, Detroit, Chicago or Kansas City?" Nathaniel asked.

"No, but—"

"No school in the world beats the education of travel. Besides there will be a tutor right with us. Now, can you possibly be ready to leave Monday?"

"Well, I don't—"

Vance decided to play his highest trump, "Reeda, I'm asking for your help. You should know me well enough by now to know, I never ask for help unless I need it very badly. Do I have to beg?"

She smiled and said, "No, of course not. The way you've been raised, I doubt you would even know how to beg."

"You might be shocked at what I can do to get something I really want." Though he returned her smile, his navy eyes were deeply serious.

That night Briley called and mocked, "So, you're going to be flying around the country with the president, himself. Maybe I should start calling you Miss Reeda or Mrs. Davis."

"Don't be sarcastic with me, Winston. If you don't like it, take it up with Vance. You saw how I couldn't get out of it."

"Tell me something. What happened when you were down at Nathaniel's place?"

"Nothing but work. How like you to ask such a question."

"Yeah, I know I'm just a dirty old man but today I saw the way Nathaniel was looking at you. Collections my ass!"

"Have it your own way. I might have known you would be the last person to believe my system for receivables would be Nathaniel's motive."

"You think he's any different from any other man?"

"I can hope! Anyway, I could care less how Vance is personally. In a career sense, he is my boss— yours too for that matter."

"Hell, he's using all the pressure the law allows to be with you."

"I don't believe that. Nathaniel wouldn't have had Tidwell and Claxton come out to his house on a fluke deal. As sharp as those two are, they would have seen though it in a New York minute. Anyway, the subject and predicate of this sentence is, I have a job to protect. At this point, I can't be concerned about all of Nathaniel Vance's motives. Or yours either, frankly."

"Never fear, you will be. Any idiot could see how bad Vance has the hots for you."

"God, I'm so sick of your insults and your innuendoes."

"I'm telling you the truth, Reeda."

"I don't give a good shit what you're doing. You're the one always insisting on no strings. So, what I do with Nathaniel Vance or any other man isn't any of your business."

"Maybe I'm making it my business."

"You listen to me, Winston, I want you to back off and I mean it! This phone hangs up just like it picks up."

His voice was contrite as he said, "I'm sorry. Forget I mentioned it. But I know Nathaniel. I put him on a plane to Atlanta. I have to catch another for Anchorage early in the morning. Starting next week, you will be making terminal rounds. You will be booked solid with Vance for several weeks. I know it's late, but I'd like to come over."

"There's no reason for that. I haven't changed my mind since the last time you were here. You haven't said anything that makes me think you have changed yours."

"Hell, I don't supposed I have," he growled.

"Then we are done." She cradled the receiver.

Within three weeks after Reeda's orientation, collection percentages rose significantly in every Alpha terminal.

As she explained again, "Nathaniel, the main problem stems from failing to insist on the regular cashier doing the follow up work on old accounts."

"How in the world did you conceive such a plan?"

"I don't think I conceived any plan. I was just doing my job. When Hank Carter gave me the cashier desk, he said to run it anyway I saw fit, but to keep the home office off his back. That was simple enough to figure. Keeping the work up and collections meeting quota was the way to make the home office happy."

"I see," Nathaniel said.

"As cashier, when the end of the first accounting period was coming up, Hank brought a casual clerk in to help and said to use her anyway I wanted. Putting her on the daily work, therefore giving myself time to call the aging accounts seemed the best way to get the best job done. You can see the logic of that can't you?"

"Of course."

"After Fred Griffith transferred to Alaska and Winston made me office manager, I was totally on my own. Hank didn't know or care a thing about managing the office, as long as the work was done right and things ran smoothly. So, I trained Helen, my replacement as cashier, to handle the desk the way I had. But it really wasn't any big deal."

"But it takes you to get it rolling," Nathaniel said.

"Hank taught me the value of giving people their heads and letting them run with the ball. If you have to supervise constantly, you're an incompetent supervisor."

"Maybe you have an incompetent employee."

"That's where I'm lucky, my clerks are competent. Actually, they are all damn good. Hank did hire good people."

"What if you hired an incompetent person, Reeda?"

"Then it would be up to me to fire that person."

"What about the union?"

"What about the union, Nathaniel?"

"It can sometimes make it hard to fire someone."

"Under the contract, I can work a casual clerk almost indefinitely before I put a clerk on regular. That gives me time to be sure the person is right for the job."

"What if a clerk somehow slips by you, gets on regular, then doesn't work out?"

"Then it's like you said about the road driver dating your daughter. Union or no union, if an employer really and truly wants to get rid of an employee there's always a way."

All her objections to being out of town had been satisfied. Good as his word, Nathaniel had chartered a plane, hired a tutor, brought Roland to keep Jamey company and they had the finest accommodations.

Leaving on Wednesdays, with appointments set up with the office manager and accounts receivable clerks on Thursdays and Fridays, they covered two terminals a week.

On those days Jamey was absent from public school. However his grades were actually improving under the tutelage of Mr. Alred. Maybe most important of all, Jamey was enjoying the trips. He loved flying, he and Roland were great pals. At the very lease, he got along well with Nathaniel.

Still, Winston's accusation that Nathaniel had more in mind than setting the accounts to rights nagged at her.

Like she told Cynthia, "I stay braced every trip, afraid Nathaniel is going to come on."

"What will you do if he does?"

"That depends on whether or not, he can take no for an answer. What would you do?"

"Well, I might go for it, if I didn't care for anyone else, Reeda. Nathaniel is a hoss of a man, if you ask me, and about the best looking thing I've ever seen."

"I should have stayed where I was safe," Reeda said, as though she hadn't heard Cyn's evaluation of Nathaniel. "In the union, I wasn't subject to sexual harassment."

"Hey, girl, sexual harassment is like air, it's everywhere."

"I mean just to keep my job."

"You'll know what to do when the time comes."

"Maybe the time won't come," Reeda said, without conviction.

"Yeah, and maybe it won't rain again. Don't kid yourself. Men are never as nice as Vance is to you just for business sake. He has to get around to asking."

"Thanks a lot, Cyn."

"Sweets, I didn't make men. Anyway, you did the right thing. Reeda, you truly didn't need to stay in the union. Drones like me need the union. I just want to work in peace. Fighters and pushers like you need the challenge of management."

Still and all, so far, she couldn't complain. Nathaniel had been the kindest, most considerate, human being she had ever known and a perfect gentleman. She could only hope it was not the big build up for the let down. There was no way of knowing and no choice, but to play it out, trip by trip.

❧✕❧

In Oklahoma City, one night after dinner, Vance smiled and said, "It's unbelievable. You take on training personnel in a new collections procedure and get it rolling quicker than all my experts, with hardly any financial background."

"Actually, the average housewife has to make every dollar count. My housewife days were very average. Robbing Peter to pay Paul is excellent money managing training.."

"Actually, Reeda Davis, there's not one thing that's average about you. You're a ten in every way I know."

"And you are very kind," she said.

The following weeks proved more and more how kind the man was. For once, she was wined, dined, complimented, and simultaneously treated as a woman, and as an equal. It was also wonderful to see that Nathaniel never equated equal with same as. As wary as she repeatedly told herself to be, a woman of stone would have responded to his charm. Reeda found herself anticipating seeing him, dressing for his approval, talking with him easily, confiding in a way she had not confided in anyone in years— maybe ever.

One night she said, "I don't expect you to understand everything I say, but I love talking with you. You're so easy for me to talk to."

He smiled and said, "My pleasure."

"Nobody, I know, feels like I do. Most of the time, when I try to express my feelings I see their eyes glaze over. Especially men."

"So much of the time, people tend to push each other around emotionally, instead of simply trying to relate to one another."

"We all start out trusting and outgoing and get it turned off by pain as we grow up."

"How do you mean?" he said.

"Like baby boys being told big boys don't cry. Half the population is on the way to being inhibited before kindergarten. And the good girls syndrome destroys the spontaneity of the other half. We all grow up being taught to keep things we need to say locked inside ourselves."

"Reeda, did you ever consider being a writer."

"Once— for a very short time. I enrolled as a journalism major in college— dropped out after Christmas."

"Why so?"

"My hormones got the best of me— I got married."

"Luckily, writing is an ambition you can take up at any point in time."

"True, if I ever get the time, I might could write some things that make me sound like an ass every time I try to say them."

"Not to me."

"Darling, you are just too perfect to be real. Money, looks, understanding— all in one male! That only happens in the movies."

"It isn't necessary to inflate my ego."

"I'm aware of that, I wouldn't if it was. I hate the shams women are taught to use on men and that so many men are programmed to believe are a woman's character."

"Like what, Reeda?"

"Like being mental half wits. Even in this day and time, too many women still pretend to be stupid. Just think, if God had sent a daughter to save the world, what a difference it would have made in typical thinking and role playing, male and female."

"You aren't typical of any woman I've ever known."

"Oh, yes I am. I am so typical, it's unreal. I just have the redneck brass to be myself."

"If that's what it is, I thank Providence that you have it."

"Maybe that's the place to lay the blame," she agreed, with a wistful smile. "I can't do anything about it— it just slips out. I challenged poor Van at every turn. Not intentionally, of course. It came out over trivial things like history dates and answers to questions on TV quiz shows. Just details that have a way of hanging in my brain."

"That wasn't your fault," he said sincerely.

"Now, I know it wasn't. But it undermined Van's ego till he hated me in a way. Being promiscuous was the one way he felt he could out do me— and did."

Friday nights came to belong to Reeda and Nathaniel. After the boys and Mr. Alred were in bed, she and Nathaniel often talked until dawn. Gradually her spirit came alive again and she could almost believe in Prince Charming and living happily ever after one more time. After a lonely eon, she had found one special person she could bear her soul to. With Nathaniel, she could be as honest as she was with herself and tried to be with her late husband. She could present her future, her past, her thoughts and ideals, the softest spots of her sensitivity, the keenest side of her intellect. He always understood.

There was genuine rapport. Nathaniel responded with thoughts from his own secret self. For the first time in years and years, she felt secure and utterly feminine. It was a new way for her to fall in love. It never occurred to her before, that disrobing one's spirit could seal a relationship just as intensely as disrobing one's body.

The sexual side of love was such a wee portion of most days over a lifetime. Putting sex first, was like settling for a grape when one could enjoy a vineyard.

When Nathaniel finally kissed her, his kiss was as normal, as natural and as welcome as her next breath. When they spoke soft mystical words of love, it was like God was near. It was like they were being soothed by the wondrous winds of heaven after years of the damning miseries of hell.

"You know you have to marry me."

"Hey, mister, it isn't necessary to inflate my ego."

"I know, but you really do have to marry me."

"Have to?"

"Of course." He kissed her lightly and then said, "I simply can't stand it if you don't."

When she agreed to be his wife there was no need to think about it or to hesitate. When it came to love, the man knew how and even in what order to say the things she needed desperately to hear him say. His compliments were boundless, her appreciation was infinite and their love was too wonderful not to trust..

When he uttered again the ultimate compliment of asking her to be his wife, Reeda could simply say, "Yes, darling, oh, yes."

When he led her to his adjoining bedroom, when he was kissing her all the while he was undressing her, Reeda felt no fear. Nathaniel was the lover, the haven, the safe place she had longed for. In his arms was where she had always belonged. She felt like a lost and lonely wanderer who had finally found her way home.

When he turned the covers back, when she lay on his king size bed, when he lay beside her and held her skin to skin, she felt no passion cooling stir of insecurity.

Thank God, she only knew the lifting, mile high feelings of sharing, of perfection and of being lucky and blessed. Seriously moving into loving him, she wondered why it was so easy to let some men in and simply impossible to let others.

And when clearly straight from his heart, he murmured against her lips, "Darling, I do love you so," it made her feel that he did beyond the shadow of a doubt.

It sounded so right when she heard herself reply, "I love you too, Nathaniel, with all my heart." She believed she was truly free of Winston. She believed without question, she loved Nathaniel truly, deeply and completely.

"I can't wait any longer to make love to you, Reeda."

"Good."

"Now?"

"Oh, yes! Please— and hurry," she said and thought, to hell with Winston Briley and his reluctant commitment.

When Nathaniel hovered over her that last small eternity of how they were and would never be again, her body rose to meet him, impatient to be one with him. With a twist of her hips she helped him and heard his gasp as she warmed him.

Looking deep into his eyes, she smiled at the bright pleasure she saw reflected. She felt so happy... so thrilled. Cyn was right—Nathaniel was a hoss of a man.

"Darling, I want it all," he whispered, "please, angel... all yourself.... all your heart."

It was such heaven giving him all of herself and all of her heart, knowing he truly would still love her tomorrow. From the start, Nathaniel had made it evident that he loved her with all of himself and all of his heart. There was nothing to doubt... nothing to dread... and nothing to compare with the love of a truly, good man.

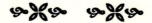

CHAPTER 18

An angry faced Winston Briley invaded Reeda's office and stood staring at her like a silent roar.

Looking as enormous as an enraged grizzly bear standing upright on its hind legs, he made her want to giggle. Knowing that would only enrage him further, she a good offense was her best defense and demanded, "What?"

"So, you are marrying Nathaniel Vance," he accused.

"So?"

"Why didn't you tell me?"

"I thought you knew."

"I knew he was attracted to you. I had no idea you were even interested in him."

"I figured you knew everything about men and women and love."

"No, I had to send my crystal ball out for repairs."

"I didn't know that. Besides, I didn't know myself till it happened."

"Seriously, don't you think you owed me that much?"

"Seriously, other than you giving me a chance at being office manager, which I have humbly and properly thanked you numerous times for, I don't think I owe you anything."

"No?"

"No," she said her eyes flat as two slate stones.

"Reeda, I thought you cared for me."

"I thought so too. Actually I did, until I saw what low esteem you hold for love."

"Then why haven't you told me about you and Vance?"

"For several reasons. You probably won't understand or agree with any of them."

"Try me."

"Number one, until lately, there wasn't much to tell. Number two, you and I have no commitment. As I recall you didn't want one. So number three, feeling the way you do about marriage and commitment, in all reality, it's simply none of your business."

"Okay, my liberated lovely, I do understand. But, no, I very definitely do not agree."

"I knew you would take my engagement to Nathaniel as some sort of threat."

"Isn't it a way to whip me into what you want?"

"Not at all. My engagement to Nathaniel is a wonderful fact."

"And aren't you proud of yourself, Miss Reeda?"

"I'm tremendously proud Nathaniel wants to marry me, if that's what you mean."

Winston's rage was as obvious as Reeda's pleasure, but his voice was controlled as he said, "I have to see you away from here."

"We hit an impasse long before I became interested in Nathaniel. We hit an impasse long before I would let myself believe we hit an impasse. Frankly, there's no point in—"

"The point is, I want to talk to you and it can't be done here. I have a meeting tonight but I'll get away as early as possible. How about your place around ten?"

"Really, it's over. The way I wanted us to be was a figment of my imagination from the start. I think we should simply let it go."

"I don't. I'll see you around ten-thirty."

That night at her apartment, his first request was, "First off, Reeda, I need a drink."

"Coffee or coke?"

"Whiskey."

"Sorry, Winston. You know, I don't keep alcohol."

"Oh, hell, that's right, I should have stopped by the liquor store. Anyway, pending brides shouldn't drink."

"This one seldom does. No one knew but Nathaniel and myself about our plan to get married. Who told you?"

"He did. Aside from being Nathaniel's right arm in the trucking business, we are good friends. Maybe I should say best friends."

"Then his plans with me shouldn't affect your feelings for him."

"Not my feelings, Reeda, his. Nathaniel doesn't know about us. It might if he did."
"There's nothing to know about us."
"Lying to yourself won't change a thing, Reeda."
"Maybe this is my night to be dense, but I don't know what you're upset about. By your own admission you're not into marriage."
"But you promised to marry him, while you still care for me."
"Don't kid yourself. Mister, you fried my little, celestial dream about you and I dead black."
"I'm not kidding anybody. I could have married you myself, if I had been interested."
"Winston, you do know how to fire a cheap shot, but that is the ugly truth and the point. Don't play dog in the manger. Get down to the bare bones of it. You don't want me pure and simple. Why be upset because someone else does?'
"I don't know. But what gets me is the fact that we would have been married, if I had been interested."
"Maybe, but you arrested our relationship in development. Nathaniel is interested in marriage. He is not only interested, he's excited. And so am I— if we are going to over simplifying."
"Speaking of over simplifying, it's time you dropped your Miss Goody Two shoes routine. Come here."
"Stay away from me!"
"You're on the verge of ruining three lives," he said, taking her into his arms. "I have to show you how wrong you are."
"Leave me alone," she commanded, moving away, but he caught her by the wrist.
Reeda resisted all her eighty pound disadvantage would allow. But in seconds she was locked in his embrace. He kept his lips on hers until resistance surrendered to helplessness and helplessness warmed to response.
When she turned as pliable in his arms as warm butter, he whispered, "You see? You do still want me."
"Actually, I hate you, Winston!"
"No, you don't. You want me as much as I want you." Gently now, he held her, waiting for her reply, confident as high noon till a tremor went through her body and told him she wept. "Please, darling, the truth of loving someone is nothing to cry about."
"You have ruined it," she sobbed.

"Ruined what?"

"My plans— all my beautiful plans! As Nathaniel's wife, I could be happy. I would make him happy. Nathaniel's a wonderful man— but you had to ruin it you bastard."

"Making you face your true feelings doesn't ruin anything. I agree with you that Nathaniel is one of the finest men on earth. For you to marry him, without caring for him, isn't what he wants or needs. It would be his ruination. That's one of the reasons I had to know for sure how you really feel."

"You say that, when you just use sex as a basis for living."

"Isn't it a good basis?"

"Sex isn't a basis, sex is a season. I learned that the hard way,"

"Does denying it make sex go away, Reeda?"

"Time makes sex go away. Love is the only thing that lasts."

"Baby, stop trying to be so logical. Some things aren't logical— they just are."

"If you don't mind, this has been a horrible day. I feel like I've been run over by all eighteen wheels of a tractor and trailer. Would you please just get the hell out of here?"

"I don't know why, you are always ordering me out!"

"I don't either— unless it's because you are always ordering me out of my values."

"I don't mean to, but maybe so," he agreed, softly.

"You really do— and I'm sick of it."

"But what are you going to do about us?"

"I don't know. I have to think about it and I have to talk to Nathaniel."

"All right, darling, I'll see you at the office. We'll have lunch and talk things out."

The next morning, for the first time since she had been office manager, Reeda called in sick. Then she dialed an Atlanta number.

After completing her second call, she took her phone off the hook and covered it with a pillow. Right now, she had all the emotional log chain she could possibly swim with.

⊱✤⊰

The passionate lyric of the love song slid off the singer's tongue like oil for the heart while Nathaniel's loving eyes transmitted their fullest meaning to Reeda. He took a sip of his drink as he appreciated Reeda's dark beauty one more time.

Reeda silently acknowledged that he was a handsome, adorable man and a rare human being. Reading his adoration, his caressing flicker of a smile, she wrapped herself in the warmth of his devotion and smiled. This was a now that would forever remain as a precious memory, preserved in the canning jars of the heart, to open and taste by remembering again and again.

It was like the love that glowed in her eyes for Van in the early days. It was the unquestioned, secure kind of love that is one of life's greatest treasures, to give or to receive— maybe life's greatest treasure. No wonder Van had never wanted her to divorce him. Until now she had never known this feeling of being infinitely loved, rather than the feeling of loving infinitely. Both had their reward— receiving it did have a decided advantage. Being loved felt so much safer. She well knew the vulnerability of a heart filled with love.

Still, rather than a sense of victory, her realization brought a sense of guilt. She had no more stomach for pulling the wings off another person's emotions than for pulling the wings off butterflies. She had spent too much time in that black valley of misery and bewilderment from loving deeply and knowing her love was wasted.

She remembered well when she had been naive enough to inwardly insist that the strength of her own loving would bridge all breaks, tie all ties, quench all thirsts. Then, finally, with no more chance than one beam holding a building, she had witnessed the love of her life, the foundation of her life come tumbling, crumbling down with all the ruins piled on her sense of self worth.

How much easier it would have been if she could have known then, that no one can earn romantic love. Only now, did she realize that man-woman love is given freely, spontaneously, involuntary, without recompense or reward except the burning, blinding joy that comes from the loving.

Beyond all doubt, she saw that Nathaniel loved her. For some unknown, unintelligible reason he loved her deeply, honestly. He loved her the way she had always wanted and craved to be loved. But— the knowing, the security, even the gratitude, did not make her love him back in a romantic sense. Whatever power motivates one human being to be in love with another had not been motivated properly in her. She wished she could find some key, some formula to make her return Nathaniel's love full measure. Winston had proven beyond any reasonable doubt that she didn't.

If Nathaniel had offered a life of mutual respect and companionship, she might could bargain but he loved her. That canceled out all the other reasons for marrying him. She loved his position, his power, his mind and she loved the man too much to marry him unable to return all he had to give. Her response to Winston proved she couldn't.

From a distance she heard Nathaniel say, "You're not hearing a word I'm saying."

"Uh... I'm sorry. Excuse me, I'll do better. What?"

"First, I want to know what has you so distracted."

"Darling, I... I don't know a nice way to say this— so I'll just say it. I can't marry you."

"What in hell are you talking about?"

"You'll never know how sorry I am but... I just can't marry you."

"You aren't married to anyone else are you?"

"No."

"Then, of course, you can marry me— if you want to."

"Nathaniel, remember that first day at Eden?"

"I'll never forget. From the moment we walked in the front door, you looked so right I knew you belonged there. And I realized at that moment the true reason I had bought Eden was to live there with you."

"Do you remember saying if you ever had a second chance at real love you would treat it like a piece of fine old crystal?"

"Yes, and I will. I do."

"If I went through with marrying you, someday you would find your fine crystal was only a cheap imitation."

"Reeda, are you saying you're not in love with me?"

"Yes. No. I don't know. I'm sorry, I really don't know what I'm telling you. There's someone else. At least there was and maybe there still is. Nathaniel, I am so sorry."

"So am I but that isn't any news. I know that."

"You do?"

"Darling, you underestimate me. You can't run a truck line and stay half a step ahead of the teamster brotherhood without knowing something about what's going on."

"I guess not," she said weakly, feeling blown away.

"And you also learn to consider the good side. Darling, I am crazy about you. And we have much in common, respect, admiration and you do have feeling for me."

"All of that doesn't spell love."

"You will, you're headed in that direction. We have talked as few lovers ever talk. Reeda, your feelings for me only need time to grow."

A man who was not good at, or used to waiting, sat waiting for an answer from a woman who was acutely interested in the pattern on the checkered tablecloth. He knew it was her turn to speak, still it took all his strength to wait that eternity of moments before she confessed, "Nathaniel, you may be totally right. I hate to sound coy or stupid, but I just don't know."

"Being older makes me impatient about love. I'm like a teenager again... don't want to wait when it comes to caring. I want it all now. But, it seems to me, if I'm willing to settle for what we have and for what we can be, doesn't that make it all right?"

"I don't think so. Every time I have settled for all right— it has always been all wrong."

"Reeda baby, those dreams and ideals of yours are mighty high. Just from the height alone, you could get dizzy and fall."

"I know— and have. But still... I have to try," she whispered, helplessly. "Can you understand, I have to try?"

"Of course. But, darling, one can be a person of principle without wearing a hair shirt constantly. The bravest warrior sheds his armor once in a damn while and the most independent women, those with genuine confidence and security in their independence know when to just relax and relish being female."

"What are you saying?" Reeda asked.

"Enjoy being just a woman. Take me and the future on faith and be my woman?"

"There was a time when I was just a woman. I had a baby on my hip, a house to clean and a husband to share it all with. Nathaniel, I thought I had my world with a string tied to it and had the string held tight in my hand. Then, somehow, while I was just being a woman, I lost the string and it all fell in on me."

"But that wasn't your fault!"

"Do you sincerely believe that?"

"Of course I believe it. Don't you?"

"Evidently not. Your saying it wasn't my fault struck too deeply."

"I don't like taking the know it all position, where people are concerned, every night's a new night. But by the time two adults meet character is molded. Couples affect each other's disposition.

Character... things like faithfulness and integrity are set before they meet. Even a hypnotist can't make us betray our basic sense of right and wrong."

"There have been so many times when I have wondered if I had been more— I don't really know, what— but, it seems I could have kept things from happening as they did if I had been strong enough or wise enough or maybe dumb enough, Nathaniel."

"Most survivors of bad marriages feel that way at times, but you can't make up with your own character what is lacking in another person's character. You will learn as your son grows closer to adulthood, he is what he is. Like right now, I would give anything if you would marry me. I would gladly marry you— second thoughts and all, Reeda."

"But don't you understand if I married you, not loving you enough, it could be a new betrayal of everything we both believe in?"

"I understand the ideal but I don't care. There's so much good between us. To put it simply, I worship you, Reeda, and I know you love me. What has you confused and maybe feeling guilty may be chemistry, but it certainly isn't love."

"Why do you say that?" she asked. He was more into her feelings than she had realized.

"I have known someone else was in the picture all along."

"And you didn't care?"

"Yes, I just couldn't do anything about it." He waited. She could only shrug. "Reeda, perhaps, coming into this world with money warped me. Perhaps it has distorted my viewpoint. However, I find it easy to let an ideal slide when love and true warmth hangs in the balance. We're too much alike and have been too close for there to be too much difference in our feelings or our thinking."

Nathaniel waited again— still she could say nothing.

"Reeda, darling, who is the bastard?"

"It... it doesn't matter. I'll get over him in time."

"Why get over him?"

"I'm won't let history repeat itself. He isn't what I want and I won't be a slave again to chemistry or old behavior inputs or whatever."

"Then marrying me should present no problem."

"Nathaniel, I respond to his advances."

"Perhaps you women have become liberated enough that you are getting some inkling what's it's like to be a man."

"All I know is that no matter how hard I resist, I respond to him."

"If you care, Reeda, go to him. I'm not a man who likes losing but I love you too much to lie to you and I know how much love means in this life if I don't know anything else."

"He wants an affair, not marriage."

"Then hold out for what you want. If you want marriage, don't settle for an affair. If he truly cares, he'll come around."

"How can you be so sure?"

"I know men. If he loves you, he will want you to be happy. He will come around. A liaison or relationship, or whatever is the nice way to put shacking up, may work for some. But it isn't for you, Reeda. And you deserve better. If the man loves you enough, he will marry you. If he doesn't, you won't be happy with him, in or out, of marriage."

"You make it sound so simple," she said, doubtfully.

"Usually is when we look at a situation head on, like rolling with a load down the highway. Get distracted by the billboards, you're going to wind up detoured or wrecked."

"However we turn out, Nathaniel, let's always be friends."

"We can always work together."

"And be friends too?"

"Reeda, I can't settle either. I'm not about to punish myself with just your friendship."

"But why not? You know how we love to talk."

"We have two remaining terminals to get orientated to your system but as soon as we finish up, I'm getting out of your personal picture and I'm getting you out of mine."

"But, Nat—"

"Reeda, we will hear each other on the watts line. We will be talking business long distance from time to time. For awhile, I am going to stay away from you. And I am going to try and forget you with another woman as soon as possible."

"But why? We will always care about each other."

"Darling, Alex taught me very well, that when I can't have something not to make it worse by whining."

"But you know we will always care about each other."

"That's true but I'm addicted. I've tasted the berry and I'm in love with the bush. If you want me, I'm yours. But for me, where you're concerned, it's all or nothing."

"Oh, now we are getting into your male ego."

"That's right, I'm past the point of no return. If I can't have you, I have to put you out of my life. I'm not going to torture myself. When we say goodbye tonight, if we are ever together again, it will be at your request. You know the conditions."

"Yes, she said softly. "You want my unconditional surrender to our marriage."

"And mine, darling. Now I think I have enough of a buzz on to eat something. What would you like?"

"Nothing, darling. I might not ever eat again," she said sadly.

"The lobster here is tremendous."

"Nathaniel, if you don't mind, to be blunt, I just really and truly feel like shit."

"Me too, Angel, but it won't make us feel any worse to have something nice to eat. Maybe you could have another glass of wine."

"That sounds good. And maybe a platter of deep fried zucchini with that fantastic dressing we like so much?"

CHAPTER 19

Sometimes it was a real blessing that working for Alpha Truck Lines could be as demanding as a cranky child. That and a weekend out of town trip helped Reeda to avoid Winston for two weeks. Then her I-need-some-time-to-think excuses stalled his invitations another two weeks. Ultimately, as she had feared, the dreaded day came.

Looking a little wild-eyed he strode into her office unexpected, unannounced and shut her door. Feeling like a cornered cat, she hissed, "Winston, I'm not at all ready for this!"

"We need to talk."

"I need more time to think things through."

"Baby, this won't go away," he said softly, reasonably.

As her phone rang, then rang again, she snapped, "Ain't a damn wrong with wishing!"

Winston stomped out of her office and Reeda's "Hello!" came out considerably sharper than she had meant for it to.

"Well, excuse me," Cynthia said.

"Oh shit, honey, forgive me. I'm nuts. Just plain insane."

"I know that's right. And Briley just stormed by my switchboard ram-rodding out of here like he was looking for a strike to break, or fight World War Three."

"I know. I'm the poor man as crazy as I am."

"Reeda, what are you going to do?"

"I don't know. I just really don't know," she answered, wearily."

"This isn't your fault. You would have already married Winston if he wasn't such a chauvinist. You really need to forget him."

"I'll drink to that, Cyn!"

"Dammit, we don't need these big bastards pushing us around."

"Couldn't agree with you more. You and Bryan having trouble?"

"What else? He never has been nothing but trouble. And, I'm sick and tired of trouble. I don't need Bryan. I make enough money to feel me and my boys just fine."

"Well, I'm glad you realize that. Y'all broke up?"

"Just about, I imagine. Last night I gave him an ultimatum. Bryan's got his choice. Her or me. I'm worn out with him trying to be in two places at one time— and me trying to pretend I don't mind. Gotta go, Reeda, this switchboard's ringing off the wall."

"Trace calls?"

"Yeah, mostly."

"Don't let them kill Patsy, or you. If it gets to be too much, just give me the overflow for awhile."

"You really don't sound up to tracing, Reeda."

"On days like today, I wish I'd never stopped tracing."

"Lord, you really are nuts!"

"I mean it, Cyn. If need be, give me the tracing overflow."

"Okay. You're the boss."

※

A week later, Winston called her from Milwaukee.

Reeda couldn't believe he was cooing, "Hey, honey, how is my girl?" as if nothing was wrong.

Hoping he had decided to turn a page, she decided to play along. "Okay, I guess."

"You haven't gone and eloped on me with the company president, have you?"

"No. Breaking the engagement signed the death warrant to any possibility of that."

"Darling, I hope you aren't too unhappy about that."

"I'm all right." Talking with Winston on the phone never gave her that awful bird-being-charmed-by-a-snake feeling that talking to him in person could.

"Reeda, you know that was best for all three of us."

"If you say so."

"Come on, you know it was or you never would have done it."

"All right, I know it was!"

"Please, darling, the very last thing I want to do with you is fight."

"Me too. So stop pushing, Winston. And listen when I tell you something. Hear?"

"Me too. So stop pushing, Winston. And listen when I tell you something. Hear?"

"I hear and I'll be back in tomorrow evening. I want to get this thing resolved, it will help both our nerves. I'll pick you up tomorrow night around nine."

"No! I have told you and told you I have to have more time to think things through."

"And I think, it's time I helped you think."

"I don't need any help thinking. We've been through it all before. I know how you feel. You know how I feel. We need to let each other go for awhile. Maybe forever."

"Woman, you are acting like a child."

"Could be we both are. You make me feel so claustrophobic, anymore. Just back off a little.

"I'll see you tomorrow night," he said, and hung up.

She listened politely while Briley drove the car through city traffic and discussed their relationship with himself. He didn't look a thing like Van, he didn't use the same words, but she felt it was just like listening to Van. In plain English the message was the same: we are doing what I want to do and you are a bitch and an ass hole if you don't agree. She guessed maybe the Romans thought the Christians were ass holes, when they bitched about being fed to the lions.

Stopping for a red light, he looked over at her and said, "I'm sure you know I would never intentionally hurt you." He waited but she said nothing. Then he said, "Don't you?"

"You know, Briley, the strange thing about pain is, it hurts whether it's intentional or not."

"I'm not trying to use you or seduce you, I just can't stand for another marriage to go bad. You do believe that don't you?"

"I must— I'm here," she said, feeling useless and defeated.

"I want you to understand my feelings and I want you to know I don't feel the way I do because I don't love you. I do love you. I love you more than anything or anybody."

Feeling this last had too many I's to let go by, she said, "Darling, I do understand. And I respect your right to your needs and your opinions. Trouble is, you have really been in management absolutely way too long for me."

"What are you getting at?"

"I think you may have been telling someone what to do for so long, you may not know anymore when you are. Winston, I don't need a supervisor in my personal life. You use the word I too much to be talking to someone you love. If you really loved me, you would be much more concerned with my needs and my opinions."

"But, darling, I am."

"Coulda fooled me! All you talk about is what you need. You haven't said one thing about we, not to mention me or my needs."

"I'm just trying to be completely honest."

"I do appreciate that. Maybe I'm taking what you say wrong but to be completely honest myself, Winston, I want you to take me home."

"What are you saying?"

"I want you to please take me home and get the hell out of my life!"

"My God! You want me to get out of your life after breaking your engagement, because of me, to one of the finest men in the world, with plenty of money and crazy about you to boot. To say I don't understand is a gross understatement."

"Winston. That's how much I loved you at one time. And I couldn't hurt Nathaniel with the possibility of still being hung up on you. But I can't live, what I consider, a slut's existence because of you. I have told you and told you that— myself, too. You don't want a woman with any brains or principles. Your first marriage proved that."

"You don't know that much about my first marriage."

"I know it failed because your wife wanted a family and because she was highly intelligent. You admitted both those things yourself. And how terrible! No wonder you couldn't live with an intelligent woman who aspired to be the mother of your child. Maybe even your children! You even had the gall to say you would probably still be living with her if she had gone against your wishes and had a child, anyway. I mean, shit, how could anybody know what you want? You don't know what you want yourself, other than to bark orders about how every detail has to be for you to be happy!"

"Never thought you, of all women, would go bitchy on me, Reeda."

"Yeah, well, surprise! That covers it all! For your information, you're the last man I would have thought would be hung up on his own image and so... pitifully insecure."

"The hell you say! I've never been insecure a day in my life."

"Yes, you are. Everybody is insecure some days, maybe even God Himself. Insecurity is all that's behind you not wanting to be married.

And I agree, you don't need a wife. A wife has needs, a wife has to be considered. You need a concubine or a Geisha or whatever those women are who sit on a shelf somewhere, waiting for their men to wind them up and set them in motion like some wind up doll."

"What if I do? What's so terrible about that?"

"Mister, that's your privilege, you're just shopping at the wrong place. It just so happens, this bitch ain't no doll and she has sense enough to know she has the right to chances and choices just as much as you do. I might could cut it if there was some reason you couldn't marry me but I can't cope with a pile of insecure bullshit!"

"I'll be a son-of-a-bitch!" he growled, and stomped the accelerator.

Like a stallion reined too hard, the car squatted in back and reared in front before lurching forward. Winston's mind racing faster than the car, blocked out the voice of the irate woman beside him.

He hoped to hell this would satisfy her. Damn it all, he was doing the thing he had promised himself never to do again— putting a ring in his nose, forsaking all those loose goodies, obligating himself to one woman and one bed. Probably, he would windup being called Daddy and staring at the tube with coffee and a pipe and house slippers.

He'd be in worse shape than a God damned gelding. It wouldn't work. Hell, as high tempered as they both were it couldn't last. Give it five years, at the most. It wasn't even logical to expect it to last but nobody could accuse him of not considering those he loved. He did! And by God he always had, always would!

Maybe— if they both worked very hard, maybe it could. Maybe, if he said his prayers and gave to the UGF and helped little old ladies across the street and got out the vote and didn't squeeze the toothpaste in the middle and could remember birthdays and anniversaries and stayed the hell out of her way when she had PMS— just maybe, God willing, it might work. It was a hell of a long shot, but maybe, this time, he could walk on water. Dear, God, please help me, because I can't let her go, he thought, braking the car.

He pulled into the drive of a house with a sign that read: JUSTICE OF THE PEACE.

"Winston, what is this?"

"You wanted to get married, so we are about to get married." He got out of the car, walked around and yanked open her door. "Come on," he said angrily, "let's see if we can wake the good justice."

Realizing how terrified he was, she cried, "This is no way to get married,"

"It's the only way I can get married. And, apparently, the only way to get you into bed."

"We need to think about this."

"If I think about it, Reeda, I won't do it. Let's go!"

She looked at him a moment in utter astonishment. Then, feeling, somehow, ashamed of herself and of him, she whispered, "I'm sorry, I can't. Marriage isn't something you back into or do to crawl in bed with someone you can't get in bed with any other way."

"But isn't this what you have been holding out for?"

"I was wrong."

"Told you that some time ago. But whatever you want, I want you."

"Winston, get back in the car."

"All right," he said, and closed her door.

When he was settled behind the steering wheel again, she said, "I don't want to be your legal mistress anymore than I want to be your illegal mistress."

"Reeda, what in hell are you talking about?"

"You honestly don't know," she said, more for herself than for him.

"I don't have a clue."

"Winston, you and I have a huge communication problem. Your involvement with a woman, with any woman, is only about sex.. No woman can occupy more than a tiny corner of your life because you are in love with the freight business. Your passion is the hot adrenaline of the grievance hearings and near strikes. You like matching wits. You crave scheming to win and fighting for power."

"You bet I do. Working with management against labor is the one thing I've found since college that is even close to football."

"Win, I can't be stuffed in a small corner of your life. I would smother to death."

"Come on now and please don't take that attitude. You know I can't help the way I am."

"I can't either because you don't even try. You are happy with the way you are. So please just take me home."

"God, Reeda, it's so hard for me to rein in with just one woman."

"I finally see that. And I don't want to hear it for the rest of my life. So, sacrifice me no sacrifices. When a man and a woman really love each other, marriage is a joy and a privilege. When it's love, marriage is no soul searching decision, it's as vital as your next heartbeat and it always, always, always has to be entered into on faith."

"In my own way, I really do want to be married to you. Reeda."

"It's too late, our time has passed."

"It doesn't have to be," he said, desperately.

"Yes, it does, Winston. Because now, I don't want to be married to you. I can't imagine how I ever thought I did when I was looking for Nathaniel all the time."

CHAPTER 20

"Miss Reeda, did you see my gold watch?"

"No, Murphy, I didn't even realize this was your last day."

"Yes'm, it sure is," he said, holding out his gold retirement watch.

"It's a lovely watch. It even has a calendar."

"Eighteen carat too, says so right on the back. It's good of the company to give us all a retirement watch and I been wanting a pocket watch for years. Just never got around to buying myself one and I'll think of all y'all, I worked with, every time I check the time or the date," Murphy said, his voice heavy with nostalgia

"I hope my health is as good as yours when I retire," Reeda said.

"I'm strong enough, but I can't believe how quick I got this old. No matter how strong an old man is, he ain't a young man. Don't do like me," he croaked, his blue eyes misty, "don't waste a minute of it."

"I won't and you still have your wife and farm and calves to look after. You have your children and grandchildren. You have many good years left and much to be proud of."

"I know. Yes'm, I sure do know I do; aiming to enjoy them, too. But all of us are bad to put things off, we hadn't oughta do that. We think there's all the time in the world but there ain't. You wake up one morning and you got old overnight, seems like. And too much has slipped by. That boy you meant to take fishing's hauling produce from coast to coast and you don't get to see him much. The trip you planned just yesterday, got put off for years and years. You don't trust yourself driving after dark no more like you used to. And, well, you just don't want to fight the road ice at all."

"But you don't have to fight road ice now or fight the dock."

"Nope, I don't and I thought the road was easier than the dock. But while I was off driving somewhere, I didn't tell my wife often enough how I loved her. Now, the years have piled up with one night sort of slipping by on top of the other."

"Murphy, now you can make up for lost time."

"I hope so but I doubt it. My wife has just sort of dried up. Kind of like a peach that didn't get enough rain."

"Women do need to be told."

"Lord, don't I know that now, Miss Reeda. And don't you be letting time go by without doing the main things you want to do. Cause one day, you'll be a lot older and it may sneak up on you that—" Murphy stopped to execute a denture smile, then went on, "you talk too much. Well, it's been a pleasure to know you and all the girls." He extended his hand, his eyes full of tears he didn't bother to try to hide.

"Same here," she said, shaking his rough hand, "and keep in touch with us."

"I'll sure enough do that."

Watching Murphy move from desk to desk, bidding the office goodbye, Reeda begin to feel contrite. Why had she not wanted him to cry? Why had she moved the conversation to override the man's sentiment? She had always favored expressing feelings. Still, she had avoided Murphy's emotion as readily as she would have recoiled from lightning. When had she become so callous? Had her own disappointments made her too insecure to show understanding? No, but Murphy's depression about retiring was repulsive to her.

After thirty-five years of pulling a freight cart, up and down, across and back, traversing the dock as listlessly as a mule at a treadmill, he ought to be jumping for joy. Thanks to the Teamsters Union, he had a great retirement package coming.

What was there to regret? Now, he could walk his fields! Watch his calves! Linger over a second cup of coffee! Pick a blade of grass! Watch a snow fall! There would be time to tell his wife he loved her every day. About to start living at his own pace, in his own way, unto his own values, how dare he weep! There was too little time in life to smell the roses to waste one moment. Anyone should be skipping to the chance, grinning like a kid going to a circus!

That night in bed she laid her book aside and thought again of Murphy's fear of retirement. Now, in the privacy of her own bedroom, she could consider if she was any wiser. Maybe she had been even worse than Murphy. Day after day she had turned her back to life like a beggar in the wind. She had become frozen, like a scared doe in a light beam, afraid to move and try to save herself. When did she become such a coward?

It was past time to admit that she had placed too much value on the sexual part of marriage while parroting ideals about devotion, communication and companionship. Now, when maybe such a marriage was still possible, because she had taken a detour and stumped an emotional toe, she was ready to ruin the rest of her life— and maybe ruin Nathaniel's life as well. What a weak little fool she had become!

It was impossible to know what prompted God to action, but when an earth child reached a certain state of mental inertia, it might be time to call it home. It might be high time to replace it with a new model with the guts to take advantage of being alive. Or maybe send it back as a dumb possum so it could sull up all the time and refuse to live with some dignity!

It was after midnight when Reeda conquered her dumb pride enough to pick up the phone. She couldn't remember ever being so nervous. Though her finger was shaking, she didn't dare stop until she had punched in all the long distance number.

And now, God, it was ringing! Once... twice... then she was hearing him say, "Hello." Her heart leapt with joy and turned to longing as he repeated, "Hello."

"Nathaniel?"

"Yes," he answered, softly.

"Da... darling, so you know who this is?"

"You know I know who this is."

"Then why so formal? I need you to help me a little."

"The ball is in your court, Reeda. Has been for some time. I'm sorry, but I can't help you with this one."

"Can't or won't?"

"Angel, I guess both."

"Actually, I can't blame you. I have been an ass. Okay... here goes. I've been so wrong— an absolute fool and I have missed you like my heartbeat. I want you, I need you and I love you more than any thing or any man in the whole world. Is that good enough?"

"No exceptions, Reeda Davis?"

"No exceptions, Nathaniel Vance."

"Then I'll fly up tomorrow and get you. We will be married and honeymooning in Bermuda by the weekend."

"But I do need some time to get ready."

"Pack a bag and grab a toothbrush. You can do your shopping after we arrive I need us together and married like yesterday. After that you will have all the time in the world to do whatever your heart desires."

"Do you promise, Nathaniel Vance?"

"Yes, darling, I positively guarantee it."

✿ THE END ✿

Printed in the United States
55224LVS00006B/1-51